MISTAKEN

THE MANHATTAN BILLIONAIRES BOOK ONE

ROXANNE TULLY

MISTAKEN

Cover Model: Kuba Walicki

Cover Designer: Betty Lankovits

To Stephanie.

*For completely misunderstanding your idea for a steamy romance...
this one is totally for you.*

ELLE

I RUSHED INTO THE VIBRANTLY LIT HECTIC OFFICE OF STARR-Bright Events. The twentieth floor of the high-rise building on the lower west side of Manhattan was still massively impressive; even on my third day on the job. The majority of the light poured through full-height windows throughout the floor. The lofty space, which expanded over two hundred meters, screamed modern-chic. White desks with red leather armchairs lined up evenly. Each desk had a pin-up board with an endless array of samples and photos of flower arrangements, space layouts and color schemes.

Not a soul so much as glanced up when the elevators opened for me seconds ago. All hard-working personnel busy exchanging ideas, solidifying venues or criticizing their cubemate's ideas. I took a deep breath, reminding myself for the fifth time that week that this was a good decision in continuing my successful career as an event planner.

Tossing my oversized tote bag onto my "new girl" sized desk, I rolled out my chair and turned on the screen. On day three of working for Starr-Bright Events I didn't expect too many messages. Other than the standard 'first week on the job' orientation-related crap like welcome videos and compliance acknowledgements. Certainly some getting used to not being the number one go-to girl for high scale events this firm was undoubtedly swarming with.

I inhaled deeply as I opened up my Outlook, prepared for yet another day of mundane 'can't believe I came in for this' bullshit.

I nearly fell out of my chair when my inbox started pouring in new unread emails. My eyes grew wider as I scrolled to the bottom of the bolded lines—the first one having a timestamp from 11:45 p.m. the night before. Most were from a few names I recognized within the firm, but nearly *all* possessed the same subject line:

RE: URGENT DONOVAN HAYES EVENT.

I double clicked on the first one which had been addressed specifically to me directly from my new boss.

From: Dean Levy
Adding Elle to the thread.
Elle - can you please handle? Thx.

Handle what? Taking the subject line at its word, I *urgently* scrolled down to the thread before I was looped in and began reading. Picking up on the matter even before reaching the bottom, I understood that a guy named Donovan Hayes was throwing a party…a surprise party…a twenty-year anniversary for his wife.

For…where was the date of event?

This Sunday?

It was already Wednesday. And they just got this account?

No way. No how. Not possible. What made this guy so special? From what I understood, Starr-Bright would turn away anyone who wanted an event planned in less than a month. Either someone at the firm screwed up and they needed to make a client happy ASAP, or this guy was a very big deal.

Someone approached me from behind and my head snapped.

Bobby Rankoff, a lanky, preppy attired tenured event planner who I understood to—at this point in his career—only passes on information, critiques others and barely do any work himself. He tossed a blue folder onto my desk and held up two thumbs, walking backwards. "Elle! Can't thank you enough. You've got this!"

Oh and the guy was also a maddening phony.

I shook my head and held up my hands. "Bobby, wait. Not that I'm not thrilled to get the work," I laughed nervously, "but what makes this guy so…urgent?"

Bobby raised his head slightly and looked around dramatically. "Donovan Hayes is the CEO of Hayes Enterprises; one of the city's biggest private investment firms. We don't turn down these types of clients, even when their requests are nearly impossible. Where there's money and recognition, there's a Starr-Bright event planner ready for the job." Bobby nodded at me and flashed a smile before pointing back to the frustratingly thin folder. "Hayes' assistant's contact is in there along with all the info she's given us last night, including budget. And Elle…use every last dime," he stressed. Then slipped into his cheerful tone again. "Good luck."

I turned back to my desk, eying the folder. My heart beat at an uncomfortable pace and feared I was about to experience my very first panic attack. And at my new job, no less. A job where I was supposed to be known as the best in the city.

Now people were acting like I was some sort of a rookie. A

sorority pledger who needed to prove her worth by doing the dirty work.

I stared at the folder, desperately trying to remember how to open a clogged throat for a breath of air. It wasn't like me to get this nervous. Why was I nervous?

Because this is impossible. Utterly impossible. And it looked like I was going to work my ass off, pulling at an endless line of strings and calling in an obscene amount of favors. All for a job I no longer truly care for.

But one I desperately needed.

"Elle?" My co-worker and next-door cube mate, Mimi called in a soft, tentative voice that snapped me out of my time-wasteful daze.

"Why me?" I whispered to her. For a moment I felt proud that my new boss believed I could handle the job and trusted me to run this important event. But it was short lived and quickly replaced by dread that wasn't going away anytime soon.

Mimi pushed off her desk and rolled close, lowering her voice. "Did you read the entire chain of emails? Everyone copied in the request turned it down. Suspiciously claiming to be too busy with projects or admitted to not having the means to plan such an event."

I ruffled through the folder. "How many people are they talking here?"

"Ninety-Seven names on the guest list." Mimi answered without blinking. Her tone dark, as if she just announced how many people were pronounced dead in a tragic accident.

"Ugh, and counting." My heart sank further into my gut after opening a fresh email update with the same subject line.

"Must have been after I was dropped off the chain. Whew."

"Thanks," I muttered.

As if she weren't near enough, Mimi rolled closer to me.

"Between you and me…I think there's a lot more to this

than just a rich guy in a *completely different industry* who Starr and Dean want to impress." Mimi spoke low. "There's definitely something they're not telling us. Something that makes this account very important."

I stared at my new friend blankly. "Something worth waiting until next Monday morning before I get too comfortable here?" I asked tentatively, biting my lip.

Mimi pressed her lips together and nodded sympathetically.

"Great," I sighed.

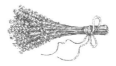

Two hours later, I'd caught up on emails, memorized the thin blue folder of information handed to me and left a message for Katherine—Donovan's assistant—to give me a call back as soon as possible. I wasn't wasting any time. First thing first; Get the venue! From what little I was given, it had to be a place well known in the city, highly elaborate, and expensive, if not by price then at the very least by appearance. And it needed to be large enough to fit over one hundred and thirteen people comfortably. I had twelve sites pulled up on my screen and started calling them immediately. Each conversation lasting shorter than the previous. By my fifth phone call, I had learned to get to the point.

I tried everything; name dropping, figures, even a threat—nothing worked. Finally, I called the one place that always worked for me in the past

"What about the Edison room?" I practically pleaded, hoping the hotel manager from my go-to venue in Manhattan would somehow make magic happen.

"Elle, I'm sorry, this is just too last minute. You know if

you had a smaller party, I could move things around, but this sounds impossible. At least for us," Gary admitted. He was the restaurant and event manager at the prominent hotel and was as close as I had to a friend most days.

"I could put you on the top of our list for high profile events," I bribed, knowing it probably wouldn't change their booking arrangements one bit.

"Even if I could move my corporate event to the smaller ballroom, I just don't have the extra staff," Gary explained. I could tell he'd considered it but just wasn't finding a way.

I released a breath I'd been pointlessly holding. "I know, Gary—thanks."

"Keep me in mind for future events...and I mean *further* in the future, Elle."

I reassured him and hung up. Keeping my hand on the receiver, I held back the threat of oncoming tears.

The hell?

I never cried when things got tough and stressful at work. These tears had to be something else.

Helplessness? The misery I still felt after losing my job at Brightman Events?

I took my usual count of deep breaths again, careful not to let anyone see my frustration on my first account with the firm.

And possibly my last.

By seven o'clock that evening, I'd left several voicemails from my little black book of caterers, florists and bands. Securing only the band. Then before signing off for the night, I made a phone call I knew I'd have to make eventually and dreaded it. This one, I made from my cell phone ensuring he'd answer.

"Elle." The sleazy voice on the other end sounded pleased and surprised at the same time.

"Shawn," I stretched, forcing a smile with my voice. "How's it goin'?"

Immediately, he scoffed. "You either need something, or you've been feelin' lonely lately. Either one works for me, babe. What can I do for you?"

"What are you doing Sunday?" I asked, getting to the point.

"With any luck—you." I could hear the smirk playing on his face.

Hang up, hang up, hang up.

Deep breath. This was going to be worth it. "I need a photographer."

"For *this* Sunday? Either you're slackin' on the job babe, or someone bailed."

"Shawn, you're the *only* photographer I know who doesn't work Sundays." I rubbed my temples, trying to remember what worked for my ex. "Would it help if you knew you were my first phone call?"

"No. But it would help to know what I'm getting out of this."

I scanned my spreadsheet and threw out the number that I budgeted for the photographer.

"Whoa, how many people are we talking here?"

I bit my lip. "Little over a hundred."

"Are you insane? Elle, I can't do that alone."

"Yes, you can. Just grab a friend and give him a spare camera, we'll only give them the pictures *you* take."

Silence was on the other end for longer than I cared for. "This is not the event planner I know, Elle. You plan perfection," he paused again. "You're desperate."

I glanced around the empty office and lowered my voice regardless. "I could lose my job, Shawn. Please."

I heard a long sigh on the other end and what sounded like tapping.

"Fine. Send me the details."

7

I breathed out a huge sigh of relief and thanked my sleazy ex. "I need food," I muttered to myself after hanging up, knowing that I wasn't going to get anywhere else tonight and may as well go home.

Still no venue, but at least the Hayes' will have music and photos.

2

SCOTT

I WALKED INTO DONOVAN'S MASSIVE CORNER OFFICE, THE bright afternoon sun glaring through the oversized windows. I always appreciated a good view, especially on the fortieth floor of a Times Square building but couldn't stand the glare. The rest of the space was primarily furnished in dark wood with a liquor bar across from his immaculate desk. Situated in the middle of the room, was a black leather sofa, two armchairs and a coffee table where Donovan conducted private business meetings that involved one to two clients he considered too important for a conference room.

I stood near the far corner of the room and watched repeats of the flashing billboard across Broadway. I checked my watch. One more minute. I never waited longer than seven for a scheduled appointment. Not even for Donovan Hayes.

"Why seven?" Kat, Donovan's assistant, had once asked me.

"Because all meetings can be wrapped up within five minutes once you know someone is waiting for you. And I tend to give two minutes leeway for travel and updating ones' assistant."

"Scott." Donovan entered his own office and tossed his jacket onto the sofa.

"Another thirty seconds and you would have had Kat chasing me down the corridor."

"How's the new investment?" He moved straight to the bar, ignoring my empty threat.

I rolled my eyes and turned back to the view. "I haven't signed anything yet or written any checks."

Donovan raised a hopeful brow. He was against this latest venture of mine from the beginning.

"But I will," I reassured.

"Sure you won't reconsider a few other investments I have in mind—guaranteed a sure thing?"

"No, Donovan. I've had my eyes on Starr-Bright Events for months. I've already explained why and I'm not getting into it with you again."

"I know, I know—all those charity events they do at firm cost only. Not very smart those two, you know."

I bit the inside of my lip and turned away from my long-time friend and occasional business partner. The guy loved to see small businesses fail, especially ones working towards the interest of others. And people thought I was the ruthless one.

Regardless of how Donovan felt about the small business, he still offered to have Starr-Bright Events throw a last-minute anniversary party for his wife, Elaine. *Very* last minute. And I knew why he did it too. To try and prove to me they're not up for challenge—which would mean they will ultimately fail when I move in and start telling them how they need to run their business.

The fact that he was using a forgotten anniversary to do it… that was one I wasn't going to touch with a ten-foot pole.

I was the last guy in the city to offer advice or criticize someone with regard to their romantic gestures.

Part of their outstanding reputation was the fact that they were one of the few firms that provide their services for zero-profit when it was for a good cause. There weren't many in the city that still did that.

"They didn't have to plan this rubbish party for you by the way. They could have turned you down."

"It's Elaine's surprise anniversary party," Donovan reminded. He stood from his chair and went to sit on the sofa. "Besides, it's *you* they wouldn't turn down."

"They could have. It wouldn't have changed my mind."

"Then why did you ask?" Donovan prodded with a smirk.

I took a breath and shook my head. I wasn't sure why I asked. I guessed it was to please my old boss who had helped me throughout the years to become one of the most successful venture capitalists in Manhattan.

Hayes Enterprises focused mainly on real estate investments, which sometimes meant Donovan buying out small businesses and their properties in order to help the big dogs get their space. Back when I worked for the man, I'd taken comfort knowing that these businesses had at least been suffering and a buy-out was their best option.

Now when there were firms that Donovan would take little interest in, he'd bring me along to handle in my own way —which was to save them from ultimate destruction and offer funds to help with growth or recovery for a piece of the profits once they have.

More recently, I was looking to take on another firm. Partner with Starr-Bright Events and provide them with business strategies to support their success rather than let them sink in their inevitable failure at the rate they were going. I reviewed their business plans, income and expenses, and payroll increases while services offered remained at a fixed rate. Those two were definitely doing something wrong.

"How's that going by the way?" Donovan finally asked when he didn't receive a reply on his last question.

I shrugged. "I don't know. Let's find out." I walked over to Donovan's desk and dialed on speaker.

The other end answered after two rings.

"Dean Levy," a busy voice answered.

"Dean, it's Scott."

"Scott, how are you?" The voice turned more prominent and aware.

"Listen—I'm here with Donovan Hayes, the client for the event you're planning this weekend."

"Assuming I'm on speaker then—Mr. Hayes, how are you? I know we haven't had a chance to speak yet and I wanted to thank you for putting your trust in us to handle your event."

Donovan rolled his eyes and took a sip of his whisky.

I ignored the rudeness. "Dean, we're calling to see how the planning's going."

"It's going great. We've got our best on the job."

"Where is this happening anyway? Have we got a venue yet?" Donovan called from halfway across the room.

I heard vigorous typing in the background before Dean answered, stretching every word. "As a matter of fact, we do. We just booked *The Square Landing*. It's right on the water with impeccable views."

"Yeah no, I've heard of it...it's not a bad spot." Donovan rubbed his jaw and glanced at me. "We couldn't get *The North Plaza* huh?"

"Actually Mr. Hayes, the North is limited on their accommodations no matter when you book your event. They haven't updated their menu in years, or their decor. And I imagine it's rather burnt out with some of the guests you're expecting," Dean replied, rather confident.

"Uh-huh...and uhh, the guest list, nothing's gone out yet as far as invitations?"

"We don't send any details out to guests until every last aspect of the event is booked, solid and vendor deposits are made. Once that happens, changes are nearly impossible. Your planner has sent out a save the date email to everyone on the guest list. With a 'details to be provided.'" More typing on the other end of the line. "Which my...updates are now telling me...should be sent out by Saturday morning."

Donovan nodded slowly but said nothing.

"Thanks Dean. Looks like you've got this covered," I praised, feeling relieved that this impossible task was being efficiently handled.

A knock sounded at the closed door and Kat peeked in. "Donovan, Mr. Morris is here for you."

Donovan nodded once at his assistant before she disappeared behind the double wooden doors, and then turned back to the speaker phone. "Mr. Levy, it was great speaking with you. I'll see you on Sunday."

I picked up the receiver when Donovan left the room. "Dean. I'm impressed and have to admit, I was a bit skeptical."

"Scott, you can trust my team. We're prepared for any job."

I chuckled. "I hope you don't make promises like that in writing." I shifted my weight, curiosity getting the best of me. "Who'd you assign this to anyway? I'm surprised one of your best was available on short notice."

There was a pause on the other end which normally would set off red flags for me. Hesitation was easily spotted in his line of business.

"Elle Rybeck," Dean answered flatly.

I always considered myself to be a great businessman, and after nearly thousands of business meetings, I'd learned to read people very well. Reading a change in tone by phone was elementary to me, especially in someone as vulnerable as

Dean Levy. If the guy didn't sound so suspicious, I probably wouldn't have given the name a second thought. But then I did a mental scan in his head.

"Rybeck? I don't remember seeing her on your payroll from two weeks ago. She another partner?"

"No, no. It's just me and Starr Howard. But Elle...Elle is terrific, Scott, she's a great asset, really. You won't be disappointed."

I stood silent, leaning on Donovan's desk. Glaring into space, almost as if Dean were five feet away from me rather than on the phone. I was waiting for a better answer, which I'd better get in the next three seconds.

"She's new, Scott," Dean admitted with a sigh following the deafening silence.

"You've worked with her in the past?" I asked evenly, after a short pause.

"No but I've seen her work. We don't hire amateurs, Scott."

"You shouldn't be hiring at all, Dean. This is exactly what we discussed at your office last week."

"I've been copied on nearly all communication and receive hourly updates on this event." Dean took a breath. "I wouldn't have given her the job if I didn't think she could handle it, Scott."

I gritted my teeth and took a breath myself. I hated when I said things that sounded like my old boss. "There was *no room* for her on your payroll, Dean," I waited a moment. "If Sunday doesn't go remarkably smooth, I imagine you'll take care of that problem on Monday?"

Another sigh.

"Yes, Scott. If there's so much as one hiccup, we'll terminate her effective immediately."

3

ELLE

I PULLED OUT THE BLACK EVENING GOWN THAT I WORE TO ALL my fancy events and slung it over my arm before walking out of my apartment late Sunday afternoon.

The client, Donovan Hayes, had insisted that he didn't want this to appear like a production to his wife or guests. Dean told me this was a popular request from clients of his stature. They never wanted it to seem as if they were trying too hard. Donovan's assistant said they didn't want to see anyone but the caterers on the floor. No security, no venue staff, and definitely no planners walking around with an earpiece telling someone to refill the vodka on table three.

That wouldn't be a problem. That kind of visibility wasn't my style anyway. I had a special way of blending in with the crowd, which included the seven hundred-dollar Armani dress I'd invested in a few years back for such occasions.

The dress had been pre-rigged years ago when I wore it to an Oscar party. One of the laced-in flowers was slightly trimmed on top to allow enough room for a crazy glue stick and some safety pins. I also sewed in a pocket covered with a chiffon drape which typically carried a small white-out stick that was held in a silver lipstick compartment and, of course, actual lipstick.

As certain mishaps became more regular at events, I updated the items I'd need to make room for in my go-to gown and the small purse I'd carry. Unfortunately, my purse only had room for a cell phone, multi-purpose pen, mini-flashlight and the event's contact list.

I ran down my list of 'Day-Of' follow ups; confirming arrival times for vendors and checking in with Starr and Dean as well as Donovan's assistant.

The Square Landing was a beautiful venue to hold an anniversary party. It was just off the Hudson River pier, shaped like a yacht, but built on the ground. The entryway was already lit up with hidden tree lights, even though the sun hadn't set quite yet. There was a mock ramp lined with red rope and a doorman dressed as a captain of a ship standing guard.

I introduced myself before walking in and handed him a card with my number in case there was a problem with the guest list.

Inside, the cabin-like lobby was dark with low ceilings. There was a small stairway that led down to the lounge, rest rooms, dressing rooms and the kitchen.

I arrived exactly two hours before the start time indicated on the invitation. After storing my garment bag in one of the dressing rooms reserved for staff, I grabbed my clipboard and headed to my first check in.

The kitchen was immense. There were two large aisles with at least six cooks and the head chef I'd been in contact with. I spotted Frank, the caterer coordinator who was tasting a pastry and smiling at one of the female cooks, and approached him.

"Hi Frank," I greeted the man whom I'd met on Friday to discuss details with.

"Elle, you're here early." He seemed alarmed.

"Why what's wrong?" I asked urgently.

"Nothing, that's good." The short man with slick black hair stepped back and held up his palms. "Chill girl, we got this."

I rolled my eyes and held out tonight's menu to him. "I need you to confirm everything on this list and initial here, please."

Frank took the menu and scanned it—twice. A second longer and I would start freaking. Finally, he initialed and handed it back to me. "We're good," he said before turning back to the blond assistant, filling the pastries.

Irritated, I dug into my pocket and tapped him on the shoulder.

Frank turned back. "What?"

"I won't hesitate to leave you a terrible review and put you on the 'do not hire' list at our firm if you continue to be difficult throughout the night." I handed him an earpiece. "Put this on, keep it on and please don't delay any responses," I huffed out before walking over to the head chef to check in. Paul was a much more pleasant person to interact with. He was direct, honest and took his work seriously— much like me.

"Keep it on mute unless you need to respond or ask me something," I instructed minutes later after handing an earpiece to the head of security.

There was some commotion upstairs—which was strange since guests weren't to start arriving for another hour. I glanced down at my black slacks and gray pullover and decided to take a sneak upstairs to see who it was.

"Dude, I told you back at the studio, you don't hold a camera like that." Shawn—of course. My deceitful, yet always on time ex was here. I watched him step away from his equipment to carefully adjust his friends' hands around the expensive piece.

He spotted me and pointed accusingly. "If he drops and cracks my lens, you're paying for it."

He introduced me to Danny, a lanky redhead who looked like he might have been in his seventh year in college. He nodded with a 'sup' and turned back to Shawn, holding up the camera. "There's no film in this," Danny complained.

"And there won't be, please be careful with that." Shawn shot back. Shaking his head, he muttered, "Should've handed him a fake."

"Please figure this out before anyone gets here," I hissed and tossed Shawn an earpiece which he caught while eyeing my outfit. My ex-boyfriend didn't need the rundown on how to use the device. This wasn't our first job together. But I was sincerely hoping it would be the last.

"Is that what you're wearing?"

"Of course not," I snapped and turned to head back downstairs to change.

At exactly seven o'clock, the doors to the ballroom spread open and a small group of elegantly attired elders strolled in. Not many of whom seemed to be surveying the opulently decorated room. I now stood three inches taller, patted down my extra-long evening gown, flipped my carefully styled waves over my ear to cover the earpiece and slipped out of sight.

Two hours later, I breathed a sigh of relief as the toasts and dinner had gone without a hitch and all that was left was dessert and handling any drunken stragglers.

There was always at least one of those at every party.

I quickly shot out a text to Dean to let him know all was going well and I'd check in again in an hour.

Quickly emerging from the secret back door, which had a narrow stairwell to the downstairs; I did my casual walk-through near the band, eying the desserts being put out. There were a handful of them that the host's had requested, and I did a quick scan to ensure they were all there. I told the Chef he could get creative with the rest.

I frowned and quickly tapped my earpiece. "Frank, what's the red object on the white chocolate mousse pastries?"

Please tell me they're cherries, please tell me they're cherries.

"A drop of blood, what do you think it is? They're raspberries."

I hid behind a stage curtain. "Raspberries? You mean the *one* ingredient I asked *not* to be used?" I spit out, feeling my face burn as I watched the guests approaching the desserts.

"Where does it say that?"

I heard paper shuffling on the other end of the conversation.

"Frank, Elaine Hayes is deathly allergic and this was one of her dessert requests."

"Hold on."

Hold on? There was no time to hold on. A moment later I heard more shuffling and arguing in the background.

"Elle, this is Paul, it seems someone wasn't paying attention." Paul sounded as if he was gritting his teeth at someone in his kitchen. "Listen, I can send someone to pick up the platter."

"You can't, they've already been laid out—it will look like something went wrong and I can't have that."

"Elle what's the big deal, just take it off the floor," Shawn suggested. I'd forgotten that everyone I'd given the earpiece to could hear the conversation.

"You take one thing off the floor, people will notice and think that something is wrong in the kitchen, and they'll question all the other table items. Not only that, I know

Donovan's assistant is here somewhere watching and I can't have anything go wrong or questioned."

"Shoulda guessed," Shawn said before clicking off.

I ignored the passive-aggressive slight and moved on. "Thanks Paul, I'll just take care of it myself." I muted my mic and reached into my purse, pulling out a small *thank you* card and scribbled a short 'congratulations and thank you for your business' note.

The guests of honor were on the dance floor and barely approached their table since the desserts had been put out. It should be an easy trade off.

4

SCOTT

"Gotta hand it to your buddy there, Westy," Donovan stepped away from a nearby guest and approached me. His head slightly cocked to one side and a glass of scotch in his right hand. My old boss nearly stumbled as if what we were standing on had been an actual moving boat rather than a stationed façade.

"Don't call me that," I muttered for the fiftieth time in the ten years we'd known each other. It was a name I had refused to let myself get used to every time Donovan had a few drinks.

And I wasn't quite ready for his white flag, admitting that I might've been right about Dean's firm. I was still judging the venue for myself, the staff, detail and overall timing of the event. I looked for anything that might appear sloppy; a miscount in chairs, delays in food preparations, and—given the time crunch to put this whole thing together—any indication that something was planned with little effort. If Donovan felt shortchanged in the least, I'd never hear the end of it. I hated feeling like I was working—especially when it came to pleasing Donavan, but I needed tonight to go smoothly.

Saving the firm that put this together was important to me. I needed another cause-worthy investment. Something that was more than just about saving jobs or making more money. Something that served a bigger purpose. A selfless purpose. Somehow, I'd trailed off from my focus on saving firms that built an honest business. The ones that actually cared about what they offered the public.

If anything were to go wrong tonight, I'd have to pull out. I didn't favor being harsh on struggling businesses I invested in, but I couldn't risk an 'easy-going' reputation either. And I most certainly wouldn't be taken for a fool.

Not to mention Donovan would start to question my judgment and second guess tipping me off on worthy opportunities.

"Oh, lighten up. You drinkin' enough?"

"Just this one." I held up my near empty rocks glass.

Donovan shook his head. "Would you stop *working?*" He leaned closer to me. "There are about half a dozen women that have been eying you all night. Just look around, they're easy to spot."

I didn't bother and looked down at Donovan. "Oh? And how would you know?"

"Cause I've been eying them," my friend shrugged with no shame.

Thanks, but I'll pass tonight.

The type of women I would meet through work-related events were hardly of interest to me. I'd entertained the occasional model or business associate, so long as they weren't in close connections. The types who didn't expect anything but one to two nights tops. I'd rarely met anyone who was worth more than a fraction of my time—not that I thought they weren't good enough for me, but my work was everything and distractions were costly.

No one could say I didn't honestly try at one point or another to have something more. But most of the time, the women I'd spend time with wouldn't spark a damn thing—well, not where it counted.

With that thought, I turned to once again scan the hundred somewhat guests to see if I could spot *her* again—the woman in the long black lace dress. Every time I saw her, she seemed to be looking for someone or steering clear of something. I laughed to myself. It wouldn't be the first time at one of these shindig's, I'd seen someone trying to avoid an old flame.

There she was again.

This time she walked by smiling politely at a few folks and headed straight for the guests of honors' table. She glanced around before her slender frame leaned to place something in front of Elaine's plate. Her dark silky waves draped slightly over her shoulders before she stood and flipped them back.

She was stunning.

But it wasn't quite her attire or make up that seemed to have chained my attention to her every time she appeared. It was something I couldn't place. Was it her eyes? I couldn't see their color from the distance, but the innocence in them, one could see from way across the ballroom. Or was it her high rosy cheekbones that made their way to the corners of her eyes every time she feigned a smile at another guest? Something about her made it impossible to look away.

Before I knew it, I stood about a foot away from Elaine's chair, where the mystery woman still lingered. She turned somewhat in a hurry and jumped when she found me standing there, watching her. The woman brushed the sides of her dress down and picked up her purse, raising her head slightly.

"Hello," she greeted.

"Hi there, I'm sorry, I didn't mean to startle you. You just caught my curiosity."

She stood straighter and lifted her head higher, as if to prove confidence. I knew the move all too well.

"Not at all, I was just sneaking in a quick note for M— Elaine." Her cheeks blushed and she beamed a brilliant white, yet nervous smile. "I don't see her, so I wanted to congratulate the couple before I head out."

"Scott Weston." I extended a hand.

She looked down at her own, which appeared to be holding a crumpled up black cocktail napkin. She switched it to her other hand before taking mine.

"Sorry...sticky." She held up the hand apologetically.

I nodded and smirked.

"Um...Isabel."

I didn't mind her leaving out a last name. Not everyone introduced themselves as if they were someone the other person should know. I let out a soft chuckle.

Isabel glanced around questionably. "Do I not look like an Isabel?"

"No, no, it's just...well a few years ago, maybe ten, I went to a gala where some supposedly famous reality show singer made an appearance. I introduced myself as just Scott, and when the singer guy shook my hand, he said his full name." I tilted my head to the side and rolled my eyes, "Now, yes I knew who he was, but I remember thinking, geez who does that?" I placed my hands in my pockets and nodded slowly. "He was really full of himself."

Isabel laughed a beautiful gentle—and genuine laugh. "Clearly you learned never to be *that* guy."

I held out my hand to her once more. "Just Scott."

Holding a wide grin as if she couldn't help it, she took my hand with a firm grip and nodded, "Still *just* Isabel."

For the life of me, I couldn't remember the last time, if ever, I had heard a woman laugh and smile with so much life and sincerity behind it. It was refreshing. No. It was breathtaking. I gave her a crooked smile, trying to regain my usual composure and charm; not entirely sure how I'd lost it to begin with. "Who are you here with?" Immediately, I wanted to shake my head at the stupid question.

"No one in particular," she answered, her tone slightly distracted and a little bit cautious, perhaps? She held on to the black napkin. I glanced down at it, noticing her knuckles tighten around it.

"Do you want me to get rid of that for you?" I offered. It appeared whatever the hell was in that napkin, or the fact that she was holding it, was making her quite nervous. Like she'd just swiped some priceless possession with it and needed to take off with the article—asap.

Her hand shot to her ear. And for a brief moment, I thought she might pull her hair back, but she simply set her hand back down and cleared her throat and her voice picked up a notch. "I'm sure someone will be around shortly to collect the trash. I'll just hold on to it till then." She rubbed on her ear again.

I'd seen stranger things, I suppose.

"Where are you seated?" I glanced around the room.

She followed my scan of the floor and seemed to tense up for a moment—then looked back at me and smiled. "Right now, nowhere since I need to be going." With a slight lift of the skirt of her gown, she stepped off the platform and tripped on her heel. Instinctively, I reached out and caught her by the waist.

Though light as a feather and pulling her to her feet was seamless, I wouldn't have been surprised if I had fallen alongside her. Regardless of how anything but graceful the woman was, something about her was magnetic. Intense in a way that simply threw me. Her eyes were wide when she met my gaze again, her cheeks flushed and I couldn't quite place what that meant. Which was odd for me. I read people like a book from all the way across the room.

A penguin attired waiter appeared before us with an empty silver tray before either of us managed to utter a word.

"May I take that for you, ma'am?" the man offered.

She blinked and her head snapped. "Yes, thank you." Isabel placed the crumpled napkin down just before the man started to walk away.

She cleared her throat loudly and glanced down, which had conspicuously led the waiter to catch the empty glass I was holding.

"Sir." The man held out the tray.

Taking my eyes off Isabel for only a second, I turned to set the glass atop the tray and thank the waiter, then raised an eyebrow at the mysterious woman. "That was considerate of you," I said—or probed. Most of the time, I was probing. Especially when I needed to figure someone out.

Her mouth fell open before any sound came out and her eyes wandered for a beat. "Well I—" she recovered with a breath and locked her eyes into mine once again. Zero hesitation. "You caught me. It was just a gentle reminder that he should focus on the *male* guests as well."

His mouth curved into an innocent smile, so I played along. "Hmm, well maybe you could drop a hint to the photographer, because he seems to be focused on you at the moment too."

Her eyes darted to the dirty blond pony-tailed man in the all black suit holding the camera. He not so swiftly redirected his focus on a couple a few feet from us.

"See, and here I thought that you were just hinting at buying me another drink," I continued, studying her.

She jerked her head back playfully. "Are they no longer free for the evening?"

My brows jumped dramatically. "Have your drinks been free all night? That does it, the next time I go to one of these, I'm wearing lipstick."

She laughed again. "Mr. Weston, this has been fun, but I need to be going," she repeated, stepping back with more caution this time and then turned to walk away.

I blinked. *This was new.*

"Another party?" I called after her.

She turned her head back, but barely glanced at me as I followed her across the hall between the crowd. "No."

"Curfew?"

Hearing my voice grow closer, Isabel stopped and turned to face me. She seemed as though she were about to respond, a slight hint of a smirk made me believe a witty retort was coming. But her mouth fell silent and eyes wandered faintly— as if she were trying to hear something. After a short moment, she looked up and immediately switched gears on me again. "Just ready to call it a night."

I nodded slowly and gave her my best cordial smile. That was all I was going to do. If I said anything at this point, it would be to stop her from leaving.

And that wasn't who I was.

Instead, I watched her attempt to gracefully make her way through the crowded ballroom and smiled to myself.

Perhaps for tonight, I'd break my own rule.

5

ELLE

"Where are you going?" I heard Shawn ask through the earpiece.

"Why don't you focus on someone else, Shawn?"

"Hey, remember this was a favor, Elle."

"I'll be back in fifteen minutes," I stammered before muting my earpiece.

As soon as I can get someone to let me in through the back door, that is.

I let my eyes flutter closed and released a slow and steady breath. As much as I loved early fall weather, late evenings tended to be a little too cool for my comfort, especially in this get up. A sweater would have been nice right about now. But I supposed I should enjoy it before I could get back in there—back to the rushing and sweating and of course...panicking. Because what on earth was going on in there without my supervision?

I sighed.

What was it about this job that I loved? Or *used* to love?

There was a thrill to what I did, that was for sure. I couldn't deny it. Took too much pleasure in it. Some of my friends, ones I rarely spent time with much anymore, would tell me their carefully laid out weekend plans and I'd tell them all the ways it can go wrong.

I wouldn't say I *adored* the planning exactly. It was stressful and, more often than not, involved working for impossible people. Sometimes I just wished I could call people, tell them what to do over the phone and hang up. Skip the hustle and bustle. Skip the runaround, the begging and calling in favors, the behind-the-scenes efforts to make sure everything went without a hitch. You know…the dirty work.

But that didn't pay.

"It really fucking should though," I muttered and laughed to myself at the idea of having a hotline for party planning advice.

"Something I said?" the familiar voice called just before he stepped beside me on the curb.

Scott. It was the tall, green-eyed charmer who basically chased me out of the venue. Like it wasn't bad enough I struggled to find my tongue when he approached me earlier, which by the way, I choked up to be because I was afraid I'd been caught in my damage control act. And *not* because he was incredibly handsome.

Did I say *handsome*? I'd been sucking in way too much of this pretentious socialite air.

I meant heart-throbbing gorgeous. Rugged features, chiseled jaw, wavy brown hair, and a crooked smile that lit something in my stomach I wouldn't admit twice. Though it could have just been that innate confidence in him that I'd kill for most days.

Days like this. When I was caught completely off guard and felt interrogated by the man instead of…well, pursued.

Caution alarms went off in my head. *Don't engage.* This

man was the reason I was out here, standing outside the venue instead of in it. Pretending to be a guest waiting for a car rather than what I really was—an overdressed staff member trying to figure out a way to get the hell back in there.

I smiled politely and responded honestly. "No, actually it was something I said"

"Ah. I'll try harder next time," he looked past me and whistled, holding up his arm.

I turned in a daze, blinking as the yellow taxi pulled up in front of us and waited. I stood frozen—my usual quick thinking failing me.

Scott stepped in front of me and opened the door. "Just Isabel, it was an unbelievable pleasure meeting you tonight."

You can say that again, I breathed silently.

My frozen features somehow warmed into a smile, not my usual plastered on polite grin, no. This one was a reaction to me being...charmed. Which rarely—no—never happens. I was a world-class expert at dodging, evading and casually slipping away unnoticed.

I was the one who charmed my way out of a sticky situation. How the hell did this man manage to get me to lose so much control that I ended up waiting for a cab on the curb *while* I was working? "Scott Weston, the unbelievable pleasure was all mine." I avoided shaking my head and slid into the waiting car.

Scott closed the door once I was in and I gave a quick wave as the driver pulled away.

I released a breath and sank in my seat.

Finally.

Wait. I'm leaving? I can't leave.

I needed to get back. There were...guests to see out, gratuities to be paid, and I still had all my stuff back there.

I told the cab to go once around the block and take me

back. I was no amateur. Even from around the block, I could handle all the necessary wrap ups for this evening. I tapped on my earpiece and began operation damage control of the century.

This time, it was one I caused all on my own.

The next morning, the driver in the black BMW made it perfectly clear he wasn't stopping when I raced in my heels to catch the city bus.

Growing up in Manhattan, I knew when it was a safe bet to cross, and when it was best to wait.

Today however, I may have misjudged. Which can happen easily when running late for work...and it was barely my second week.

I could have sworn the angry sedan brushed against my flared skirt as I just barely made it across the intersection and onto the bus.

The night before, I had to wait until it was confirmed that every last guest had left the venue before going back for my stuff, which unfortunately hadn't been until nearly one o'clock in the morning. And I couldn't risk one of those guests —a certain Mr. Weston, who I noticed speaking with Donovan Hayes—to recognize me wandering about instead of being halfway home. Especially after the brief internet search I'd done on the man. Besides being first on the Hayes event guest list, the man was as close as anyone could get to the CEO of Hayes Enterprises. And Donovan Hayes himself, seemed to be a big deal to the firm that currently employed me.

Yeah, too close for comfort.

You couldn't just be a nobody, could you, Mr. Weston?

Though there was one drunk straggler I escorted out myself since the staff was mostly gone. He was mumbling incoherently and smirking the whole time. I ignored him and politely walked him out.

I hopped off the bus and glanced around before running straight into the building. I'd already be just under a half hour late to work so stopping for coffee was no longer an option. Not to mention how obnoxious it would appear to the tenured employees if I strolled in late, with a venti latte in hand and not a care in the world. I didn't need or want that kind of reputation. I didn't like any kind of attention, much less the negative kind. Heck, I'd made a career of staying out of sight.

The elevator doors opened to my floor. I trailed in swiftly, making a beeline for my desk—all the way in the back.

"Elle," Dean called from the doorframe of his office. I spun and watched him motion toward his office and then disappear behind the frame, leaving the door left open for me.

Man don't they give a girl room to breathe here?

"Dean, I just walked in the door," I sputtered, surprising myself with my irritated tone.

God I need coffee and quick—my job just might depend on it.

"Yes, I see that. Please come in, tell me about last night."

I couldn't exactly tell him this was a less than optimal time for my full report on the night. I needed to sit, gather my thoughts…and recover from lack of sleep.

Nonetheless, I was a professional.

I might be able to explain this to Dean. Heck, maybe he'd find it hilarious. After all, though we weren't exactly friends before I agreed to work for him, we were more than just acquaintances.

Dean and I had both been in the industry for years. I'd often give him updates and reviews on new venues, give him warnings on vendors and send him all the necessary "beware of..." articles that may be of use to him and his firm. We first met at the Conrad Ballroom less than three years ago when a new manager of the elaborate venue double booked their event, and after having some unfriendly words, we ended up teaming up to make it work. I came up with decorations that blended and worked for both parties and walked his clients through the changes delicately and flawlessly. Dean had once told me my magic may have saved his firm that summer.

When I was laid off from my job at Brightman Events over a month ago, I casually sent him another useful article and signed the email, *"Free Agent"*. I wouldn't think of asking for work, no matter how embarrassing my savings were looking these days.

But wasn't that Dean anymore...he was now my boss and I needed to remember that. And if my new boss needed the lowdown on the long night right this moment—I'd oblige.

"Cocktails went off without a hitch. I had previously arranged for extra valets so there wouldn't be delays. The party didn't start one minute late, but there were some stragglers when it ended. Mr. Donovan left a generous staff tip which I distributed as per my gratuity allocation chart. No damage was done at the property. No allergic reactions. The musicians played at an acceptable volume and appeared to be highly admired."

"Excellent. And no one saw you on the floor?"

"Not a soul."

"Great work," he mumbled, already focused on his emails.

That's it?

I pulled off the nearly impossible and all I got was "great work?" Meanwhile, the musicians—who lost their gig for this past Sunday and were therefore available for the event, got thanked profusely from Dean with a huge tip and a promise to repay the favor.

I shook my head—probably visibly—and turned on my heel. "I'll go now."

"Oh–hey sorry to cut this short, I wanted to ask you more about how you've liked working here so far—"

"Oh well..."

"But I have an important meeting I need to prep for—so we'll catch up later."

With a single nod, I walked out the door and to my desk. My head as high as I could manage. It was enough that I was proud of my accomplishment this weekend. *I've still got it.*

I slumped down in my chair and debated on turning on my computer just yet. I was not ready for anything else today. A day off would have been nice. Sure, nearly everyone at the firm worked weekends, it was the nature of the job, but I worked overtime to get this event perfect.

From the corner of my eye, I caught Mimi pushing off her desk to wheel up to me.

"Congrats." She raised an eyebrow. "Looks like you're here to stay."

"Hmm?"

"You know if you didn't pull this off, you would have been gone today, right?"

How could I forget the top secrecy of why this particular event was so vital to nail to perfection, down to the very last non-raspberry-filled pastry?

"Thanks for the official welcome." It was always appreciated to be reminded of your current situation; broke and practically fighting to keep a job.

How did everything get so screwed up?

I was so much better than this. I was a brilliant planner—one of the top at my last firm. I knew the business; knew all the secrets; knew all the hits and misses of event planning history.

Even socially—I worked the crowds, befriended each and

every client that walked through my private office, giving them the step by step of how I was going to throw them the party of the century. No one walked out without signing with me. And no one was ever unhappy with the turnout.

How I missed having it all together. I was never well off, but I made a decent living and *loved* my job. Until the magic carpet I'd been riding for seven years had been ripped from under me...and I'd been falling ever since.

"I knew you'd pull it off."

"You don't even know how it went," I pointed out.

"I don't need to. I heard you run with it from day one and had to hand it to you. You knew what you were doing. I had no doubts."

I narrowed my eyes. "You know, you're right, I did kind-of kick ass with this one, didn't I?"

Mimi leaned into me and glanced around. "You stole the damn show around here. No one wanted it because it seemed impossible... but not for you." She leaned back in her chair and studied me. "Something tells me Dean already knew this about you."

"What makes you say that?"

Mimi glanced over her shoulder and lowered her voice again. "Because about a month before you started, the firm went on a hiring freeze."

I frowned. "What? But then why..."

Mimi looked me up and down and shrugged holding her palms up. "Now you understand the catty looks and judgment you've been seeing around here."

I stared at her and blew out a steady breath before glancing around at my surrounding colleagues. The invisible walls suddenly closing in on me. My time here was limited. There was no doubting that. "I need coffee; I'll be back in a few."

6

SCOTT

I TOSSED THE FILE BACK ON THE COFFEE TABLE IN DEAN'S LARGE office; correction, Dean and Starr's office. They shared the spacious room, occupied by the two clean wooden desks directly across from each other. The room thankfully had roller shades down, reducing the glare from the enormous windows which covered most of the rooms' back wall. The relatively new business center on the lower west side was managed by a well-known developer who welcomed firms to lease by floor at the minimum. The rent was astronomical and nonnegotiable.

"Consider me impressed, Dean."

Dean clapped his hands together and plucked himself off the front of his desk where he'd been leaning. "I knew you would be. I never doubted my team."

Starr crossed from where she stood by the window to the sofa and sat uncomfortably close to me. "Scott, last night's event is a terrific example of what we do here. We craft amazing, unforgettable events for all our clients and sometimes," she glanced at her partner enthusiastically, "we make miracles happen."

I breathed in deep and shifted as soon as I felt the woman, who was wearing a fiery red dress, brush her leg against mine. It didn't take much to catch the warning glance Dean shot Starr.

Starr was a fierce and bold business owner who had let her success blind her on keeping her firm running without threat of going bankrupt. About a decade older than me, she managed to maintain some youthful features, but regardless, everything about the woman screamed cougar. I sighed internally. It's not like I couldn't handle her type. Most times I'd actually enjoyed it. But not when I was strongly considering going into business with the so-called power non-couple.

I stood, grabbing the folder I'd been reviewing of the Hayes event and cleared my throat, "Noticed you stayed within budget, too."

"Came under, actually," Dean corrected.

I nodded, absently.

"So, should we draw up the paperwork?" Dean rubbed his hands together. His confidence rising high after last night's questionable success.

I stared at the man I once considered a friend. Dean and I went to grad school together nearly a decade ago, with a focus in Business. Dean went into entrepreneurship, taking course after course on running your own business. Back then, Dean was just as cocky, insisting he'd never work for anyone. He'd hit the ground running the day he graduated. Sure enough, the guy started his firm, building it from the ground up, eventually partnering with Starr in order to expand. Now here he was, needing a bailout—and by the looks of it, he needed it fast.

I, on the other hand, hadn't been as sure of what I wanted when I graduated. I wasn't as eager and didn't picture endless dollar signs every time I chose my courses. I studied business intelligence and management. Hayes Enterprises was my first job out of grad school and I never regretted a single move.

Don't get me wrong, I liked Dean, but his ego was his downfall. Even now, when he was practically begging me to become a private investor in his firm to save it from shutting down, the man stood before me with his head held high. As if this were part of his business plan all along.

I shook my head and ran a hand through my hair. Being an old friend, I didn't feel like I owed Dean anything. But I appreciated the idea behind his non-profit charity event planning, and wanted to see it thrive, despite how I felt about the owners of the damn place.

"My lawyers will do that part, but not so fast," I answered. "You both need to understand that this isn't just about throwing a good party. I'm sure your staff is amazing, every last one of them, but there's much more of my advice that you haven't even considered." I hated getting frustrated—never needed to work this hard. Desperate business owners were eager to follow my guidance. Albeit, they might have considered them *demands*, but still followed. These two were a bit too headstrong for my liking.

"Listen, I like what you guys do and I want to help, but I'm not investing in a business that demonstrates they don't need to be saved. A business that uses its resources to do charitable events *at cost*, can't be granting raises, hiring, and running their operation out of such a prominent location," I circled in place and waved my hands around, "You don't have clients coming here, you don't need all this."

"With all due respect, Scott," Dean started sluggishly, in a *"you still have a lot to learn"* tone, "Starr and I worked very hard to get to a point where we can have such a location—for five straight years. And as for our employees, they are important to us, and they're loyal. So yes, to show our appreciation, we do compensate them competitively." Dean hesitated then continued. "You don't know this trade, Scott. By limiting the number of employees we have, we limit the projects we take on."

"With all due respect, *Dean*, I may not know much about the event planning business, but I've also never been in a situation where I need to shut down and start over. Which, I don't know if you realize this," my lip curved and head tilted to the side as I pointed out the door "once that happens—they're all walkin' right out of here with you." I straightened, watching my old friend stand speechless. "You cut two today, you save eighteen for at least another few months until we figure out a new strategy."

Dean raised an eyebrow. It was his defeated expression. He glanced at Starr, who motioned an arm toward him, giving her partner the decision. "Fine, we'll consider some layoffs," he muttered dryly before adding "*along* with other strategies, which we will come up with together."

I glared back at Dean for a long moment. "I'll have my lawyer draft something this week," I moved to the door. "But nothing is getting signed until I start seeing some effort on your end. I won't have my money drained in a business that refuses to make changes."

"Understood," Dean nodded, unenthusiastically.

"Scott," Starr, who'd been awfully quiet for most of the discussion, came up behind me and turned me to face her. "I agree, perhaps we have been too loyal to our employees, but it might be a good idea for you to meet them, maybe individually or an official group introduction right out on our floor." She peeked at Dean, who looked as though he was about to come out of his skin. "Of course once you're officially part owner of the establishment."

I knew she was right. Knowing your staff helps in a lot of good business decisions. Not knowing who does what exactly is where the downfall usually originates. "Very well," I agreed. Perhaps the woman should speak up more often. "The employee that worked on the Hayes event last night," I turned to Dean, "You said she was new and supposedly somewhat of a somebody in the industry?"

"To those *within* the industry, yes. There aren't many venues in Manhattan that haven't heard of Elle Rybeck."

That surely was impressive. So was the night she'd thrown together; questionably flawlessly. "I'd like to meet her."

"I don't think that's a good idea. We haven't exactly made it public knowledge that we need—"

I held up a hand. "Relax, I just want to thank her without telling her my connection to this firm, and start on *my end* of our deal—get to know the staff." I winked at Starr.

She stepped in front of Dean and held a hand to his chest. "I'll take him over to her desk."

7

ELLE

THE BEST CAFE WITHIN A TWO-BLOCK RADIUS WAS *Blue Reserves*; a bright, modern establishment, where the exterior is primarily made up of glass windows. Located on the corner of a busy intersection just across the street from my office building.

It typically had a line out the door and around the corner; almost reaching the next nearby coffee shop. But at this late hour of the morning, it was a reasonable fifteen-minute wait. I had only been a consumer of the place on two other occasions, but the coffee was beyond exceptional. The elite cafe mainly had business attired clientele and served pretty, high-end healthy choice pastries to complement their coffee. I had yet to hear anyone order plain coffee here. It was either a large cap, or red-eye, or cinnamon latte. I just wanted a large coffee to go.

I yawned.

Make that extra-large.

I overheard the barista telling a young woman that they

didn't serve decaf and can offer her a decaf *Americano*. At nearly double the price of regular coffee, the customer reluctantly accepted.

What kind of coffee place doesn't serve decaf?

I quickly scanned the menu before it was my turn to order. I needed something strong, hot and foamy.

"Try the Censored Hot Brew," a deep voice murmured over my shoulder.

My chest seized at the slight feeling that I might recognize the voice. I spun and there he was—Scott Weston.

And from what I'd Googled about the man...*Just Scott* was definitely not appropriate for him.

He wore a crisp, solid white button-down shirt with a tan blazer. His hair, the same golden brown and slightly curled ends that I found mesmerizing the night before. And that killer slow smile when my face settled into recognition.

"Isabel," he acknowledged with a slight nod.

So sophisticated.

I smiled back and was just about to say God knows what, before the barista abruptly called out, "What can I get started for you?"

I turned back on my heel. "Ah, large *censored* hot brew —please."

Scott's lip curved and he glanced at his shoes.

"I'll take your word for it," I said without barely a glance in his direction.

He slipped in front of me in line, and now faced the cashier, handing her a clear plastic card. I realized that he was paying for both our orders.

I narrowed my eyes. "I didn't even hear you order."

"I didn't. They know my usual."

Usual? Oh no, does he work around here?

"So what did I just order?" I asked. For some reason, I felt like I needed to keep words pouring out of me as though if I didn't, he might see through my...well, whatever the hell it was I was hiding. I wasn't sure anymore.

God he's gorgeous.

"Exactly what you wanted," he replied casually with a small shrug. He picked up my drink at the counter. "You take sugar?"

Definitely. But all I could manage was a meek nod. "How did you..."

He handed me the drink with a grin and cleared his throat. "Your strong, hot and foamy, madam."

I stared at him as chills ran down my spine. "I said that out loud, didn't I?" Not that it was so terrible, but what else could I have subconsciously said out loud?

Saying my thoughts out loud was an unfortunate lifelong habit and got me in trouble one too many times.

Again, Scott grinned at me. In that 'knows he's sexy as all hell' kind of grin. And I bit the inside of my bottom lip. "It's a strong roast covered with foamed steamed milk. Hence the 'censored'."

I licked my lips because well, that sounded heavenly, and nodded, appreciating the sensual creativity of the name.

"So you work around here?" I asked, and then immediately regretted it, since all that would do is prompt him to ask me the same.

"No."

Strange. How does someone get to be served their 'usual' when they didn't work nearby? "Oh. You live here." It came out almost matter-of-factly.

He chuckled this time. "No, I know the owner. What about you?" He gazed at me, admiringly.

Dammit.

I bit my lip and moved aside from another customer who was trying to push past me.

"Here, do you have a few minutes? Let's sit." He motioned

to an empty small round high-top table, and we took the two seats across each other. I was quiet and maybe even a bit fidgety as he studied me and held up my cup as if it were enough to hide me. This wasn't like me. I never weakened at scrutiny.

Maybe he would forget he asked and we'd move on to something else? I took a slow sip from the steaming cup, knowing he was waiting for an answer.

Let's see.

Well, I was running late this morning because of the detour you made me take last night in the middle of my first event on the job. So I snuck out to grab a decent cup of well-deserved expensive coffee. I am the newest and least respected employee at the firm across the street that served the hors d'oeurves you had yesterday at exactly 7:15 p.m., because that's the time they were scheduled to be served!

"I'm actually just on this side of town checking on a client." I took a sip and smiled politely.

Umm...vague much?

God, this wasn't going anywhere good. And though I made a mental note that lying was okay since I didn't intend on ever seeing this man again, I kicked myself for my lack of creativity with the response. I could have done way better than that.

He eyed me intently. And I had to say *something* to derail him from asking anything more.

"Forgive me for not focusing on the current topic, but I'm extremely concerned to find that I am thinking out loud." I said, desperately trying to avoid another blatant lie. "What other secrets have I revealed to the world, unintentionally?" I held a hand to my chest and bulged my eyes in exaggerated horror.

"Well lucky for you, you only muttered a G rated secret." He winked. "How's the coffee?"

I bit my lip and tapped a fingernail on the plastic white lid. "It's perfect. Thank you." I rubbed the hot cup between my palms and stopped when he glanced down at them. Was it me or did he seem to notice all my nervous ticks? "So, tell me about your friend. Is this a franchise?"

He seemed to be considering the question. "Oh, the owner. Not exactly a friend. Stewart is more of a business acquaintance."

Of course.

"Well please let him know that I'm not only impressed with the taste, but the creativity of the name of my new favorite drink."

"I'll be sure to let him know that *Just Isabel* is a big fan."

I offered a single nod and refused to take the 'I don't know your last name' bait. Then another thought crossed my mind and I felt my face fall a little. Was he implying that my opinion wouldn't matter to the owner?

"I really should be going." I'd already been gone from the office for over twenty minutes.

"Oh, do you have an appointment nearby?" Scott asked.

I glanced at my phone to see a handful of emails come through. I scrolled down, making quick mental notes to myself about each one. I jumped out of my seat when I saw an email from Mimi with the subject in all caps; WHERE ARE YOU?

I clicked it and read. Apparently Starr had brought over someone who *'looked very important'* to meet me and my boss was irked that I wasn't around.

Scott stood and nodded toward my phone. "Is that work?"

"It's my assistant," I didn't miss a beat with my response. It was a reflex of having to deal with head managers and owners of some of the most prominent venues. More often than I enjoyed, I needed to sound like I was coming from the top. I was used to leveling myself with people like Scott Weston. My old boss, Ron, used to remind me that 'with a slight raise of your head, no one will ever be the wiser'.

Except when I tried that with Scott last night, his lip turned up as if he could see right through that.

"She's just reminding me of my busy schedule today." I smiled politely. "Thanks for the coffee," I repeated, ironing out my skirt so I could take another second to decide if I should extend a hand. It was something I typically never thought twice about, but this man…stirred an uneasiness in me that I just couldn't shake off.

I cleared my throat and extended my hand with my head held particularly too high for it to look natural, I was sure of it. "It was a pleasure running into you."

Scott stood and took my hand, but didn't shake it. He held it and locked eyes with me. It was as if he *knew* what he was doing to me.

"Same," he said simply. "I think it would only be fair if you bought the next round. Say, tomorrow?"

Was he asking me out? I sighed, because I knew what my answer had to be. I mentally searched my library of witty and respectful turn downs for when clients asked me out. The words were there; I had a slew of them.

That's so flattering, but not for this busy bee; I would in a heart-beat, but just can't afford the distraction right now; Absolutely. Why don't I give you a call; we'll plan a celebratory lunch after the event.

But none sounded right in my head.

Not for Scott Weston.

I realized I may have been staring at the man whose features were pure perfection and just uttered, "Um…"

"Come on Ms. Isabel; don't make me ask around about you."

God his eyes were really something. And the way he was looking at me; as if challenging me to say no. When he probably damn well knew I couldn't.

I let out a breath. "Tomorrow huh? How about 12:30?" I fought the urge to bite my lip.

Suppose I could substitute my lunch break for a cup of coffee.

He flashed an all-knowing grin. "Perfect."

"Don't you need to check your calendar?" Men like him always had a calendar to check. Then again, it wouldn't be the worst thing if he canceled last minute. Because I had absolutely *no* business seeing this man again.

He opened the door and winked at me just as I passed him. "I'll move some things around."

8

SCOTT

"HARRISON, I NEED TO SEE STRATEGY," I INSISTED FOR THE FIFTH time that week after Todd Harrison, a multimillionaire entrepreneur, reached out to me with what sounded like a worthy investment proposal.

I leaned back in my chair in my home office, despite Donovan granting me full access to my old office at Hayes and use of his resources. But I enjoyed my own space and working on my own—with zero chance of people walking in unannounced.

That and the fact that I hated distractions more than I hated a poor investment. Which was exactly what this guy on the other side of the line was starting to sound like.

The man wasn't drowning by any means, but his family-operated business certainly was. When numbers started dropping at his large enterprise printing organization last year, Harrison got anxious and *stingy*. Firing his well-paid GM and promoting a senior associate with little experience to run things. I was surprised by the stupid move by someone who was supposed to be in the top five of New York's printing organizations. A move like that usually meant the guy was desperate and taking advice from amateurs.

I met with Todd and his senior officers a few weeks ago and looked over some quarterly reports. After I made my own assessments on where it went south, I generously pointed them out and gave him one week to come up with a strategy before I consider signing.

Typically, the next step was for them to let *me* know what they planned to do to fix it. It wasn't a game I played with future partners. Nor was it a test. But before I committed to a partnership, I needed to know that the firms I was bailing out had in turn planned a well-thought-out business strategy that would potentially skyrocket numbers in the coming year. It didn't need to be a sure thing—I knew every investment had its risks.

But I needed to see real effort. I needed to hear that they're willing to try anything and would take action almost immediately. Time is money and I didn't plan to waste one dime of it.

But if the guy had nothing, then neither would I. It was as simple as that.

"Look, my team is trying. But some suggestions would help here."

"I'm not a problem solver, Todd."

"Well then how do you know if what we come up with will work?"

"I take chances on people with a plan. People who think and don't give up. You stop thinking—you've given up. I'm not investing." I was about to hang up but thought better of it before I blew an opportunity. "And I'm at my limits with these useless phone calls; call me when you have something solid."

I never said I was nice about it.

I took a deep breath and looked at my watch for the seventh time in the past hour. It was almost time to meet her.

A small but unmistakable spark went off in my chest and I frowned.

I was *excited* to see her.

The realization made me grit my teeth and for a moment I wondered if I should call it off. I enjoyed a life where nothing meant anything, and people were easily forgotten.

Something told me Isabel was not a woman who would blend well with this lifestyle.

I tapped my finger on the wooden table.

Rats. I didn't get her phone number. And if there was one thing I certainly didn't do, was keep a beautiful woman waiting.

"Apologies for my tardiness," I said at the sight of her long dark hair and slender frame. Isabel was standing outside The Blue Reserve café one hour later.

She turned and once again, my breath caught. It was the third day in a row I was seeing this woman and yet the mere sight of her still took my breath away. She looked positively radiant and yet somewhat reserved and cautious. She was wearing a black dress that angled on one end, barely touching her knee, and a sapphire blue cardigan. And of course, that warm smile that was always too polite and formal.

Like I was a client or something.

Surely, she'd thought we were on better terms than *that*.

"I take it you haven't eaten lunch yet?" I asked, holding out an arm.

Her face fell and she glanced at her watch. "Well, I..."

"I didn't think so; of course a busy woman like yourself

couldn't possibly stop to eat lunch. I bet your assistant grabs you a usual salad assortment from somewhere *very* specific."

Isabel seemed comically offended by my assumption but still gave me her hand. "That is *not* true. I like variety just as much as anyone."

I tugged her closer with a grin to the point where she'd nearly stumbled, like she hadn't expected or been prepared for the playful gesture.

"Ever been to Grainy Tavern?"

"I have not…" she shook her head and turned back to the coffee shop, now halfway up the block. "I really thought I'd just buy you that coffee and be on my way."

Why does she keep doing that?

I narrowed my eyes at her. "I don't believe you'd come all this way to do just that." I challenged, surprising myself, it was definitely something I rarely did with women.

"I'm not coming from very far."

At this point, the vagueness came at no surprise. But I decided to try my luck and toyed with her anyway.

"Now I know your business dealings are on the lower west side." I winked, stopping us in front of the restaurant and motioning toward it.

She released a breath and turned to me, staring me down with a 'well played' smirk. "Fine, I'll have lunch with you. But I'm not answering any questions about my business dealings." She held up a finger. "Or falling for any more traps."

I nodded once in agreement to her terms and held back a laugh. "It's only fair."

Isabel offered the same swift nod before breezing past me and into the restaurant without another hint of hesitation.

The hostess seated us at a table for two by the window and handed us two lunch menus.

"Are you going to suggest something here for me as well?"

Isabel asked after taking a moment to scan over the menu. A menu I barely glanced at. Heck nothing seemed to exist when she was sitting inches from me and there was so much about her I wanted to know. Like where he hell she came from, how she knew Donovan, because I swore I knew each and every one of his clients and heavens knew this was no personal friend of his.

I grinned and tried to look lost in my own menu. "That depends if you'll start mumbling cravings again." When she didn't respond, I glanced up finding rosier cheeks and a small smile.

"Smoked salmon bowl." Isabel set her menu down.

"Great choice."

"It has capers, so I'm sold."

"Salty foods. Impressive." I glanced at her.

"Most women are into salty foods," she said with a matter of fact.

"But they don't show it."

"That's silly. What? Do they order a bowl of kale and just for color, some cherry tomatoes?"

I laughed. She'd met half the woman I'd been on dates with. Which, while an average male my age might consider too few, I considered too many.

"So how do you know Donovan Hayes...and or Elaine?" I asked, setting both our menus down to signal the waitress we were ready to order.

"I don't."

I frowned. "I'm terribly sorry, are you not the gorgeous woman I had the pleasure of speaking with for seven whole minutes the other night?"

She shrugged and looked away, taking a sip of her water. "I crashed."

I laughed out loud. "A Donovan Hayes party? That wouldn't be possible."

"Okay I'm lying. I was insisted—invited," she corrected, shaking her head. "But it was very last minute."

"You'll be happy to know, everyone was invited last minute."

"You're kidding. How'd they pull it off?" The corner of her mouth turned up.

I let my eyes wander from Isabel for the first time. "I'm still trying to figure that out."

She arched a brow.

"If you ever need event planners, Starr-Bright Events are your people, by the way," I threw in.

"What about you?" she asked almost instantly.

"I'm in short-term investments."

"Stocks?"

"Businesses."

She watched me, waiting for more. So I went into a very high-level description of my work and my investments. I didn't bore her with details. "They let me in cheap to save themselves. As soon as they manage to make it on their own, I pull out with my original investment plus a percentage of current assets."

"That's brilliant."

I smiled. Her compliment seemed so genuine. My smile faltered when I then remembered our deal of keeping *her* business private so instead of asking, I waved down the waiter to give him our order and turned back to find Isabel studying me intently.

I tilted my head when I could tell that she'd finally reached a question she seemed hesitant to ask. As though searching for the right words.

It wasn't a talent; it was more of a curse. I couldn't remember the last time I had a conversation without reading someone's undertone and expression, even the ones they tried to hide. It was part of the reason I rarely dated for too long.

The women in my life either thought too much or not enough.

"What was the inspiration of your first save?"

"My first save?"

"Every superhero has an origin story. What's yours?"

I raised a charmed brow to her analogy. It was one that I'd never considered. In fact, I thought the opposite. Often my involvement resulted in layoffs or smaller spaces, taking a few steps back in order to come back stronger. And most of the time, they did. Once in top shape, those firms worked on expanding. But only the stronger ones who learned where they went wrong in the first place would end up flourishing toward the end.

"That sounds like a second date response." I winked again.

Isabel eyed me and twisted her lips. "Hmm...do I really need to know that badly?" she mumbled.

I laughed, nearly choking on my water. "I worked for a firm whose sole mission was to dissolve smaller companies that were in the way of larger ones from growing. In other words, these mom and pops were keeping the rich from getting richer."

"And your job was to aid in the growth of monopolies."

I frowned at her harsh description of what I used to be a part of and unfortunately, couldn't disagree. "I watched my firm aid in hostile takeovers, negotiating buyouts with downright threats, and... well, I didn't like it." I arched my back slightly to allow a young man to place our food out in front of us.

"I was sent on a mission to get a CEO to sign fifty-one percent of the company to another, with the advice that their future didn't look good. And the guy—knowing his company's undeniable fate—refused. Said his father wouldn't want it sold. He'd figure out a way to get business moving again, and if not, he'd go down trying." I focused on my water glass, turning it in place as I remembered the Blake Brothers accounting firm. Truth was, back then, I couldn't stop thinking about Richard Blake and his small but loyal staff. Real people. They were a family and would have been demolished by selling out.

I glanced up at Isabel's waiting, genuine eyes and shrugged. "I wanted to help. I looked into their finances and business plans and figured out a way. My boss, a certain Donovan Hayes we both know well, refused to listen so I invested my own money."

She swallowed but seemed to recover quickly at something I'd said. "Didn't that cost Hayes Enterprises an account?"

"It *did*, but Donovan was more interested in the turn out. I knew it was a risk, but I saw what they were doing wrong. Anyway, they thrived over the next fiscal year, and I pulled out less than two years later with enough profits to make it on my own, saving small businesses without ruining lives."

Well, without ruining too many lives.

"What about you and Donovan?"

I chuckled. "I'm one of his favorite people. He acts like I still work for him. Occasionally he'll tip me off to a company that has potential, or just not worth his time. I prefer to think the former."

Isabel watched me with curiosity and maybe even a little fascination, as if discovering something new about me that she appreciated. "A superhero in Armani ties."

I hesitated. "Except, I'm not always very heroic to those I rescue."

"They never are," Isabel waved a hand and picked up her fork.

"Aren't they?"

"No. Most of the time, superheroes are arrogant and dismissive and they almost always think they know best. The *sure* way to win." She shrugged. "But most importantly, they learn a valuable lesson at the end."

She was spot on until the lesson at the end part. I bit the tip off a breadstick and then pointed it at her. "You watch too much television."

Isabel tossed her head back with laughter. "I'm not kidding. It's a Hollywood formula. You've seen it. The hero always makes the wrong judgment of how to stop the villain because of...let's use the example of *rash decisions*...because he didn't stop to listen to his knowledgeable—but not as powerful—sidekick. Who typically ends up being right, because of something our *hero* was not seeing to begin with."

I listened with amusement to her analogy. There was a grin on my face that I couldn't suppress, no matter how hard I tried. "So, I'm no hero after all?" I tried to sound disappointed, even though I never believed I was for a second.

She sat up and continued with a hint of enjoyment. "Oh no no, you are still very much the hero. You have to remember; without you—the one with the power to save others—in your case an excess of funds—there would be no one to save the victims of...the bigger fish of Manhattan." She shrugged, popping a cherry tomato in her mouth. Which, all in itself, almost made me lose focus.

Dammit. I was doing it again; *staring* at her. I rarely found anyone that captivated me. And what the hell was it that she'd just said? Painting what I did as some necessary evil for all the good I do? I couldn't figure out why it meant so much to me. I almost wanted her to say it again— the validation of my often ruthlessness.

It was rare for people to see me as anything other than a man who only saw dollar signs in his ventures.

9

ELLE

"So, I'll stand by my word that I won't ask you about your business dealings. But can I at least ask what you do and how you know so much about what makes up a superhero?"

I sighed, knowing full well that I needed to answer that question—and how strange it would be if I didn't. Not to mention suspicious as hell.

I could do it. I could tell him that I worked for the firm that was hired to plan his friend's anniversary party. And that if he had spotted me an hour earlier that night, he would have found me in black ankle pants with traces of powdered sugar on them, a fanny pack, my super worn but still oh-so-comfortable Toms and barely there makeup.

I could just tell him that, and something told me he'd probably get a kick out of it.

Yeah, out of you being a joke.

No. He'd find it hilarious. I was sure of it.

Yep, and he'll probably share this "funny" story with his best bud—Donovan Hayes. And sure the Scott Weston I was having the pleasure of dining with might be one hell of a charmer, but who knew the real him behind it all?

The man I'd read about seemed like he could do some serious damage to my career.

Or…he could be the hero I hadn't been waiting for.

Don't be ignorant, Elle.

Even if I wouldn't get fired for being caught out on the floor, I'd blow my whole "party-goer damage control" ensemble that will no doubt get around. My new colleagues would mock the hell out of me for months for my back up plan when things couldn't be taken care of *off* the floor.

"Vendor management," I answered half truthfully.

"And what do you do with these vendors?

"Negotiate."

His green eyes locked on mine with an unreadable expression. Then, a slow crooked grin began to spread across his face. "Spoken like a true businesswoman."

"How's that?"

"With little to no detail."

I was by no means ashamed of who I was or what I did for a living. Not in the least. I'd had a successful career that in no way would ever make me a millionaire, but I enjoyed my job. I enjoyed working a color palate and running with not-your-everyday themes just as much as anyone else in the business. The last-minute changes that sent everyone into hysterics while I problem solved—that was getting closer to why I went into the business.

Not just the typical "florist is late" and the "bakery delivered the wrong cake" kind of problems. I had a reputation of making *miracles* happen. There was a solution for nearly every scenario. And when there wasn't; that was when I had the most fun. To put it simply; I loved it when shit went wrong. My old boss, Ron once joked; "I'd love to see what you'd do in a runaway bride situation," Clearly implying if I'd go as far as taking the bride's place just to save the day.

Needless to say, and considering I was twenty-nine, single with no children; my career was *everything*. Busy as a bee was how I liked it.

And now...*him.*

I huffed out a short laugh. I hated to admit I enjoyed these encounters—all of them. The last three days. In a row. I couldn't remember the last time I saw a man that often that I was actually *dating*. Much less, someone I needed to stay the hell away from.

Even though I teased him about it, there was nothing heartless about the man; at least not when he smiled. And he had a show-stopping smile—the kind that made a woman focus on it and stop breathing for a good four seconds while everything else became hazy. His voice was smooth and always seemed game for anything I threw his way.

And had I really called him *Superman?*

I shook my head and rubbed my eyelids.

Charming to all hell...and not meant for you.

Someone snapped their fingers near my desk making me jump.

"I'm sorry hun, didn't mean to startle you." Bobby didn't sound apologetic at all.

"There's a team meeting in the main conference room. Five minutes."

I clicked on my calendar. "I don't remember seeing…"

"Just popped up. Starr asked me to make the rounds—make sure everyone is aware and can accommodate." He looked me up and down. "Good thing you got back from your extended lunch break in time," he sneered and sauntered off.

What was that supposed to mean? I never had to justify my lunch breaks before to anyone. Least of all, a co-worker who was by no means someone I reported to.

Moments later, I stepped in to the larger of the two conference rooms on the entire floor. The room held an extended shiny wooden table and was surrounded by at least a dozen black leather chairs. All of which had already been occupied. I lined myself against the back wall along with a few other employees. Every soul in the room was babbling away. But the undertone was easy to pick up.

They were nervous. Exchanging rumors heard.

Some asking about a man they'd seen walking in and out of the office a few times in the last two weeks.

Mimi's warning email from the other day came into mind.

The chatter quieted almost instantly when Starr and Dean walked into the room a moment after.

"Thank you all for meeting on short notice. We appreciate you—" Dean started.

Mimi hurried in and muttered a quick apology as Starr shot her a look.

Dean clapped his hand once. "I believe that's just about everyone, now. Let's just get started. As you all know, Starr-Bright Events has been moving up to be well known and respected as one of the industry's lead non-profit charity event planners. Now the fact that we offer non-profit services is what got us the recognition." He glanced at Starr. "That said, it is important we remember that it is not *all* we are. Our organizational reputation for corporate and social events is just as important to maintain." Dean paused for a deep breath. "Starr and I noticed that over the last two years, nearly sixty percent of our staff—yes, you guys—picked up *solely* non-profit charity events during the holiday season."

Either I was imagining it, or at that moment, approximately sixty percent of the room shifted and glanced around the room.

Starr took a step forward. "As grateful as we are to your commitment to prioritizing these charities that depend on us —it is simply unacceptable to make them your *only* focus during the holiday season," she added. "We have been losing hundreds of projects for large-scale events because we're just not making them a priority."

"Well, that is changing this year." Dean stepped in again. "In order for us to continue doing well and helping charities run their events at little to no cost, we need to back up our revenue. So, starting November, when the calls start coming in, unless you have a profitable corporate or social event project, you are strictly prohibited from accepting any non-profit events until January."

One of the staff members I remembered as Brian called out. "So what are we supposed to do when they call us to plan their event again this year? Returning customers is another thing the firm takes pride in, isn't it?"

Good for you, Brian.

"Yeah, like the Children's Hospital Santa Party," the blond sitting next to him called out.

"Or Hillard's gift wrapping bash?" Someone from the other side of the room called out.

Dean held his hands up. "No one will get turned away. You will forward the request to either myself or Starr and we will assign it accordingly. Look we're not trying to take annual events away from you." He glanced at Starr again. "We're just aware that these nonprofits are very easy to get, especially in December, therefore we haven't been working as hard to get those profitable ones on our calendar. And that is where we need our focus to be this season."

A few more simultaneous call outs and mumbled chatter

began before Starr appeared to become frustrated and spoke. "If anyone has a problem they'd like to bring up, then maybe we can separately discuss if this is the right place for you."

Silence instantly filled the room. Finally, Dean thanked everyone in a softer voice to counteract the mood, and promised a follow up meeting in the weeks to come.

I walked back to my desk. A few folks had gathered around cubicles, whispering away. I was still too new to join any one of them. Not that I could say much anyway. Dean and Starr made a great point and the fact that people frowned at it as if they'd just canceled prom night, told me I wasn't at Brightman anymore. Where we were all professionals. And thrived at a good challenge.

I sat at my desk for barely a second before seeing Starr stride into the elevator with her coat.

It was rare for Dean to be in his office alone. And given his recent speech, I needed to have a few words with my new boss. His demands were of little concern to me since I *never* had a problem landing a deal. But *something* was up that he wasn't quite sharing. And that was a big problem for me.

After losing my job at a week's notice, the last thing I needed was secrecy if the company was in trouble. Which Dean failed to mention when he offered me a position here.

Before even giving myself a moment to think about how to approach this, I was at his door. "Dean?" His elbow was resting on his desk and he rubbed his forehead.

His eyes shot to me. "Elle, not a good time," he mumbled.

I didn't assume it was. But to hell if that was going to stop me. His firm was clearly facing a downturn and after what I'd just been through, I was supposed to just ignore that?

"You know, Dean," I started after letting myself into the office and closing the door behind me. "I wish I could have said 'not a good time' when I lost my job before reaching retirement, but life doesn't always work that way." I shrugged with my palms pointed up, and gave a polite grin.

For a moment, Dean seemed as though he was going to throw me the *I don't know what you're talking about* card, but when I shot him my cold glare that I knew Dean remembered from when we argued over who got to keep the booking at Conrad Ballroom, he blew out a strong breath and stood.

Dean's eyes flashed outside the glass walls just before he pointed to the chair in front of his desk. "Have a seat."

I didn't intend on having a full sit-down discussion, but followed his instruction and planted my butt on one of the chairs, silently wondering if I should have just kept my mouth shut.

But as Ron Brightman would tell you, you'd think I was running the place the way I'd always interfere with business management.

Dean dropped back down into his chair and started shuffling paper on his desk, frowning at them and mumbling quietly. "I'm making it look like we're discussing a project, so please play along." He shot me a look and then pointedly glanced outside his glassed-in office where certain staff members may be prone to notice a non-project-related conversation.

"Elle, I know how Brightman used to operate. His entire staff had a quota. And not just on the jobs his staff pitched and accepted, but also in the ones he made his employees *turn down*."

That was true. Ron was solely focused on being the lead in the industry by turning down mediocre parties so that his talented staff only worked on high profile events.

I didn't show any sign off agreement and waited for more.

"He was a man who cared more about the name he made for himself rather than the numbers," Dean continued.

I raised a brow and shrugged since I found no fault in that.

"I guess that would be an accurate description of my old boss, yes."

"Well, we don't work that way here. We don't have quotas, we accept every job no matter how small or who the client is. And while Starr and I may not have money to throw away like Brightman did, we've done everything we could to get to be the third best in the city," he paused and took a breath, probably because he realized he was raising his voice.

"I want you to know that none of what I said in there affects you. Your capabilities are highly valued here, and while no one else might appreciate your history in the industry, I do."

"Thanks, but I'm not concerned about what I'm able to bring; I'm more curious about what you think you're accomplishing by changing expectations on your team and not giving them a reason why."

He leaned back in his chair; clearly not expecting to be challenged and glared at me as though I were an intern implying I should be put up for vice president. "Your concern is appreciated," he finally stated. "If there's nothing else, I need to prepare for a meeting." He straightened in his chair, adjusting his jacket.

I stood, accepting my current position—as the nobody I apparently was—and walked out.

10

SCOTT

"I have to hand it to you, Weston, I thought you'd bail on Levy—and what's her name's thing by now. But you're darn set on bailing them out instead," Donovan said that Friday afternoon at Smith's Hotel bar around the corner from Hayes Enterprises. It was an end of the week ritual for us ever since I became a senior executive at H.E. Mainly it was Hayes' way of winding down and talking about the week's biggest wins and deals. And it was something we continued long after I left his firm.

With the way the man treated me, you'd have thought he never had children. But he did. He and Elaine had three successful children. Though neither wanted any part of real estate capitalism or anything else Hayes Enterprises did. After his two older daughters went to med school, he held out hope for his son, who was the youngest. Alfred ended up moving to L.A. two years ago to become a filmmaker.

"They stand for the good of humanity," I said dryly. Knowing exactly how that sounded to my old mentor.

"What they stand for isn't making them money. And it'll make you lose yours."

"I'm not putting that much in." I lied.

"Still. It's not nothing. Every dollar will be a waste."

Why do I bother with this man anymore?

I felt like I knew the answer to that. But I'd deny it to every living soul. Donovan took more of a chance on me from day one than my own father ever had.

"Thought they'd win you over after Elaine's party."

He sneered. "Oh yeah, blowing up some balloons and calling a caterer is nothing short of impossible. And they came through without a hitch!" Donovan pointed a mocking finger at me. "Impressive."

I rolled my eyes and glanced at the old man's glass. Still about a third full, which meant another good half hour of enduring his cynical and interfering ways.

I did well on my own and didn't need his negativity. But Donovan had been a great mentor and gave me opportunities I would always be grateful for. Regardless of how he treated most of his employees and how scared shitless I was when I first walked into his office nearly ten years ago, he saw something in me he valued and had kept me as his right hand ever since.

"You're on your own next time you need a favor." I stirred the contents of my own glass before taking a hefty sip.

"I did you a favor," he countered. "You wanted to test the waters and I happened to have a time sensitive matter."

I was silent for a moment, then caved, choosing to take advantage of the topic. "Did you know everyone at the party?"

Donovan's amused eyes watched me. The ones I hated when I gave away more than I'd intended. "Mostly," Donovan replied simply with a slight grin. I inhaled but didn't say anymore. "Curious about a certain dame in a black lace dress?" he pried.

"You know her?"

"Look, Elaine cohorts with a handful of females from the club, she doesn't really do much else, so I had to fill the ballroom. I asked Kat to pull some business contacts and invite them to the social gathering. Served two purposes." Donovan weighed out his hands. He always looked to see how things would help his business and was quick to eliminate everything that didn't. A quality I admired.

I shook my head. "No, she had to be a friend of Elaine's."

Donovan chuckled. "She was no friend of Elaine's."

"She had to be, I think I saw her leave a note by her chair before she left."

Donovan jerked back. "What's gotten into you? We never talk about women when we're drinking."

I never talk about women at all.

I licked my lips, irritated.

Donovan must have caught it. "Alright look, she was probably involved in one of my transactions in some way at some point," he shrugged and then his eyes drifted.

"What?"

"Woulda thought I'd remember someone like her."

I snickered and stared at the rocks glass in my hand. It had been a long week—and three days since I'd last seen her. Her long dark hair, full rosy lips with a hypnotic smile that crept into my head more than I cared for. She had once again refused to give me a phone number, a last name or what she did for a living.

It was cool. She was different. She valued her privacy. Most importantly, she wasn't clingy with expectations.

Luckily, she also agreed to meet me again Saturday night. This time, a date was definitely implied. And I intended to find out much more about the only woman I couldn't stop thinking about.

11

ELLE

THIS WEEK WAS MOSTLY QUIET AT THE OFFICE. SINCE STARR AND Dean's threat, everyone had been seemingly busy and insanely focused. There was a lot less chatter and much more business-related calls. I hadn't heard so many pitches and follow up calls since my days at Brightman.

Brightman, where every single employee genuinely meant business. We were the most highly respected professionals within the industry. No one ever had a problem landing an event. Instead, we competed over who got the biggest.

I poured myself a glass of red wine. It always helped calm my nerves. And it was exactly what I needed on this quiet Friday evening. I planted myself in my favorite corner of the sofa, pulled a throw cover over my legs and flipped through on-demand movies.

I found myself wishing it was Saturday night. Which wasn't good. I was supposed to be sitting here thinking of ways to get out of my date with Scott Weston. Not daydreaming about seeing him again.

A loud buzzer from the hall jerked me out of my daze. I set down my glass and pressed the intercom.

"It's me. I brought food." I heard before smiling at the voice and holding down the button to let her in.

I glanced around the small apartment. I lived on the third level of a walk-up on the lower east side. When you made your work your life, living anywhere outside the city didn't make sense. It was pricey, but worth it. Not the apartment— the commute. And getting around quickly was essential.

I lived in something slightly better than a dump but was nowhere near the quality of the luxury rentals they were starting to build across the street from my sad little brownstone.

Regardless, it was home and I'd made it my own. Art that hung on my walls came from event giveaways. Each piece reminding me of the nights' success.

I evened out the throw pillows on my pale blue tufted sofa, picked up two articles of clothing from the floor I'd slipped out of after work today and tossed them to the side when I heard footsteps walking up the hall.

I pulled the door open for my best friend Char, and she walked up in her high heels with a smile too wide to be real and a big brown paper bag.

"Thai?"

Hmm. Char's comfort food. I narrowed my eyes at her. "Why?"

Char blew out an exasperated breath. "Mark broke up with me."

"What?"

"He said his parents didn't like me."

"You mean his mother didn't like you."

"I haven't been known to be moms' favorite, Elle, you know that." Char walked the bag across the foyer and into my open kitchen. "And he told me all this after I reheated take out, because, as usual, he was late."

"Would you rather he waited till after you fed him?"

"I guess not. So, hungry?"

"For secondhand Thai? Sign me up."

Char laid out cartons on the coffee table while I poured a glass of red for her, covertly happy for the company.

"How's the new job?" she asked.

I sighed. "Impossibly bearable."

Char raised a brow.

"I just mean it's impossible some days, but I need the work."

"Hmm…"

"What?"

"It's just this job never used to be *work* for you," Char pointed out.

"Tell me about it. It's not the same. Now they're making everyone hunt down high paying events to work on along with the non-profits they typically book through the holiday season. Which clearly means that they need to start bringing in revenue and fast. Chasing down work to keep working is not what I signed up for." My cheeks began to burn with fury all over again.

Char watched me. "Why did you take this job again?"

"Besides being on the verge of eviction? I'm good at it. I'm a good planner; a problem solver. And I am certain there is a better way than sending their entire staff on a project hunt frenzy this time of year."

"Have you tried sharing your thoughts?" Char dug into a dumpling.

"I don't have any ideas if no one tells me what's going on. Besides, Dean would hardly listen to me. And why should he? My job has already been threatened twice since I started."

Char frowned at me. And I immediately felt guilty, rambling on about my first world problems while she just had her heart broken. "But enough about work. Tell me what happened with Mark."

"I just did. He ended it."

"That's it?" I didn't know why I even asked. Char didn't talk about her feelings. Mostly because she rarely gave men much of her heart to begin with. If any of it at all. She mentally and emotionally held them at arm's length. It was no wonder his mother picked up on it right off the bat.

"That's it—maybe after the second glass, I'll have more to say, but right now, I need distraction."

Boy, do I have one for you...

"I don't know what's going on with me, Char. I've never been so unhappy and so afraid to lose work."

"Welcome to the real-world, Elle. Not everyone has a fantasy job where their boss treated them like a partner and every project felt like walking on air."

I took another sip to keep me from coming out of my skin. Then I thought of the one bright side to the entire disaster my new job ended up being.

Scott.

Charmingly sexy and completely off-limits. Somehow, during our three separate encounters, I managed to break away from his inviting charisma.

And unfortunately for me, on every occasion, it was because I needed to get back to work—that was *my* lifestyle. Not his.

"What was that? Where'd you go?" Char broke into my thoughts pryingly.

I cracked, knowing damn well, I could use the advice. "Remember that party I worked last Sunday?"

"You mean the 'make it or break it; take one'? Yes."

I went on to describe nearly every detail of meeting the devastatingly gorgeous billionaire at the Hayes event. And then again the next morning. Followed by the trick lunch date the day after that. And… the one step too far. "We're going out tomorrow night."

"Wow. I'm in the wrong business to meet men." Char was a lawyer and a badass one at that. Besides being tall, blond and basically a knockout, she was also quite intimidating. So the fact that she didn't meet the right men had zero to do with where she worked. I too would be afraid to go anywhere near her when she had her high heels, black rimmed glasses and a vibe that screamed 'I will crush you in there'.

"That was stupid, right? I shouldn't have agreed to see him again."

"See him again? You are downright dating the man, Elle." Char sat back as if assessing the situation. "Who thinks you're what again?"

"I never said. He just…assumed."

"Assumed what?" Her sharp tone made me flinch a little.

"That I was one of the guests at the event—which was full of high-powered executives and socialites. He probably thinks I'm a VIP of some major organization…oh hell, I don't know what he thinks, Char."

"I *wonder* whatever would make him think that." Her prosecutor tone was in full effect.

"I am not a fraud," I practically shouted. "I never lied." I turned away from Char's glare. "I just let him believe something that isn't true."

Char tilted her head to the side in her best effort to show compassion. "Sweety, if he's that into you, it shouldn't matter."

"It does matter. For so many reasons. And I don't even know why I agreed to this date. I was running to get back to work. I had to end it somehow. He kind of sprung Saturday night toward the end of lunch. What was I supposed to say, sorry this was incredible, but I can't see you again?"

"Of course not. But now, you don't have to rush out to get back to work. Now you can tell him the hilarious misunderstanding."

In a matter of five seconds, I managed to consider all the horrendous outcomes of telling Scott that I was nothing more than the party planner dressed above her means. And when he noticed me, I was merely trying to avoid disaster by clearing an accidental raspberry from Elaine's dessert plate. He would most certainly laugh. And not in a good way. He'd probably run and tell his friend-for-life Donovan Hayes—who for some reason, was an extremely important client to Dean and Starr; and would no doubt fill them in on this 'hilarious misunderstanding'.

And I would not only lose my job, but would become the laughing stock of the office. And if there was anything that I couldn't bear more than anything, it was the wrong kind of attention.

I breathed out a shaky breath, which made Char pull herself off the sofa and take my wine.

"Whoa. Hey. It's not that big a deal. Listen, if you can't do it—you can't do it. No need to break a sweat here, hun. Just… be careful."

I sank into the couch. "Char. I think I just realized what a mess this could be. Event planning is my life. I don't know anything else and my reputation would be toast. And not the kind you put butter on and eat; the kind you throw out because you left it in the toaster too long and it's burnt to a crisp."

Char shrugged. "Some people like burnt toast. Some people might use it as breadcrumbs on salmon. Breaded salmon is a big step up from toast with butter."

"What?"

"I'm saying when you're no longer cut out for what you think you're made for, there's something bigger and better out there for you."

I grimaced. "So, can I still go on my date tomorrow?"

"By all means. Just be careful."

12

SCOTT

Saturday night, I waited for Isabel inside *Cooks Place*. The small, secluded restaurant was a best kept secret on the lower east side. Somehow, I thought Isabel would appreciate a more private yet equally high-end atmosphere.

I tended to read people well, and one thing I picked up on my mystery woman was that she preferred to keep a low profile.

She hadn't given me a phone number or taken mine for reasons that she merely spoke around that Tuesday at the Tavern. But thankfully, she accepted my dinner invitation.

"When can I see you again?" I had asked after our lunch.

Isabel had appeared to be considering. I wasn't used to that; *anticipating* a response from a woman. But I couldn't just let her disappear. And something told me she would. I let her get away that first night and was miraculously given another chance the morning after. So I had to think of something.

"Okay, I propose this. Either you give me your phone number, or meet me Saturday night at eight o'clock at Cook's

Place downtown. Should I sweep you off your feet for a fourth time, you give me your phone number."

"Is there a third option?" she had asked, pursing those luscious lips I couldn't wait to taste.

"Something tells me you've already made up your mind about Saturday night. So, I'm nixing option three. And thank God because I really didn't like option three." I flashed her my cocky all-knowing grin.

And she took the bait. Even though it completely felt like *I* was the one on the hook.

She'd blushed, stood and simply said, "Cook's Place... eight o'clock."

I smiled and nodded once at her before she walked out of the restaurant and raced off again to wherever the hell that woman fell out of.

And then my vision of her faded. Replaced suddenly by a burn in my chest at the thought that she wouldn't show. Isabel wasn't terribly late, but this feeling, this *disappointment* bothered me, and that fact in itself was enough for me to consider leaving before she had a chance to break me.

I pulled myself off from the padded bench just as the host, an elderly man in a tuxedo, approached, pulling out a chair across the table.

"Mr. Weston, your party has arrived." He moved aside and there she stood. Her expression blank, yet there was the faintest sign of a question in her brows.

Her flowy black dress came down just above her knees. An orange scarf draped over her shoulders.

"Isabel." I considered standing but refrained. I didn't typically do that with anyone else. For some reason, the chivalrous move felt natural when it came to her.

Her...whose last name, job and phone number would remain a mystery for God knew how long.

"Were you leaving?" she asked.

"I was considering it."

"You're honest to a fault I see," Isabel took her seat and glanced at the wine on the side of the table.

"Why would it be a fault? Wine?"

"Yes, please." Her response came almost too quickly.

I poured a small amount for her to try. "If you don't like it, we can get something a little less dry, but this one..."

"It's delicious." Her expression suggested she wasn't appeasing me, either. She twisted the bottle at the base to look at the label and looked up at me questionably. "You're telling me you're an honest businessman?"

"There's no other way for me, unfortunately. I don't like the idea of having to remember who I said what to." I took a sip myself. "Nobody's worth a lie."

Her brows creased. And then a slight nod, as if she were analyzing me.

When she stayed silent, I elaborated. "Telling a lie implies you care about what people think. Or that their feelings matter to you."

"Ah. So, you've never told your mother that you *meant* to call?"

I blew out an audible breath and watched her with some amusement.

"What?" She jerked back.

"We've been on this date for five minutes and you're already asking about my parents? Rushing things a bit, *Just Isabel?*"

"Ooh...oh you're right. I should be careful—you might decide to flee if I get too clingy. Just so I know, where do you draw the line?"

I laughed.

Her eyes shined in the dim light as she smiled brightly at me. "No, really. Tell me. I'm genuinely curious. Calling you on an hourly basis? A singing telegram on our two-week-aver-sary?" she laughed along.

I watched her for a moment. "I draw the line at lying. I don't tell them and I don't tolerate them."

I noticed her swallow and set down her wine glass, which made me frown. *Shit.* I was so used to the upper hand and setting people straight off the bat, that I answered her without a second thought. I hadn't meant to offend her.

"I am so sorry. I just crashed our party, didn't I? Here, have more wine." I topped off her glass. This seemed to win her over at the start of the night.

She simply smiled and held the stem of her glass out to me. "Thank you." She attempted to regain composure and looked at me. Despite the hesitation in her eyes, I noticed how beautiful she was. Gold tinted lights illuminated her skin. Her dark hair rested over her shoulders, highlighting the sheer beauty of her face.

She took a long sip and a deep breath, shooting a polite smile my way before lifting the small menu off the side of her plate. "What do you like here?" her tone suddenly formal.

Just as she asked, a server approached, placing our appetizers on the table.

"I preordered the apps. I hope you don't mind," I told her. But it didn't do much to her mood. She simply nodded and placed down her menu. Her eyes everywhere but me.

I'd lost her. Had I really screwed this up in the first ten minutes? I could fix this. But how? Trying for a woman wasn't something I ever needed or wanted to do.

In this case though, it was both.

"Can I ask you something?"

Her eyes darted up.

"Would you go into business with an old friend?"

The question seemed to have thrown her off. "That seems odd. Would this friend be someone I've always been close with and trust or have I not seen this friend in some time and happen to now be involved in a business transaction with them?"

I was impressed with how quickly she followed. "The latter."

Her eyes wandered as she considered. "You're asking the wrong person. I've always put business first."

I tapped my fork on the lined table, satisfied with her response. "Actually, I think I've asked the right person. And thank you for confirming my initial thought."

"Ah, so this wasn't hypothetical?"

"Not for me at least," I answered.

"Well, to tell you the truth, I'm going through something similar. I just uh…signed a deal with someone I considered… more than an acquaintance but not exactly an old friend."

I raised a brow since she appeared to be regretful of the decision. "And?"

"It's not easy." Her eyes wandered up and around. "He can be very…secretive about his business plans and I don't like to work that way, you know?"

"Sounds like you might need to cut that tie loose."

"Also, not easy. This…uh, deal, happens to be my…highest paid, currently."

I watched her, running a thumb across my bottom lip, taking a moment to try to make sense of what she was saying. Not because it didn't make sense but because she was talking around something. Like coding certain words.

I needed to snap the hell out of this before I say something stupid again.

"Anything I can help with?"

She gave me a hard stare while shifting the pendant on her necklace back and forth.

"Sorry, forgot the rules."

She rolled her eyes. "I don't have rules. I just don't like to mix business with pleasure. If I tell you what I do, it would be hard for you not to think about it."

I leaned forward. "I'm super intrigued now."

"I'm just Isabel. Single, yes. Live in New York City, of course, and I tend to dress for success."

"Well, I thank you for those three wonderful facts, Isabel— and full disclosure, I only found one of those facts kind of wonderful."

She blushed and I grinned in response. I knew I could turn it around.

"This dish was truly delicious," she commented.

"I'm glad you liked it."

Something dark flashed in her eyes and her smile faded. It was so sudden and whatever it was, it was bothering Isabel. She lifted her palms abruptly and shook her head. "I don't know why I said that."

I drew back. "So you didn't like it."

"No, I did." She looked back at me from her plate. "I don't think it was truly delicious. I thought it was very good. I especially enjoyed the olives. And the wine. And the breadsticks."

Normally I would have frowned at such peculiar behavior, but everything about Isabel just intrigued me, and I only wanted to hear more. A slow smile spread across my face as she went on.

"I don't think I've ever uttered the words *truly delicious*, that's not who I am, to be honest," I laughed at myself and leaned back in my chair. "And quite frankly, I'm pretty full and I think I would prefer to just walk with you and maybe even stop for mint chocolate ice-cream."

ELLE

My heart beat like a thunderbolt. Why the hell did I let Char get in my head? I—no *Isabel* had always been smooth, swift and easy with Scott. Now I let Char's stupid condition of being myself ruin everything. I really wasn't hungry for an entrée or anything else for that matter. Although this place was so perfect and romantic, I'd just felt claustrophobic suddenly. But jeez, did I have to insist on ice cream?

Sure you don't want to add that you'd like it in a cone, Elle?

But to my surprise, the man didn't flinch. He barely took his eyes off me. Scott lifted a finger slightly, and the waiter was at the edge of our table within seconds.

I wanted to bury my head in quicksand. I'd managed to screw up a date with the man of—well, someone else's dreams.

Scott slipped a few bills to the waiter. "This should cover it. Thank you."

"Thank you, Sir." The waiter began to reach for the plates, when he noticed Scott glare at him and scurried off.

I was pretty sure I stopped breathing when Scott stood. But then he reached out a hand and spoke softly, "I know just the place."

With my hand in his, Scott crossed us to the west side of the street to hail a cab going downtown. He asked the driver to take us to Hudson River Park, which was beautiful during the day, but I'd never been there at night. Knowing the city as well as I did, I was sure it was just as amazing lit up from all over including the passing cruise ships and Jersey lights across the river.

Not much was said during our commute. But the fact that he didn't want the date to end was obvious and also somewhat nerve-wracking for me. What was I getting myself into?

"There's an ice cream shop up the path here. He's open all year."

I nodded. "I'm sorry about dinner," I blurted out, needing to break the ice.

He grinned. "Oh, please don't be. Perhaps it was a bit more formal than it needed to be."

"Perhaps," I repeated. "You've just been awfully quiet since…"

He glanced at me. "I've been trying to remember if Pat's Parlor has mint chocolate chip." His tone was casual.

I smiled, and probably blushed, I couldn't be sure. Tonight felt so strange. It was everything a first date should be and yet my thumping heart and guilty mind made it everything it *shouldn't* be.

"So why ice-cream? I mean don't get me wrong, it was a stellar idea. But just curious."

"Honestly, I don't like to eat much on a first date. I like to walk. The wine was spot on though. Sometimes I need it to…" I glanced at him, "feel more at ease...when I'm unsure of something. And the ice-cream, well," I shrugged, "that's just my sweet tooth."

Scott slowed to a stop beside me, turning me to face him. He gazed at me for a moment without a word. As if seeing me for the first time. I swallowed, trying so damn hard not to get lost in his eyes as they searched mine. Was he trying to figure out what the hell my issue was? Or was he as drawn to me as I apparently was to him.

Suddenly his hand fell from mine and he glanced away. Just when I thought I'd lost him for a moment, he wrapped a strong arm around my waist, scooped me off my feet and spun me onto the other side of the pavement.

"Thanks man," a now distant voice called.

A bicyclist had zoomed past us and would have crashed right into us in the dark had Scott not pulled us out of the way. Almost immediately, his eyes were glued back to mine but now, his arms were wrapped tightly around me. And not just protectively, it was almost possessively, as if he'd been waiting too damn long to hold me like this and had no plans to let me go anytime soon.

I released a breath. "Whew. Thanks, I um—" I swallowed, suddenly very much aware that my heart was hammering against his chest. And not because I could have been trampled a moment ago. But because I didn't want him to let go either.

"Are you alright?" he asked softly.

I nodded.

Scott lifted one hand off my waist and cupped my cheek, his thumb stroking my skin. "I want to kiss you. I *need* to kiss you, Isabel."

My eyes dipped slightly to his mouth and I pressed my lips together. Knowing I had no right. Not like this.

I nodded in spite of myself.

His fingers moved and wrapped the back of my neck, pulling me towards him and pressing his lips to mine. His grip was strong but even if it softened, the intensity wouldn't wane, because I felt glued to him with this kiss.

Our tongues collided and I moaned at the taste of him, melting into him, slipping my hands around him and gripping at his shirt. His fingers laced into my hair and pulled at the strands as his tongue circled around mine.

A bell chimed at a nearing distance and he pulled his lips off mine glancing in the direction, ready to shield me from any more reckless bikers. There were two this time and they rode right past us. One of which I thought I heard call out 'get a room'.

"Teenagers," Scott muttered.

I giggled. "Um, we're the ones making out in the park."

"Touché." He smiled, reached over to straighten out my hair and took my hand in his before walking us further up the path.

After taking a moment to recover from that kiss, which

apparently only *I* needed, I spoke. "What were we talking about?" My hand jerked to the bottom of my lip.

"Clearly something that made me want to take you in my arms and become one with you for an unfair forty-seven seconds."

I blushed as Scott's mouth widened on one side.

"But essentially you were telling me things that made you become real and no longer something that I imagined couldn't possibly be true." Scott looked out into the distance in front of us and we were silent for a moment.

"So tell me, Superman, why do you doubt going into business with an old friend?"

Scott shrugged. "I knew the guy on a personal level years ago and…I guess he thinks that he doesn't need to oblige with my expectations."

Okay, now I was genuinely confused. "So why work with him?"

He scoffed. "I'm an investor. I won't always trust or like who I work with, I just need to take interest in the business. And I expect my advice to be followed, since at the end of the day, I'm…"

"The one with the money?" I finished.

"I was going to put it differently, but yes." He winked. "I'm careful about who I choose to help and where I invest. Naturally, I need to believe there's potential for significant profit. I look into their competition, how much stronger they are than those competitors, and finally, what the hell these guys plan to do to keep up with the market," he paused. "I admire the service this firm provides to the public. They focus on those less fortunate." He glanced at me. "There aren't many who do and I'd hate it to be the reason that they drown. But the guy is just being very difficult to work with and he's refusing to follow some of my demands."

"Demands?"

"Of course, I need to make a few in order to ensure my investment isn't wasted. Just by looking at their statements and business strategy, I can tell where they're going wrong."

I nodded understandingly. "So, you know how their business should be running?"

Scott shrugged. "I have an idea...but it's hard to say when the owner is keeping me at arm's length."

"Well I think you should forget your history with the guy and follow your instincts on wanting to save the business for what they stand for. Or send one of your associates while you oversee things from a distance. But I don't think you should consider backing away. And who knows, there might be a hefty return."

"But in order to guarantee that, I require full cooperation and immediate fulfillment of my demands."

My head jerked back. "I don't understand, is this a hostile takeover?"

"Of course not. But what they're doing isn't working."

I threw my hands in the air. "Then find out why. *They* are the industry professionals. Not you. You might have the funds and good business knowledge, but they know what works for them. I think you need to find a way to work together."

"You're going to single handedly be the reason for my first loss."

I laughed, then paused. "Wait, your first?" My eyes bulged. Maybe the guy *did* know what he was talking about. Also, he didn't become a billionaire at age thirty by making all the wrong decisions. Still, it sounded extremely one-sided. "I suppose you already attempted to look into why they're sinking?"

"Overstaffed, for one," he murmured.

"Ha. I may have to agree with you there. Most entrepreneurs almost never know what their employees do. They'd probably be surprised to know just how uneven workloads can get."

Scott grinned through the side of his mouth. "Sounds like you see right through it."

"I tend to keep a closer eye than most," I admitted.

"Do you have a big team?" he asked.

I eyed him and decided not to dodge the innocent question. But it would still be a lie. I cringed. Keeping my promise to be myself was becoming more impossible every minute.

"No. I can honestly say, I do not."

Scott nodded and smiled favorably at me. "Perhaps that's why someone like you might never need saving." We reached the ice cream parlor and he pulled the door open for me. The place was brightly lit and cooler than it was outside at the end of October.

Scott approached the counter. "One mint chocolate chip, please, double scoop. And…" he placed a hand on the frosty glass enclosure and eyed the choices. "I'll have the Superman." He turned back to me and winked.

13

SCOTT

MONDAY MORNING THE ELEVATOR DOORS OPENED TO THE Hayes Enterprises floor. And I was not in the mood. Donovan had the nerve to require my presence at a client meeting.

"Hey Mr. Weston," Donovan's quirky assistant called as I rushed past her."

"Hey Kat," I mumbled, then backed up a few feet. "Who's he meeting with now?"

Her eyes bulged and she struggled to shrug. "His calendar says 'private.'"

I narrowed my eyes and stepped toward her. "Kat, you know I can tell when people are lying to me."

"Ms. Heart," she corrected quickly.

I cursed, pulled on my collar and took a deep solid breath as I redirected my anger at the door at the end of the hall.

"She's not here yet though," I heard Kat call behind me.

"With any luck, I'll be out of here before she is," I called back. Fists clenched and anger boiling under my jaw, I pushed

Donovan's door open and stormed into his office. "You called me here for a meeting with *Claudia?*"

Donovan leaned back in his chair, a sly smirk on his face. It irked the hell out of me every time I saw it. It only meant one thing. That Donovan needed me on a new deal.

And it had to end.

"Look I know how you feel about the woman. I just wanted you to hear her out. It sounds like she's got something we could both use."

"I'm not on the market for new projects. I've got my hands full."

"Then you need more hands." Donovan stood and crossed to his bar at the opposite end of the large room. He poured two glasses of scotch, tossed a thick ice cube in mine and handed it to me.

I crossed to the massive window at the far end of his office. Every time I did since last weekend, all I would do is wonder where in this busy bustling city she was. Isabel was all I could think about since I left her Saturday night. The evening had been one for the books; fun, pleasant, honest and more than anything, unpredictable. It wasn't often a woman was real with me. And if they were, I'd prefer they weren't. Isabel was rich with grace and warmth. She took my breath away. And that wasn't something I thought possible.

"Look, I'll sit in and advise if you need me to," I pointed my drink at Donovan, "for a fee," I added. Not that I needed Donovan's money, but whenever I felt like my time had been wasted on stupid shit, I'd get pissed and send Donovan and his assistant a bill for "advisory services".

"You know I'm good for it, Weston."

I turned back to the window. "So what's this about any—"

The door flew open as the devil let herself in. I glanced back to the window then faced the woman in the ironically appropriate red dress.

"Gentleman," Claudia practically sang out. Her long legs strode to the center of the room to greet Donovan with a kiss on the cheek. Her platinum blond hair was down today, nearly reaching her elbows. Large gray eyes, full lips I wished never kissed—or had wrapped around my cock, clouding my judgment. She was an alluring woman, no doubt, to anyone who didn't really know her.

"Hello Claudia," I muttered, in the most bored tone I could muster.

"Pleasure to see you as well, Scott." She turned to Donovan. "You know I don't like to waste time, so I'll get right to it. I have a proposition for you."

I knew her proposition plenty and refused them all; except for that one time. Which I'd lived to regret.

"I'm hosting a fashion show in December. We have the models lined up but I'm looking for a few more sponsors for the event. I need big names. No startups."

Donovan chuckled, "What kind of business do you think I'm running here, advertisement?"

"Surely you have clients in need of *great* exposure?" Claudia looked back and forth between the two of us.

"Don't look at me," I said, "My aim is to keep firms from losing their name, not spending an enormous amount of money for a spotlight at a fashion show."

Claudia was co-founder of *Empire Fashions,* one of the largest organizations to promote and showcase the biggest names in the industry.

"Look this event needs funding and more importantly a display of sponsors preferably from reliable sources."

"Who do you have so far?" Donovan asked.

"Rim's Athletics, County Trust Bank, and of course they'll have a display of some vendors. I can't use any of our modeling agencies or designers."

"Of course not, they're all involved," Donovan agreed

absently. I could already hear the wheels turning in his head.

"We need to show we're backed by trustworthy organizations," she pleaded.

"Hayes Enterprises is a private firm. We have no business sponsoring a fashion show for exposure."

"And you don't need it, either," I mumbled from where I still stood by the window.

"Fine," Claudia said. "I'd figured as much for Hayes Enterprises. But surely over the last few years, you've made millions for a large stack of accounts."

"Those were privately managed and not up for display or commit to sponsoring," I barked.

Claudia rolled her eyes. "We are all about being discrete and noncommittal aren't we, Scott?"

I turned away from her.

"Look, I'll leave this list for the two of you on what we ask per size and location of the ad," Claudia was a relentless woman. She didn't typically give up after merely ten minutes of a proposal. She laid it on Donovan's desk, which he picked up and looked over.

"You've got quite a list of spots available."

"Don't get too excited over the little ones. Most of them are going to be vendors. We're looking for sponsors to use in the main room and the tables, gift bags…"

My ears perked. "You don't have them lined up yet?"

"No, that's why I'm here. We still don't have a gift bag sponsor, which of course would be the biggest. Someone willing to—"

"I meant the vendors," I interrupted.

"No, we leave that part to the event coordinator."

"Which is?"

"I'm not sure yet. Our go-to firm recently folded; Brightman."

I gritted my teeth at the name. "And no one else comes to mind?"

"I believe the search for one is mid-flight."

I couldn't believe that there was only one event planning firm that came to mind for one of the biggest fashion events of the year. Starr-Bright Events were clearly on no one's radar. And if no other firm seemed to be either, then they still had a shot. The job and the exposure might be just what we needed.

Donovan raised an eyebrow at me; the man always knew an opportunity where one presented itself.

I pushed off the window and walked over to the bar. Claudia's drink choice was typically vodka. I scooped a generous amount of ice into a glass and added the strong clear liquid, then handed it to her.

"I'll tell you what. Donovan and I will come up with two or three of one our biggest clients to sponsor the event. In exchange, you hire a firm I've recently signed on with to plan it."

Claudia opened her mouth to protest.

"I just had them plan Donovan and Elaine's party of over one hundred people and they did an astonishing job."

Claudia eyed Donovan as if to confirm. "Thanks for the invite," she mumbled. "Who is it?"

"Starr-Bright Events."

"Done."

"I'm not," I continued. "In addition to them running the event, you give them a spotlight. One of your top three. At *no* cost."

Claudia's jaw dropped. "You've got to be joking. We've reserved the floor lineup for our biggest names. Starr-Bright is nowhere near—"

"And my job is to get them there." I shrugged and motioned my hand toward the exit. "Think about it. Call me."

"Fine. I'll consider it. But if I do hire them and give them a spotlight…I'll have conditions too."

"I don't doubt that."

With her signature raised brow and pursed lips, Claudia set her drink down and walked out.

Back in my apartment, I thought quite a bit about getting involved with Claudia again.

When I met her, she had showed up at Hayes Enterprises looking to outsource some of her company's divisions to cheaper firms. Considering that the plan was to outsource about half her company's departments, it was quite a project. One that required some late-night calls with international vendors and an overseas business trip.

Claudia was indeed a beautiful woman. Naturally, our attraction was inevitable. One night of passion turned into a few consecutive ones.

Next thing I knew she was making decisions on my behalf on certain deals that I was overseeing. She'd broken deals with vendors that I'd personally hand-picked and formed relationships with. She has ultimately *used* Hayes Enterprises resources and ran the deals herself, in the end breaking some of my most important connections. I tried to set her straight, but she clouded my judgment in every way that worked. Ways that I… was ashamed to admit. It is no wonder people say never to mix business with pleasure.

I didn't doubt one bit that Claudia would fine-tune the agreement to her liking. But Dean and Starr needed the exposure; especially since they weren't even considered after Brightman folded.

Ronald Brightman.

The man had stubbornly refused my help for a bailout. Especially since Ron felt that if he couldn't save the business on his own, without my bailout investment, it wasn't worth saving.

"And what? You'd come back in three to five years and save it again? No thank you. I think it might be time for warmer climates for me anyway."

For some reason I thought of Isabel. She seemed so wholesome and warm. Unlike any woman I'd ever met; especially not someone like Claudia; who was an opportunistic liar.

I couldn't imagine that a woman like Isabel would have anything to do with Hayes Enterprises, where the types of people I typically dealt with were usually as devious and cunning as Donovan and Claudia were.

I pulled out my phone and considered calling her. Saturday night was incredible, but she left it strange and cold. Something was on her mind.

This wasn't good.

I needed to pull myself together. Maybe it was best to see her from a distance. Avoid getting too attached. After all, I still had no idea who she was.

'Just Isabel' was not someone to be trusted...yet.

14

ELLE

I DIDN'T MIND A BUSY WORKDAY. I WAS GRATEFUL FOR HOW motivated and eager everyone had become since Dean and Starr's announcement to get with it or get out. All of a sudden, every minute of the day counted. There was no longer any idle coffee chat; no one commenting on other's planning strategies. Well everyone except for Bobby, who still believed he was untouchable. And maybe he was. I began to wonder how much the worthless wonder got paid.

But I quickly snapped out of it, I needed to focus now. I pulled up a long list of connections from when I worked at Brightman. Surely they'd all heard about the great Ronald Brightman folded after twenty long and hard working years— having built an empire from nothing and becoming one of the fastest growing names in the industry, with the largest staff and most well-known clients. How he got himself into a state he couldn't get out of was beyond me.

I'd drafted a crafty professional email with a slight

personal touch to each of my contacts that typically held annual winter or holiday events. I only needed to solidify one, after all.

I thought of Scott, and immediately buried my head in my hands. Rubbing my temples at how odd that whole thing turned out to be. I tried to convince myself that I didn't have an amazing time with the man on Saturday night. And how unfair it was that I'd finally found the perfect man and I was starting it off all wrong.

"Stressed for a profit event?" Mimi whispered, pulling her chair behind mine.

I popped my head up and just knew I looked hopeless. "Huh? Oh. No. I'm actually not concerned."

"Ugh, of course you're not. You could probably get a job anywhere if they cut you."

I shook my head. It was appalling that this was all the staff could think about these days. In the meantime, they did still all have events lined up through the next few weeks. There needed to be more thought to go into this. A better strategy all together. Not strike fear into their souls. "How's your search going?"

"Oh terrific, can't you hear my phone ringing off the hook?"

I shrugged. "I'm happy to help if you need it." I grinned and swirled in my chair back to my computer.

"Hey if you're looking to share some ideas, you should come to the 'planned to perfection' meeting we have twice a month here. We just kind of brainstorm off each other and help with gaps. It's kind of like a workshop that Starr hosts, but I swear, it's just another way for her to keep track of what we're working on."

"Oh, Starr did forward me the invite for that. It's tomorrow right?" I clicked on my calendar.

Mimi pushed her chair back toward me. "So about that guy you were thinking about?"

I sighed. "How did you know?"

"If you're not concerned with work, then you were there pulling your hair out over some*one* who's been on your mind."

I sighed and glanced around us. "His name is Scott; I met him at a party. He doesn't know my real name. Well, he knows my real name; people just haven't called me that since grade school. I didn't think I'd see him again, but then I did and he's really sweet and hot and so…not meant for me. My best friend is being super uptight about it. Anyway, there are things…I can't really take back now, and I need to figure out a way to not see him again."

Mimi nodded. "Okay, I didn't understand half of that. But what I would like to know…is why you can't just tell him you don't want to see him again?"

I looked up at her with guilty eyes and bit my lip.

"Oh you don't *want* to stop seeing him. I see." Mimi shook her head. "Then honey, you'd better hurry up and give him the low-down on the real Elle Rybeck and give this guy a chance." She gave me one last encouraging look before swirling her chair back to her desk.

My eyes drifted to my phone. "Maybe I won't have to," I mumbled.

It was entirely possible that all the over thinking was for nothing, since he hadn't called except for a quick text on Sunday thanking me for the date.

Ugh, who does that?

So naturally, I'd been speculating. And I really shouldn't have been speculating anything about Scott Weston. I should've been glad that he hadn't suggested we see each other again. Or how he couldn't stop thinking about our kiss and that he couldn't wait to do so much more of that.

This should have been a huge relief. A dodged bullet. A way out.

Maybe in a few days I could change my voicemail greeting back to my common name, the one that everyone knew me by, instead of the generic, yet super professional nameless recording I'd switched it to after I'd given him my phone number.

At eleven thirty, I'd finally finished sending out pitches to old clients and even got a decent amount of research on my latest assigned project. I leaned back in my chair and threw a hand over my furious stomach, since coffee and half a chocolate frosted donut was about it for me early this morning. Perhaps some fuel would be a good idea right now. I reached into my tote bag searching for my wallet, but instead, pulled out my vibrating phone, the display making my stomach flip.

Scott.

I glanced around and crouched down in my chair before answering, feeling as guilty as though I'd been having an affair with the President. I evened my tone, "Just Isabel speaking."

"How was the rest of your weekend?" There was a smile in his voice.

"Simple. Yours?" I answered honestly.

"Sunday is typically the only day of the week I like to go dark...therefore complicated."

I laughed. "To what do I owe the pleasure, Mr. Weston?" I smacked myself on the forehead. Marilyn Monroe's voice and '*Mr. President*' was clearly on my mind.

Why couldn't I just have said, "*what's up?*" It was like I was stupid pills when I talked to this man.

"I had a great time Saturday night, and I thought I'd tell you that."

"Ahh...somehow you knew I'd be up all night thinking about it. Well thank you for the reassurance," I teased.

"It's my pleasure," he said matter-of-factly.

I rolled my eyes.

"I was also hoping you were free for lunch today."

I glanced at the time display on my PC. "Bit short notice, isn't it?"

"Business typically is."

"Business?" my brows creased.

"Yes. I was hoping to pick your brain about... vendoring."

"That's... not a word."

"You see? I have so much to learn." There was that smile in his voice again.

I had to fight to keep my own lips from breaking into one when I answered him. "What do you need to know? It's not that big of an industry."

"I'm a little disappointed you think so. I disagree and think I should better educate myself in the trade, should I plan to invest in such a business as yours."

"It's super simple, Scott. You find something you can't do yourself and outsource to someone who does. For example... balloon animalist."

"Balloon animalist?"

My eyes bulged at the nonsense that kept coming out of my mouth, and I waved one arm in the air as if I could pull a better answer from midair. "Or a financial... data...vendor." I squeezed my eyes shut wondering how on earth this man was going to take *that* combination.

He was silent for a moment. Not as quick witted or confident as he was when I first picked up.

Way to go Elle, what else you got in that wacky brain of yours?

"Okay, see now I'm super confused. And *twice* as curious as to what type of services you provide," he laughed, somehow setting my body at ease. "So, noon?"

"I have a one o'clock that I can't—"

"The Wyatt Hotel across Central Park. There's a bar in the lobby. Noon. I'll be waiting." The phone clicked and there was an endless dial tone.

Whoa.

Something definitely changed in his tone when I'd started to turn down his invitation for lunch. And the way he abruptly ended the call...razor-sharp and demanding. I guessed that's how Scott Weston handled business; to the point and never taking no for an answer. I was almost afraid to be late to this so-called business meeting.

"I'll have whatever this drink is. Has cucumber in it, sounds refreshing," I told the bartender, pointing to an item on the drink menu.

"It's similar to a margarita, only better. Made with rum and cucumber."

"Sounds perfect." I smiled and turned back to Scott. "Is your office around here?"

"I don't have an office. Don't need one. No staff either. I handle my own business. My own way. On my time."

"Entirely alone? Not even an assistant?"

He shook his head with some amusement. "Too much of a cliché."

"So what do you do? Work out of a coffee shop?"

"Those who don't have prospects or actual business might work out of coffee shops. I have a small computer I only bother carrying when I'm digging into a new firm and their financials. But I mostly work out of this." He held up his cellphone; then pulled out another one. "And this."

I laughed. "Is that so you can be on a call while focusing on something completely off topic?"

"You've done this before," he grinned and took a sip of his amber drink.

I nodded and took a bite out of the cucumber garnish. "'Fraid so." His eyes lingered on my mouth as I chewed, the lust in his eyes nearly making me squirm. "So what's the deal with that? Are you trying to save money?" I questioned, in an attempt to turn the attention back to business. Though how I could focus on anything but kissing him again right now was the real question.

And given that Scott had stolen glances at my lips at least four times since I'd walked in, told me it was on his mind too.

He chuckled. "No. It's because I never know where I'll be. I'm in and out of meetings with firms I have deals with. Some days I might choose to work out of their office but if I do that, it's mostly so I could scope the place out."

"What do you scope for?"

"The staff. The management. Get a feel for what they spend time on. What their focus is. And what they envision as a future state."

"And you do all that...alone?"

"No sidekick for this superhero." He smirked.

"Is it because you don't think you need anyone to be a fully functional operation?" I asked, only part joking.

"It's because I know I don't. But I also don't trust anyone—or rather, very few I should say, when it comes to consulting on how I operate my business. And those I do, again in the very low—single digits, already have an empire of their own."

I nodded absently at his words. Something triggered an article I'd read about him that first night I met him and needed to know everything about exactly who I was dealing with.

I hesitated, then after a long sip, decided to say exactly

what was on my mind. "So, I'm not going to deny looking you up on the internet, especially when you so graciously introduced yourself as though you won the most recent Oscar."

Scott's head cocked to the side as he watched me, looking part intrigued and part guarded.

I wavered, and then decided to follow through. "You tend to have pretty high expectations; especially when it comes to downsizing. There was also someone who quoted you saying '*the risks we take with the working class*'." I raised an eyebrow at him, not bothering to hide my judgment at such a statement.

"You read that on the internet?"

"I might be paraphrasing," I pursed my lips.

"From what?" he seemed genuinely horrified as he whipped out his phone.

I put my hand over Scott's and his eyes immediately shot to mine. "Look it up later. What I'm saying is that your expectations might be a little too demanding. You want people to know that you try to work with them, not disintegrate their core values."

"Which is?" He pocketed his phone.

"Their employees," I answered softly. "This may not be a reality to you or Donovan Hayes, but eighty percent of entrepreneurs *value* their staff. To walk into a business and tell them *they're* the problem...might send the wrong message." There was no biting my tongue on this one. I meant every word here and he needed to hear it.

Scott inhaled deeply through his nose and leaned back, seemingly frustrated. "I suppose that was just more paraphrasing?"

I sensed a drastic change in his mood and second guessed my response, which was somewhere along the lines of, *no, that was all me.*

But it seemed he'd already guessed as much considering what he did next.

Scott checked his watch and raised a brow. "Looks like you could still make your one o'clock in plenty of time." He motioned to the bartender and stood. Looking back at me, he said, "Thank you for meeting me today, Isabel. It was a pleasure seeing you again." His tone was formal, distant, one I had yet to hear.

And one that was telling me everything I needed to hear to know this was ending.

The bartender returned with a card and a slip. Scott pulled out a pen from his inside pocket and signed it, nodding once at the other man.

My mouth dropped but couldn't settle on any combination of words. Had I meant to apologize? Did I even want to? My mind ran wild with an infinite inner debate as I watched the man try and flee from me.

After running through a short list of possible triggers of what set him off, I decided it didn't matter anyway. I needed to stop playing the role of someone who *would* know what they were talking about when it came to business.

I let my mouth run away with me again. Because the truth was, I was speaking as someone from the outside, as a representative of this "working class" and if I were being honest, I knew his methods were wrong, or just needed some work.

Still, I'd basically called the man immoral and I needed to say *something*.

"Scott, I—"

"I'm sure we'll be seeing each other again soon," he interjected, with barely another look in my direction, before grabbing his jacket and taking off.

Slowly, I turned back to my half full cocktail. "Don't count on it."

On my way back to the office, I pulled out my phone and sent a quick text to Mimi.

Elle: *Thanks for covering; I should be back before one.*

A short moment went by before my phone dinged.

Mimi: *Anytime. How was lunch?*

Elle: *My cucumber was delicious.*

15

ELLE

"Events don't just happen," Bobby lectured at the team meeting on Thursday afternoon. "They take a considerable amount of time to create and develop."

Funny, I was just thinking what a considerable amount of time this pointless meeting was taking. Since Scott had run out on me the day before, I'd been focused on projects and booking myself solid through the end of the year. Most of those bookings came from my pitches earlier in the week. Nearly all replied with plans to book an event and some even put through a deposit to hold the dates until they had more details.

At least three of those contacts had jumped for joy to find out that I was working in the city again after Brightman.

I wouldn't be able to handle them all in the month of December. I should have been at my desk starting my game plan on these rather than sitting here, listening to some over-confident and fruitless employee try to act like he'd invented the damn industry.

"I put together a list of some helpful techniques. I think you could all benefit from keeping this handy when working on a project," Bobby continued, handing out printed copies to the eight-plus people in the room, who I swore looked just as annoyed as I was.

"You have got to be kidding me," I spat out before I could stop myself.

Bobby jerked back, dramatically. "Is there a problem?"

"I'm sorry, I thought this was a meeting to brainstorm off each other on upcoming projects and discuss goals."

"Yes, well, Starr was unable to make today's meeting. She said to carry on without her and she'll try to join later. So why don't we go around the room and you can all discuss what you're working on where you think your weaknesses are."

I addressed the others in the room. "Is *this* what these meetings are usually about?" If so, then I certainly didn't belong here. I could be holding seminars on how to do this shit.

Bobby blew out a slow breath as if to remind himself that he was dealing with a child. "These meetings centralize on learning from each other, becoming more efficient and," he eyed me, "trying not to be so defensive when critiqued." He turned to head back to the front of the room and glanced back over his shoulder. "Welcome," he added, with a smirk.

I looked at Mimi, who just rolled her eyes and shook her head.

Bobby looked around the room. "The focus this week is creating the perfectly planned pitch for the perfectly planned party. I know many of you are still trying to book yourselves for the holiday season."

Well, I'd heard enough. Jumping out of my seat, I stormed out of the room muttering "This is bullshit," and marched towards Dean's office. Char's warning about losing my job be

MISTAKEN

damned. I'd worked way too hard my entire adult life to listen to this.

With me, I had the folder of emails confirming the events I had lined up in less than twenty-four hours to book me through January.

Angrily, I pushed the door open, and practically ripped the sheets of paper out of my folder before slamming them in front of him. Dean pulled back, blinking. "Is this what you're trying to get out of us?"

Dean barely glanced down. "Elle, what on earth—"

"You think I need some sort of lesson on how to be a planner?"

"What? Where would you get that idea?"

"From the guy who thinks he's due to become a partner here," I barked breathlessly. Half shocked at my own actions. I'd never even gone this far with Ron.

He sighed. "Is it the planned perfection meeting that Starr holds?"

"Take a look at these, Dean." I pointed to the file I threw at him. "I pitched them all less than a day ago. Seven out of ten already responded. Looks like I'm going to have my hands full. Unless I email them all back right now and tell them that my boss doesn't think I'm capable of handling their event. He thinks I could use *training*."

"That's not what those meetings are about, Elle. I can assure you. What did Starr say that made you think that?"

"She wasn't even there," I shouted just as Starr walked in, and Bobby behind her.

Dean focused on the first email in the pile, then flipped to the next one. Bobby appeared smug, while my high-heeled *other* boss looked highly irritated.

"Elle, did you walk out of my meeting," Starr demanded.

"You weren't even there," I repeated.

"I was a little late and surprised to hear about your

outburst. Elle, these meetings are essential for our success. Yes, there's sharing your ideas and brainstorming, but there's also a lot to learn."

Was this woman serious?

Eight successful years in the industry, and I was answering to these imbeciles? I turned to Dean who was not the least bit engaged in the conversation. He was clutching the emails like a lifeline, skimming them over again.

Bobby turned to Starr, "I appreciate your support. It was just extremely disruptive and completely counterproductive," he spoke low, making me sound as though I were an irrational maniac.

"Of course it was. Elle won't be disturbing our meetings anymore," Starr started.

Dean shoved the email print-outs back into the folder and stood, coming around his desk and handing them back to me. "No, she won't be. She'll be leading them."

I was definitely *not* expecting that.

Starr glared at Dean. "Excuse me? Dean this is—"

"Highly unacceptable that Bobby doesn't appreciate Elle's history and knowledge. There's plenty you can all learn from her experience." He turned to Bobby whose mouth fell open. "Bobby, have Erica reschedule today's meeting to Monday." He handed me back the folder. "You're in Monday, right?"

"Of course."

"Great, let's talk about these tomorrow." Finally, he turned back to Starr who had both hands in the air. "Starr, if there are other meetings you think Elle would benefit from, I'd like to be consulted first."

I looked at Dean. I was never the ignorant type and didn't like people assuming I was. I placed the emails back on his desk, gently this time. "You should hold on to those and disperse them as you like. I'll keep searching till I find something I'm interested in." I glanced in Starr's direction, "You'll also need it to justify what just happened here."

I walked toward the door and stopped in front of Bobby. "Please try not to be disruptive on Monday. Oh, and… *welcome.*"

I speed-walked to my desk needing desperately to hide in the tiny confines of my cubicle before I did anything that stupid again.

Yes, it was slightly invigorating to be able to march into the boss's office and give him a piece of my mind but only because it ended up working out in my favor. And *only* because I waved a handful of new leads in front of his face while half the staff was struggling to get *one.*

My heart dropped to my knees when I thought about where I was before I started this job. Nearly two months unemployed and considering moving in with Char.

I plopped back into my chair and rubbed my temples, pausing when I heard a chair roll up to me.

"You got a secret trust fund or something you planning to fall back on?"

I lowered my hands to look at her. "No."

"Well it sure sounded like you were trying to get yourself on the top of the list."

"What list?"

"The list of people to get canned once Dean and Starr finally fess up that this firm is seeing its worst days."

I frowned. "Did you hear what went on in there?"

"Everyone heard. You left the door wide open when you stormed in there."

I felt myself turn beet red and lowered my head again. "I don't know what came over me, Mimi, I've just had it with the bullshit, I guess." I was going to add something else about my being better than this place, than what's being offered to me here, but I didn't want to offend her.

I cringed at that thought, as visions of Scott and his tight jaw and distant eyes brushed past me yesterday when he left me alone at the bar.

I hated how hurt I was as I finished off that drink, wishing I'd never said a word. I hated that I let him make me believe that there was more to him and that maybe this could work. Most of all, I hated that I missed him.

16

SCOTT

"This looks good Harrison." I took the conference call from one of Donovan's private office suites on the Executive floor Friday morning. I scrolled down the spreadsheet and business plan as the man on the other line spoke. It still showed less effort than I expected but it was something. "More realistic timeline and I like the switch to less expensive vendors. Have you had anyone on your team research any of them?"

"Of course," Todd answered almost too quickly. "I feel like we've done as much as we could on our end, Scott. And we're not stopping there; I've given some serious thought to cutting our staff."

I sat up in my chair. "Why is that? Do you feel you're over-staffed?"

"Well, no I actually think we're adequately staffed and pretty consistent with our clientele."

I shook my head, swallowing hard. Because I knew the

answer to this but had to ask it. "Then why are you giving it serious thought Todd?"

He went silent for a brief moment. Then spoke in aggravating circles. "I thought...maybe that was... what you typically—"

"Understood," I mumbled and shook my head. "Let me give you a call back, someone just walked in. Thanks." I disconnected and rubbed my eyes before running both hands over my face. I was cutting this guy way more slack than I should have.

This woman was getting to me. She was making me rethink my business strategies. How the hell could she have done that? No one, not even Donovan, had ever successfully shifted me off course. I never made the wrong assessments. I could see what the problem was after just one review of financial statements and business plans. And able to fix it— fast. The less time I spent on an account, the quicker I could get out and move on. Donovan had once joked that it was the same way I preferred my women. In, out and move on.

I personally would have given myself a little more credit than that. There were a handful of women I had given more than a single thought to. Well, more than a single *night* to. I didn't do much thinking when it came to women. And apparently, I wasn't doing much thinking when it came to Isabel, either. Luckily, she reminded me why I steered clear of women who got too involved in my life, personally *or* professionally.

Who was she to basically tell me my business strategies were immoral?

And the only reason I couldn't stop thinking about her was because of the insensitive way I bolted from our lunch date. It was out of character for me. That was the only reason I'd called her this morning—to apologize. But she didn't answer, and it was for the best.

I stood and paced the length of the office. I'd never met a woman like her before and if she got in my head in a matter of minutes, then seeing her anymore would be sheer suicide to everything I'd built myself up to become.

Kat peered into the office. "Mr. Weston, you asked me to remind you when it was almost eleven."

I glanced at my watch and sat back down, mentally shaking off the hurt look in Isabel's features. "Thanks, Kat. Please let me know when Starr Howard gets here. Oh and before you send her in here, please ask her if she has new plans for me to review. Otherwise, reschedule with a location TBD."

"Noted." She began to slip behind the door.

"Kat?"

Instantly, she appeared back in full view.

I rubbed my forehead. "What do you women expect men to do when they screw up?"

Kat seemed taken aback by the question. "Um...I..."

"Like say a guy did something that was messed up...you don't respond to his messages. So, what do you expect him to do? I mean I know there's that whole 'sending flowers to your office' thing..."

"Um, sure, maybe ten years ago..." Kat said honestly. "But the modern-day woman prefers something more...I don't know...creative, I guess."

I stared at her. "Creative," I repeated.

She narrowed her eyes. "There isn't one solution really. It depends on who this woman is. How you met, details you know about her. What kind of things she likes or appreciates."

"Thanks, that's really helpful." It might have been the biggest lie I told all week.

"Of course." Kat didn't seem so sure she believed me anyway.

My cell phone vibrated and my eyes darted to the screen.

A pang of disappointment followed by anger hit me just before I reluctantly answered.

"Hello Claudia."

"I'm sending you a budget for the planners. This number should take into account all expenses and the fee," Claudia stated firmly.

"I take it you're accepting my terms," I leaned back in my chair.

"I'm still negotiating the spot they can have on the floor."

"Excellent. Let me know when that's confirmed." I went to hang up with zero hesitation until I heard her on the other end.

"Scott, we're running out of time."

"Not when it comes to Dean's team. They've already proven that. I've got to run, call me when their spot is confirmed."

"They can have the centerpiece," she blurted.

A slow smile spread across my face. "I'll let them know and we'll be in touch." I hung up and called Kat to let her know to have Starr come in regardless.

17

ELLE

"Why is everyone all of the sudden so chatty with me?" I asked, walking up to my desk from the copier on Friday afternoon.

"You forget yesterday's events already?" Mimi teased. "Earned you some respect around here."

I rolled my eyes and unlocked my computer, refocusing on the team meeting agenda I'd been working on.

"I'm still shocked as hell you did that. Especially with the rumor about the cuts."

I tried to hide the lump in my throat of possibly having to go through losing my job again. I seriously needed to find another line of work. "Well, I'm not surprised. This is a pretty lavish office for a firm whose main focus was charity events. And, no offense to you or anyone else here, but I don't see the kind of work ethic I used to see at Brightman. I also see a lot of time wasted on unnecessary meetings and cube talk."

"Okay, first 'cube talk'? And second, you mean like the meeting you're creating a mile long agenda for?"

"Oh, this?" I nodded to my computer screen. "I don't intend on discussing half this shit. This agenda for Monday's meeting is purely to piss off a certain cocky and feckless individual. I mostly want to focus on pitching and see what's been working for everyone and what hasn't. And then if there's time, how to juggle multiple projects efficiently." I shrugged, "It's sort of my specialty."

"I've been meaning to ask you," Mimi began cautiously. "You have quite the reputation for being one of the top five planners in the city. You clearly know what you're doing and could probably run a place like this."

I swallowed, knowing where this was going.

"Why did you end up taking this job?"

The answer to that was something I still hadn't been able to understand. Char thought it was my eagerness to secure a job asap instead of looking for something more managerial.

"I just want to do what I do best."

And keep a roof over my head.

My phone vibrated loudly on the hard surface and my heart skipped a beat. I reached for it and swiped to see a new message from Char saying she was in the neighborhood and wanted to take me for coffee nearby. I was always up for a few minutes with my friend, but my shoulders sank regardless.

Get over it, Elle, it's for the best.

We came from two different worlds. And his dumping me in the middle of a pre-lunch cocktail proved that he was no better than my exes. Just with more money and social status.

"Everything okay?" Mimi asked.

"Yeah, I'm just going to call it a day an hour early."

My computer pinged and I looked down to see an instant message from Dean asking me to stop by his office.

Terrific. He avoided me all day and now when I was about to head out, he wanted to chat?

"What's up?" I pushed open Dean's door, meaning to come off a little more polite but failing.

He stood, holding up the folder I handed him the other day. "You said you weren't interested in any of these, is that right?"

"Nope, they're all yours. I'll find something else."

"Something bigger?" Dean walked around his desk and approached me with a smirk and a slightly raised brow.

"Exactly."

"How about Empire Fashions year-end wrap up?"

"Empire Fashions?" My interest was most certainly piqued. "A handful of my old colleagues worked with them during fashion week, but they've never held a year-end wrap up that I knew of."

"Empire's CEO is hosting a gala-style fashion show at the end of the year. They plan to showcase their biggest designers, this year's most talked about designs and are promising sneak-peeks for next year's styles. Starr was only able to get a few details but it's looking like the guest list is expected to be close to three hundred. The who's who in the industry are expected; designers, models, buyers, producers, celebrities, and of course the media."

My mouth dropped. "This would have been huge even for Brightman," I breathed, then narrowed my eyes at him. "How'd you get this?"

"Starr had a meeting this morning with...an old friend with connections. The details are still being ironed out and I believe we're even being given a promo spot on the floor. But I wanted to give you a head start to begin planning Elle," he said. "I think there's no question who I'm giving this—"

"I'll take it," I interjected. Finally there was something worth my time; something worth getting excited about.

"Not alone. You'll need help."

I let out a huff. "Dean, you know I work alone. I don't have time to babysit an assistant."

"This one is too big for one person and we can't afford *any* mistakes. None. Zero. Mimi will assist you."

Well, if anyone... "Alright." I lifted my head and walked to the door, turning back for a moment. "Let's catch up when you have details."

"There's nothing to tell," I insisted as we crossed the intersection on the way to Blue Reserves.

"So he hasn't called?" Char asked.

"He called. Once."

"Huh."

"He's not the blow up your phone kinda guy," I shrugged.

"No, I guess he wouldn't be," Char agreed.

"Could we not talk about him anymore? You were the one who told me I should be honest. I couldn't do it. And it no longer matters. I'm moving on. What are you doing on this side of town anyway?"

Char narrowed her eyes. "I said you should be careful. There's a difference." Char paused, then shrugged. "Anyway it's Friday. Thought we'd get some dinner or happy hour or something."

"It's a good idea. I'm happy to see you. But I'm pretty sure at some point you compared my situation to a roasted fish," I whispered with a grin as we entered the Blue Reserve café.

Char laughed as we took our place in line. "Okay, you did not get my crusted salmon analogy. And it had nothing to do with your billionaire."

The woman behind the counter handed the customer in

front of me back his card and then turned to me. Her features immediately brightened as if she'd recognized me from last week. "Oh, hello. Thank you for coming by again. Will you be having the Censored today?"

I blinked. "Um...yes, thank you."

"Of course, and for you?" she asked Char, who rattled off a pretty specific order given she'd only had thirty seconds to look at the menu.

Char leaned in to close. "So, you come here often?"

I shrugged. "Just once, I guess they really know their clientele." I pulled out my wallet.

"You're all set," the barista said as she bent behind the counter and pulled out a cellophane wrapped insulated coffee mug with a small envelope attached. "Your coffees are on us today, and Mr. Weston left this for you earlier. Come back with this tumbler anytime and we'll fill it with a beverage of your choice at no charge," the young woman announced cheerfully.

"Um..." I stood frozen and stared at the wrapped gift.

"Your drinks will be ready at the end of the bar. Enjoy the rest of your day." She turned to the next customer.

"Thank you very much," Char said from beside me, steering me away from the register. "I'll wait here for our drinks, and then you can tell me what just happened," she said in a tone that was part excitement and part 'I want the whole truth and nothing but'.

What did just happen?

I quickly scanned the place cautiously as I chose a small table by the window, then pulled the sealed note from my unexpected package.

.   .   .

"Most of the time, superheroes are arrogant, dismissive, and always think they know best! But more importantly, they learn a valuable lesson at the end..."

Dearest Isabel,

I might be living proof of this Hollywood formula theory you have. I made a rash decision (or two) and have come to learn something others knew all along.

I hope you'll give me another chance to take you to lunch. I'll be waiting for you tomorrow at Bryant Park at noon.

Your hopeful date for tomorrow,

Scott

I tried hard not to be charmed by the note and set it down.

Char came over with our beverages. "Okay, what was that?"

"This was the cafe where I ran into Scott the day after the party."

"Oooh. Wait a second. That doesn't explain how he could just buy you lifetime coffee at this place. I didn't even know that was a thing."

I sighed. "It's not. He said he knew the owner."

Char glanced down. "What's the note say?"

I pushed it aside, dismissively. "It's only a note. It doesn't change reality. What he did the other day just proved we're not compatible. I had no business pointing out his flawed strategies. He's clearly done just fine without my advice."

"You don't need to be a billionaire to know how to run a business, Elle."

I looked out the window. "I think people like Scott just don't even consider a work-around for layoffs, there *are* other ways. Although, I don't know, I think Starr-Bright Events could definitely benefit from a few less unproductive employees." I shook my head and turned back to Char, noticing her reading the note. "Hey."

"Wow," Char's jaw dropped and she slid it back to me. "You read that note again and tell me you still never want to see him again."

"I do. I just *can't* see him again," I grasped my best friend's hand, hoping she understood.

Char frowned for a fleeting second as if she had a thought that never occurred to her, then her expression turned neutral. "You're right," she sat back in her chair and threw her arms up in the air. "You should just stay home tomorrow. Maybe look for a job that might be more fitting for you, because let's face it, Elle, you've grown out of this one. Then you could turn on one of your silly romantic comedies and go to bed feeling sad and alone after watching someone else's happy ending..." Char sat up as if she were making her point with a row of jurors. "Or you could go and *live* yours."

My heart ached. Not because of the possibility of living out my own happily ever after. But because of just how impossible it was.

I sat up. "I plan on living mine out. I do. But not with Scott. He doesn't know how far down the chain of social class—"

"Who cares about your social status and what you do for a living. You guys are *into* each other. Stop hiding behind a job you're not even sure you want. Tomorrow night you're going to Bryant Park."

I nodded reluctantly. "Fine. But only to tell him the truth and be done with it."

Char tried to hide her chuckle. "Sure. Totally done. End of story."

18

SCOTT

I SHOWED UP AT BRYANT PARK A LITTLE EARLY ON SATURDAY afternoon. I couldn't remember the last time I waited for a woman, much less wondered if she were going to show up. Midtown was particularly busy this afternoon. With the weather being sixty degrees on the last day in October, it didn't surprise me.

I climbed the short steps up into the block long park and removed my sunglasses, taking a glance around. She wouldn't be hard to spot, even here.

I hadn't even considered what I would say to her about running off the other day. Blowing it off like I would with anyone else wouldn't work. Not with a woman like Isabel. Every time she looked at me, it was as though she were analyzing me, but never scrutinizing. As though she were dissecting her own presumptions and figuring me out.

Now it was time to figure *her* out.

And she'd be here. Anne from Blue Reserves was one of the few I trusted at the establishment. Only she would remember the woman I was there with the week before. There's no doubt she would have made it a professional and seamless delivery, without calling attention to it.

Isabel hated too much attention. That much, I could tell from the moment I laid eyes on her.

So when Anne called me later that day to tell me it was done and—from her point of view—well received, I was relieved. Now all I had to do was wait. I wouldn't call again. Or text to make sure she'd come.

No.

I needed her to know that I'd be waiting regardless. I let my ego get the better of me the other day and I never did that.

Isabel was refreshing—but at the same time, terrifying because I'd stepped out of character for her more than I cared to admit.

As if feeling her presence, I turned and found her at the top of the steps just a few yards from where I stood. She was watching me. With most of the trees close to bareness, the sun shined unevenly in her pathway as she hesitantly made her way to me. A smile fell easily off my lips and I closed the distance between us.

"Too late," I whispered, sensing that she was rethinking coming here.

Her tense shoulders released and she turned up a brow. "Don't be so sure of yourself, my back up plan is supposed to call me within thirty minutes."

I huffed out a breath. "Okay, that was a terrible ice breaker. I'm going to try again." I cleared my throat. "Isabel, I am exceedingly sorry for lunch the other day. I clearly do not take well to criticism from people I like." I narrowed my eyes at her. "Or are trying more than usual, to impress," I added honestly. "Thank you for giving me a chance to make it up to you today."

She broke our gaze and walked ahead of me. "Of course,

but could we keep lunch light?" She glanced back, "I had a burger before I came in case you bailed again." She pursed her lips to keep from laughing.

My head dropped, half in shame and half laughter at her candidness.

"It's really okay," she offered when I caught up. Her voice seemed distant and she was avoiding my eyes. It was almost as though she were trying to get this over with.

I wrapped a hand around her arm and twisted her to face me. "Isabel," I started, "I want you to know that you can trust me. I imagine that it's unsettling when someone you just started seeing is easily pushed away by a simple comment, but I'm glad that you're here and giving me another chance to be…"

"The hero?" She blinked, her tone almost sad, as though she didn't believe I could be…but wanted it.

"I realize I may come off… intimidating, I hope you know I don't mean to be, it's just—"

"Your nature?"

"Well, no. Not always." I paused, scanning her over once. I licked my bottom lip and continued. "It seemed you'd already made up your mind about me and there's just nothing I can say to change it."

If I weren't looking for it, I may have missed it, but her brows furrowed ever so slightly at the thought that I might be giving up.

I extended my hand. "Good thing I love a good challenge."

She smiled through the hesitation in her eyes… a look that made me think that perhaps it wasn't anything I'd said.

"Unless there's another reason you're wavering?"

She nodded slowly. Her contrite expression made my chest tighten and I narrowed my eyes. "You're not ready to say?"

She shook her head.

"Good." I slipped my hand into hers and pulled her against me, my voice low as spoke against the corner of her lips. "Because I'm starved."

The moment I'd done it—looked the other way when it was clear she was keeping a secret—I knew I'd fucking lost it. My control, my need to dominate every situation. Out the damn window, because I wasn't ready to let her go.

I almost went back on my word until I felt her relax in my arms and the smile I'd been waiting to see for days finally emerged. "Lead the way, Superman."

Any fucking doubt—gone.

We walked through to the restaurant on the opposite end of the park. I stopped in front of the entrance and turned to her. "I hope you were kidding about that burger. This place has an exquisite menu. You have to come hungry."

"Exquisite huh? In that case, I'll save any more comments about you until the end of the meal."

I held open the door for her. "To be on the safe side," I agreed and winked at her.

The restaurant was as busy as any weekend. Luckily, we wouldn't be dealing with the crowd. "Right this way, Sir."

I took Isabel's hand again and followed the host. We made our way to the back and up the stairs where the noise finally quieted. The upstairs was clean and empty, save for a few guestless round tables and chairs. The rooftop had a parted wooden plank ceiling, with plants and tree lights raked through.

"Um... I'm sorry, doesn't the rooftop close in late September for the winter?" Isabel asked the host, who glanced at me.

I turned away to let the woman answer. "Yes, it is ma'am. Please, right this way." The host seated us at a single small table against the far end of the roof near the double railing. There was one heat lamp behind Isabel's chair, which I'd requested—in spite of the gorgeous weather. She seemed to appreciate it.

Once the host left us alone, I turned to her, trying for the fifth time that day not to let her beauty throw me off. "So how often do you come here?"

"Here? I've actually never eaten here. Why?"

"You seem to be well versed in their seasonal rooftop schedule."

She laughed and waved an arm. "Oh that's most New York City restaurants…probably." She swallowed and looked away.

"Well yes, they do close in September. But I wanted a private quiet setting with a spectacular view. And my apartment might have been too forward, so this was the next best thing."

Her smile was back and she turned back to me. "Where is your apartment?"

"If you really want to know, you'll have to come see for yourself."

Isabel threw her head back in a quick laugh. "What happened to not being forward?"

"Out the window since you brought up my apartment."

Her mouth fell open. "You brought up your apartment."

"Could I start you off with drinks?" Our waiter appeared by our table.

I held up one hand while tugging at my collar with the other. "Well, I don't know…it sounds like we're about to skip to dessert."

Isabel threw her hand over her mouth laughing then looked up at the waiter. "No no, we're going to go straight for the entrees please. In case my date takes off again mid cocktail."

I blew out a shameful breath and picked up the menu, suppressing a smile. "Do you like oysters? We'll start with the oyster platter, and we're fine with water for now, thank you."

With a single nod, the waiter turned away.

"Thank you for the coffee," Isabel blushed a little, rubbing her napkin. "That was a very...unique gesture."

I licked my lips. "It was a bit of a long shot you'd be there that day. But I somehow got the feeling you were in the area quite often so my odds were good."

"Did I say something to make you think that?"

"Well you mentioned that you just found your favorite new coffee place, which would be an odd choice to make if you were never around. But also, when you emailed your assistant back, you mouthed 'five minutes' as you typed. Now this may be a dead giveaway that I was indeed staring at your lips but I'm hoping you take that as my avid attention to detail when it comes to women."

Isabel narrowed her eyes at me. "But in the note you said 'meet me tomorrow'. You didn't say Saturday, specifically. What if I came on Monday?"

I grinned. "Regardless of when you got my note, I'd be meeting you the next day."

Her lips parted for a brief moment before she spoke. "That's an awful lot to go through for someone who offended you."

"I completely agree." I glanced at her, before picking up my glass of water. "Smart move skipping to the entrees."

Isabel laughed and did the same.

"Feel free to order a cocktail, I just can't because of an afternoon engagement that I need to be sober for."

"Business?"

"Not on a Saturday. There's a Halloween fundraiser I attend each year. This year, it's at the Center Theatre uptown. It's staged like a carnival with various activities, games, prizes and mini staged skits. People come and participate in random auctions, buy boxes of candy or soup cans to be delivered to the organization, who then distribute it as needed." I set down my glass. "Or they just come to watch the joy it brings and donate from the goodness of their heart."

Isabel's eyes lit up. "That sounds amazing." She bit her lip. "Can I... join you?"

My grin was wide. "I was hoping you might."

19

ELLE

THE HALL AT THE CENTER THEATER LOOKED AS THOUGH
Charlie Brown's great pumpkin had thrown up all over the
room and its seeds grew into mini pumpkin babies as they
hung from the rafters. Paper bats about as scary as any
origami hung in any empty space left by the pumpkins. The
black and orange combination was fitting for the obvious
theme of the day. An enormous paper mâché witch riding a
broom took up an entire corner of the large atrium, aimed as
though she were about to launch head first into the crowd.

It was perfect.

My heart skipped as a new parade of excited costumed
children poured into the hall, most holding square orange and
green felt bags. Scattering in all different directions, they were
welcomed by random carnival vendors, which were appropri-
ately set up in a U-shape facing the entrance.

"Oh, Mr. Weston," a well-dressed elderly dark haired
woman dashed over to the front door where Scott and I stood
in a short line at the collection table. "Please, please come in,"

she insisted, shooting a warm smile my way before taking both our hands and guiding us away from the line and into the heart of the festival.

Scott slowed the eager woman, "It's good to see you again Patricia, but we haven't yet purchased our tickets." Scott motioned back to the front table.

"Oh don't be silly. We wouldn't be here this year if it weren't for all your generosity, Mr. Weston."

"Patricia, this is my friend Isabel, she's very interested to see what the festival is all about. Please show her around, I'm going to go back to the table and rejoin you two in a moment." When the woman opened her mouth to object, Scott held up his hands, walking backwards. "If it makes you feel any better, I promise to cut my way to the front of the line."

The woman shook her head then turned back to me, her eyes beaming with pride. "Patricia Rodriguez. I'm the host and lead coordinator of Harry's Hallowfun Run."

I took her hand, but was nearly speechless—my eyes still struck with the scene. "Y-you did all this?" I twirled slowly around the space. "Ms. Rodriguez, this is spectacular. I've been to a good number of charity events and fundraisers and never seen anything quite like this, especially for an entrance fee of only five dollars. How did you get the space?"

Center Theatre wasn't typically open for public events like this one. The elaborate building that took up nearly the entire block was made up of theaters, banquet halls and reserved for upscale events, such as operas or galas. The Hallowfun Run seemed more of a neighborhood affair at the local YMCA.

"Mr. Weston didn't tell you? We're typically a lot further uptown and the community spaces are only large enough to hold the volunteer carnival vendors, but not spacious enough for all the neighborhood children to be able to participate and enjoy the entire day. We would have to limit the entrance to two hours and then switch out the crowd to people waiting to get in. The event has become so popular over the years that it's been getting a little hectic at the door. Of course we couldn't raise our ticket rates; it would defeat the purpose that all are welcome. A few months ago, Mr. Weston spoke to Harry, the founder, and said if we'd be willing to move our fundraiser this year, he'd offer to arrange and rent out one of the larger halls of the Center Theatre so that there's no time limit for any child to enjoy the carnival."

I blinked twice, wondering how on earth the man I'd read about, the man who'd on more than one occasion had proved that he was as ruthless as they get, could be the same man in Patricia's story.

My gaze turned to Scott who was writing out another check beneficial to the organization. My heart swelled and then dropped to the pit of my stomach at the thought of walking away from him.

Get it together.

"Ms. Rodriguez, do you have a business card?"

"Please call me Trish," she said, handing me a card. "Here, let me show you around." She tossed her head back at Scott. "He's probably going to be tied up for a bit, anyway."

I turned back to see Scott talking with an older gentleman in a mediocre suit. "Yes, I'd love that." I followed Trish to the first tent at the far left of the atrium. The tent was completely covered with dark purple velvet curtains that hung at the entrance. In front of it, was a folding table with three children and a volunteer event worker, who were all wearing disposable plastic aprons. The children were decorating medium sized pumpkins and the volunteer was helping with the carving.

"How sweet…and sticky," I commented with a smile to the volunteer.

"This is Becky, she always does the jack-o-lanterns table," Trish said then moved to pull open one of the blackout

139

curtains and held it open for me to peek in. "There's no one in there, but once the pumpkins are carved, they are displayed in this tent with an electric candle. Each jack-o-lantern has a name etched on it. There is a box to vote for your favorite. It's two dollars per vote for all the contests we have here today."

"That's brilliant." I shook my head in awe. "I can't wait to see more. But you don't have to walk me around. I'm sure you are very busy." And I certainly hoped that part of Trish's job wasn't to entertain the high dollar donors and their guests.

Trish nodded distractedly and waved at someone in the distance. "I'm going to head back to the front to greet some guests. I'll let Mr. Weston know where to find you. I person- ally need to pull Harry away for other matters. That man could talk for hours."

I laughed. "Thank you so much, Trish. I hope to see you again soon."

The woman touched my arm endearingly before rushing away. I turned back, smiling to myself, completely under- standing the woman's sense of urgency.

I wandered toward the back of the atrium to explore more of the magnificent event. I walked past a few booths lined up of Halloween themed games and snacks, admiring the creativity of each one.

Then I finally reached the far end; a built-in stage that joined the U-shaped array of tents and booths. And it looked like the show was about to start.

Costumed children who appeared to have very few parents surrounding them, were becoming increasingly excited and impatient for the show to start. A young woman pranced around frantically, and seemed to be moments away from pushing the eager children away from the stage. As if on instinct, I rushed over to her.

"Hi. Can I help you with anything?"

The girl, who seemed close to college-age, looked up at

me. "The magician is refusing to put on his act until the children calm down and move back at least two feet from the stage and there is no way I can make that happen. Look at them."

I turned back to the crowd. She wasn't wrong. Even a loudspeaker asking them to move back wouldn't overpower them. I looked around for Trish but the woman was nowhere in sight.

A burning flame rose up from the pit of my stomach. I figured this had something to do with a performer who was too hot-headed to work for their attention. Looking around, I spotted the magician behind the curtain adjacent to the stage, with a demeanor that screamed, "Only approach me if you think you're worth my time." The man wore an orange felt top hat, a black and orange polka dot vest, and metallic green pants. His wheeled suitcase was open and he was absently on his phone.

Before I could stop myself. I was taping the man from behind.

"Hi there. Elle Rybeck, event planner. Listen, I've been doing this a long time. I've seen performers like you before. You're lazy and only interested in doing the easy, rehearsed part of your job. Well guess what comes with the territory of working children's parties; *taming the crowd.* You were hired to do a job and if you're not out there in thirty seconds, you're going to lose it."

"Look I don't know who you are, but I was hired by Trish. I'm here every year, and I've never seen it get this crazy."

I looked the man in the eyes and pulled out my warning tone when it came to dealing with stuck up vendors. "I work for some of the biggest event planners in the city. I'm actually here with my partner, scouting vendors for children's parties. And you just fell off our list."

The roaring of children's voices grew louder and more

impatient by the minute. Turning, I focused on the man's open suitcase and went digging as he looked on in horror. I pulled a piece of flash paper and lighter before running off toward the stage.

I stepped on to the stage, ignoring the intimidating howling and cheering of the children, who were indeed *way* too close for comfort. I marched three steps back, feeling a tingling of sweat beads forming along the back of my neck. I blew out a breath and brought the two props together, holding them as far away from my chest as my arms could stretch. A flame blazed into the air for a fleeting second. Enough to get an array of gasps and a hefty step back from the crowd. Before the cheers or demands for more magic could start, I marched dramatically to the edge of the stage.

"Hi everyone," I addressed the group of children. "You want to see more magic?"

"Yeeesss," the children cheered.

"I don't know. Could be a little dangerous. Are you sure you're ready?"

I received another positive response from the crowd.

"Tell you what, let's all take three *jumbo* steps back and see if we can get your *real* magician up here for more tricks?"

The kids looked around and were clearly lost on how to do that.

"Let's all do it together. Count with me," I exaggerated one backwards step after the another, watching the crowd follow my lead. "One…two… three."

Once they were all a good distance away, I peeked to examine the open space between the front row and the stage. After a single nod of approval from the college-aged assistant, I glanced over at the stubborn magician, who now stood on the side of the stage, joined by an astonished Trish.

Jumping off, I winked at the frantic assistant whose name I

never caught, and sauntered past the stunned magician, flicking his lighter back to him. "Crowd's all yours."

He caught it and looked back at Trish before heading for the stage.

"What was that?" Trish asked as she was joined by her boss, the man I noticed speaking to Scott earlier.

"That was a child entertainer who got a little claustrophobic."

Trish blinked, turning to her boss, "I guess I should have warned him about the bigger crowd this year. She turned back to me. "That was...incredible, thank you. Holly told me he was on the verge of leaving if those kids didn't calm down."

"Leaving?" Her boss looked up at her. "That doesn't sound like Jim. And who are you?"

Oh no. By the man's furious tone, I had a feeling I might have slightly overstepped back there.

20

SCOTT

I watched Isabel as she passed the magician I'd seen many times before at this fundraiser. Her eyes, though still showing a hint of anger at the man, flashed with self-assurance as she murmured something to the wide-eyed entertainer and flicked him the lighter she so skillfully used on the stage moments ago.

Truthfully, I never liked the guy. His tricks were vastly the same every year and he seemed to be easily annoyed by children. I'd kept meaning to mention it to Trish but decided against it.

Isabel appeared completely flustered suddenly, as Trish and Harry approached her. I didn't miss the familiar shift in her shoulders when she was regaining composure as if the last few moments were out of character for her.

I overheard a bit of their chatter—not liking one bit what I was picking up from Harry's tone and approached them. "I leave you for a minute and you're starting fires?" I winked at her and wrapped a protective arm around her waist.

Isabel raised her chin and smirked. "Putting out a fire was more like it."

I smiled. "That was brilliant."

Harry on the other hand didn't look too impressed. The man usually wasn't. His demeanor set a protective alertness in me as he looked at my date with a questionable eye. "You don't think that was at all dangerous?" Harry asked.

Isabel turned to the man with a respectful yet challenging glare. She heard his undertone; there was no doubt in that. "Not at all. Flash paper is completely safe, and I know how to use it."

"It's fire." The man practically barked.

"That goes out in a millisecond...or two."

I wanted to interfere but I was still so curious about this woman and what other surprises she may have given away during this glorious hour. Harry still seemed dissatisfied with her actions and glanced at me. I met him with an equally challenging glare. Except mine had more unspoken threats behind it.

I had no idea what those threats might be, but Harry didn't need to know that.

The man swallowed any further argument and turned to Trish. But it appeared that Isabel wasn't done. It was as though she was turned on; whatever that term meant for her.

"I'm also very familiar with the Center Theatre and their protocols on special effects. Flash paper doesn't and never has fallen under their policy of prohibited entertainment equipment or gimmicks."

Okay, now that was impressive—even if completely made up.

Trish stepped between them. "Isabel, thank you so much. We wouldn't have had a show today if Magic Jim left because he couldn't control the crowd." Trish spoke loudly, nudging her boss who looked over to the stage.

"Yes. Thank you."

I cleared my throat. "Maybe you two will consider hiring outside your comfort zone next year. I'm sure you'd find plenty of magicians who would jump at the chance to work for such a cause."

"I have to agree," Isabel chimed in. "This is a terrific festival and...uh, I'll tell ya, I'm having a flaming good time," she laughed nervously and Trish and I joined in. Harry simply nodded once and turned in the other direction.

I was still laughing when Isabel slowly pulled me away from the crowd, waving back at Trish.

Once we were alone, she swiveled frantically and grasped my hands with hers. "Oh my gosh, I'm so sorry, I must be a total embarrassment."

"Are you kidding? This is the most fun I've had in weeks. You—you are full of surprises," my eyes narrowed on her. "What came over you when you were talking to Harry by the way, it was as if you were prepared for a battle."

"Honestly, I was. I don't like being treated like I don't know any better and can't make decisions that would be best for everyone. Unfortunately, I've dealt with many Harry's in my life and can feel them from a mile away."

I rubbed my chin, not sure what to make of that statement. "Yeah, he can try to be intimidating. Especially when it comes to women. I've never liked that about him. But I do like his organization. Trish keeps him in check though."

"I can see that."

We walked by a table with apple cider and Isabel reached into her purse, "Oh those look delicious." She handed the woman a few bucks and took two plastic cups full, handing one to me.

We continued down the row of booths on the way back to the other side of the hall. "Before we go, I have to get a bag of candy corn."

"Just one bag?" I asked with a smile I couldn't help.

Isabel stopped at the candy booth, reading the sign. "Oh. This was one of the charities that donates boxed candy to foster centers." She picked up a medium-sized box to be filled and pulled a hundred-dollar bill from her wallet. As she handed both to the young woman behind the book, Isabel was given a pamphlet with a list of charities.

"You know I didn't bring you here to donate," I whispered.

"I know."

I handed the same woman a bill, picked up two cone shaped plastic bags filled with candy corn and held up a hand that no change was needed.

We finally reached the last booth by the entrance which was the jack-o-lantern tent. I paid the booth attendant behind the rope telling her we'll be making two votes and pulled Isabel inside.

The small, enclosed space was devoid of light, save for what glowed through the few decently carved pumpkins. I slipped the candy corn into Isabel's purse, pulled her by the waist and pressed my lips against hers. I brushed a hand down her cheek and cupped her jaw. Something I was dying to do from the minute she jumped off the stage, her face glistening with the heat of the flames she had drawn. She welcomed the kiss with a soft moan and fell into me.

She was so different—even her kiss. It was playful and exciting. There was something eloquent about the woman and it wasn't just her mouth. It was in the way she lived. I had a feeling there was so much more to her that would blow me away, if only she would let me in on it.

I needed to know more—but for the first time in my life—I was too afraid to ask.

We made our selections. I picked the closest one but Isabel took her time, truly admiring the detail in each one before making her decision. I swore it was just to make me wait and suffer as we lingered in the dark secluded room together.

"People will start to get curious, Isabel, and I know you don't like the attention."

She traced a finger along one of the pumpkins and cocked her head at me. "How would you know that much about me?"

"Because you ran up on that stage in the heat of the moment, but when you realized that people were watching you, you were flustered through and through."

"Reading lips, watching me sweat. I need to be more careful around you, Mr. Weston."

I put my hands in my pocket, and narrowed my eyes at her. "Yet, I still don't know your last name."

She tugged on my collar. "My point exactly," she said before pulling aside the curtain and stepping out of the tent.

Was it me or was her tone almost seductive those last few minutes? I glanced down before following her out. Needing desperately to be alone with her as quickly as possible.

We made it as far as the lobby, and I was stopped by another member of the organization on their way in. And since I could barely form two sentences, I introduced Isabel before making up an excuse to bolt because I couldn't spend one more second without having my mouth on her.

Down the long hallway before the main exit, I pulled her waist beside mine, my fingers squeezing her possessively and leaned down to her ear. "Now that we're done here, how about that drink?"

Isabel bit her lip and turned to him. "I'm having a great time today, Scott."

"But..."

"Actually, I'm not so sure there was a but...I'm just having a really great time and I don't want it to end either."

She seemed to nail the reason for my invitation for drinks. Regardless, I sensed hesitation—again.

Isabel took an unsteady breath and then swallowed. "I'm not sure if that's a good idea."

Somehow I expected to be turned down. But I wasn't used to persuasion when it came to women. Not that I was used to getting what I wanted with them either. I was always respectful. But Isabel was different. There was something more to her hesitance.

Deciding against questioning, I nodded once and motioned her forward. "Then I'll take you home."

The weather had cooled drastically after sunset. We walked a few blocks longer than I'd intended before I even tried hailing for a cab. Since leaving the building, she'd been quiet and distant. I took her hand and pulled her to a stop, turning her toward me.

She lifted her chin, hesitantly.

"I'm not sure what happened, but at the risk of being completely reckless before I possibly never see you again, I want you to know that you're the most incredible woman I've ever met. What started as a physical attraction has become something that is new territory for me and something I don't know how to react to. So if I said or have done anything to make you doubt me, I am sorry. But in full honesty, because that is what I have to offer…I would like to get to know you better. To find out more about what makes you who you are." I took a step closer. "And why I can't get enough of you."

Her eyes sparkled and she bit her lip. "Where were you going to take me for that drink?"

"I didn't really think that far ahead," I murmured.

Isabel closed the distance between us. Her wavering eyes were saying something completely different than her body as she pressed against me. "Didn't you say your apartment was nearby?"

"By the Hudson."

"Probably a great view," she murmured.

I gripped her chin and stared at her lips. "It's astounding at this hour."

21

ELLE

I was familiar with the recently developed high-rise buildings on Riverside Boulevard. The street wasn't closed off but it somehow seemed more private. He led me to the last building on the block. A sharply suited doorman opened the glass door for us as we approached, and four lobby attendants welcomed Scott as if he were the owner rather than a tenant. We reached the elevator bank at the end of the lobby and entered an empty car, silently taking it to the top floor.

"The penthouse, huh?" I raised a brow at him.

He chuckled and narrowed his eyes as he led me to one of the two double-doored units. "Would you believe this was the last apartment available in the entire building?"

I shook my head.

"I didn't think so." He unlocked the door and pushed it open for me. "It was mostly about convenience actually. I liked the way it was furnished and it had the biggest windows in the entire building."

Cautious of the delicate dark wood floors, I slipped out of

my heels. The apartment was large with an open floorplan. To the left was a modern kitchen with smooth bamboo cabinets, stainless steel appliances which were remarkably spotless, and an elongated island topped with black marble. Just as I'd imagined, the living room had a breathtaking view of the Hudson River and part of New Jersey through floor to ceiling windows. The furniture was dark and minimal, consisting of one dark gray sofa, two lighter toned armchairs, and a cut tree trunk shaped coffee table over a cowhide rug. Even the dining table looked as though it was staged for a magazine.

"You haven't lived here long," I observed.

"Two years."

"Model furniture?"

"I was told the in-house designer spent two hundred thousand furnishing this unit."

I looked around, questioning what a designer could possibly had spent so much money on when there was so little in the apartment.

"I got rid of a lot of the…extras…kept the mattress though, that alone was thirty grand."

"That better be one hell of a mattress."

"Hasn't disappointed me yet." A smile tugged at his lips. "White or red?"

"Red, please." I flushed and turned away.

Scott pulled two wine glasses from the hanging wine rack over the kitchen island and poured into them.

"All joking aside, this is a really nice place." I walked to the window, taking in more of the view. Who knew when I'd see it again.

He came up behind me, handing over a full glass. "Looks like we just missed the sunset," he muttered. "Too bad, you'll just have to come back another time to see it."

I turned back to face him. "Still an amazing view though."

"What happened earlier?" he asked after a beat.

I blinked, tensing everywhere at his question. Then held up a finger and took a generous sip of wine.

He chuckled. "At what point will you stop needing liquid courage to speak to me?"

I struggled for a moment, my mind racing back and forth between what a sophisticated socialite would say to something like that—and the truth. Needing another few seconds, I stepped away from the window and sat on his sofa. "I'm a very private person. My work is everything to me and I guess I'm afraid to lose focus."

He gave a single nod. "You think spending time with me is a distraction," he said as if he completely agreed.

Not exactly.

Hoping the next honest thing I said would be enough; I raised my head as he met me by the sofa. "I'm enjoying our time together…more than I thought I would."

He set down both our wine glasses. "And it's scaring you. The thought of losing yourself."

No, what's scaring me is that I want to lose myself in you.

I only nodded as my eyes dropped to his lips.

"I get it." He wrapped his hands around my neck, raking strands of my hair between his fingers. "More than you know," he whispered. I met him halfway in a heated and hungry kiss as our mouths collided. I hadn't taken Scott as the type of man to hold back when he kissed, but it occurred to me that this was the first time he'd kissed me when we were alone and it was so very different. So needy and passionate. He'd been holding back.

And I'd been missing out.

My heart pounded against my chest. Against his. His lips and tongue were so hot, desperate, it made me move into him, wanting to taste and feel him just as badly.

With the change of position, Scott pulled away. "I apologize. That was inappropriate. I did not bring you up here to—"

"You didn't?" There was disappointment in my voice, I wasn't sure how to hide.

"Not at all."

My eyes dropped to his chest. "Well, thanks for the view." I said before lifting them back to his. The physical connection, the need to be touched by him, to be near him is all I wanted right now.

Desire was taking over and our lifestyle differences went out the window.

So did honesty.

I wanted this man. The one who swept me off my feet on our first date when I'd thought I'd ruined it. The one who would have waited for me to show up regardless of what day I got his note. The one who generously donated time and money into a children's organization.

My chest ached when I realized I couldn't walk away if I tried.

I could fight fire with fire. Tell off my boss and an obnoxious employee. I could face the richest of the rich at galas, blend in with the crowd when I needed to, conversing like one of them—and do it well.

But when it came to Scott Weston, I could do nothing. Except for maybe telling him the truth. And while I desperately wanted to do that, the thought terrified me.

"Tell me what you're thinking Isabel. Help me figure you out."

This was it. I was seconds away from screaming out the truth and ultimately having this man send me on my way, or worse, ruin me. He'd been upfront about how he felt about lying and while I hadn't outright lied, a lie of omission was no better, was it?

Okay, so maybe there were a few fibs here and there...

Coming out of my high, I shook my head and pushed past him, heading toward the door. "Scott, I'm sorry, you're saying all the right things, I just—"

"Isabel," he called, a chill in his tone stopped me in my tracks. "Tell me why."

My head snapped back and I practically shouted. "I don't want to be figured out."

He glared at me; his chest rose as he took in a silent breath.

Feeling the sting in my eyes, I turned and slipped on my heels, my hand shaking as I reached for the door handle. A warm breath in my ear stopped me from pulling it open.

"Then I won't ask," Scott whispered before placing both hands on my waist.

"If you'd like to leave, I prefer to take you home myself. But if you'll take a chance here and stay—I promise you—you won't regret it."

"What if I could promise you that you might?"

He let out a short laugh. "No matter what the story is here," his eyes roamed over me then landed on mine, "I'm going to bet that I won't."

From what I'd read about the man, he never made bets he knew he wouldn't win. Which made his words enough for me —at least for tonight.

The tension in my shoulders released and I pressed my lips together, moving to slip off my heels again.

"Keep them on," he instructed.

I slipped my heel back into place and looked up at him. "Was there more to the apartment than just the view from the living room?"

"As a matter of fact, the roof is spectacular."

My brows creased with disappointment, until he flashed a devilish grin. "Maybe I could show it to you in the morning."

Before my judgment betrayed me again, I threw my arms around his neck, kissing him with an uncontainable thirst.

Scott's hands slipped down to my behind and he wrapped my legs around him, moving us through the apartment until we reached another large room. But he hadn't bothered to turn the lights on.

"The master suite," he said when I'd released his bottom lip from my teeth.

"Fascinating. Where I come from, we call it the bedroom." I glanced up, barely seeing anything except the general vicinity of his bed. "How do you—"

He set me down and moved across the room, spreading apart a set of dark gray drapes that reached from the thirteen-foot ceiling to the floor. He then moved the next set of drapes, letting in more light into the room from the city lights surrounding the Hudson. There were two full walls covered with windows until his entire bedroom was exposed to the night.

"Magnificent." I breathed.

SCOTT

The only thing that could have made this moment better was to have Isabel standing in the middle of my bedroom naked. I moved toward her, unbuttoning my shirt, a need pounded through me but I needed to control myself. I'd never wanted anyone the way I wanted her right now.

I placed my hand against her cheek, since her eyes had deceived me before, I needed to know she wanted this too. "What do you want, Isabel?"

Her eyes dropped to my lips. "I want you."

It wasn't enough. I needed to know I wasn't imagining it.

That I wasn't pushing her into something she was still conflicted about.

But hell if I could have stopped now. I wrapped my hand tightly around her hair and tugged it to the side, exposing her neck. I trailed kisses from her earlobe down to her collarbone, making her shudder. A good sign, but still...

"You want this. Tell me you want this, Isabel."

She raked her fingers in my hair and stroked her hips against my erection in response. Her contact immediately sent a wave of unfamiliar pleasure through me. Incomparable to any woman I'd ever been with.

"About as badly as you do." Her desperate whisper was all I needed.

"Excellent," I muttered against her lips before taking her mouth.

Isabel was quickly proving that she wasn't just another woman. She was not only sexy as hell; she was passionate, kind, smart and had one hell of a wit.

This temptation would quickly become a distraction that neither of us could afford. Especially because something still felt off about the woman that felt so damn right in my arms.

Pushing aside my endless wonder of the woman I was about to take to bed, I raked my fingers through her long hair letting my hands land on her hips for a moment before pulling her silk blouse over her head, tossing it carefully to the edge of my bed, eyes still locked on hers.

At the risk of having her second guess herself again, I took a step back to search her face, but she stepped forward and pushed my loose shirt off my shoulders. Without further hesitation, I lifted her and she wrapped her legs around my waist —the heat of her pressed against me was too good to let go. Lowering her onto the bed, I pulled back to admire her body.

Her sheer bra left nothing to the imagination and my eyes lingered on her breasts. My hands fell back to her waist and she lifted slightly for me, allowing me to peel off her jeans followed by her black laced underwear. My eyes flicked to hers briefly once she was fully naked and I lowered myself over her, kissing her, letting our bodies connect and explore each other for a while until I couldn't take another minute without tasting her.

I trailed tender kisses down her chest, her stomach, until I finally reached her mound, spreading her legs apart before pushing my tongue between her folds without warning.

She cried out with pleasure and surprise. Her hands were in my hair within seconds and I took that as a need to delve deeper. Her moans were growing intense as I licked and sucked on all her tender spots. As much as I wanted to see her go into a complete state of ecstasy, there was a better way to get her there and I couldn't hold out much longer.

"Hold tight," I whispered.

I pulled away and removed what remained of my clothing, before reaching to my dresser for a condom. Isabel was swift to lift it from my fingers, tearing the wrapper open and sheathing me slowly. When she reached the end and licked her lips, I almost didn't make it, moving quickly to her entrance and connecting our bodies.

Once we got into a rhythm, I wrapped one hand on the back of her head and the other embraced her thigh. I lifted her, flattening her back against the headboard and plunging into her.

She felt incredible; wet, hot and smooth. Her moans were growing louder as her fingers dug into my skin with every thrust. I increased speed and pressure, feeling my own climax close. She screamed in what I confess might have been the most beautiful sounds I'd ever heard, before her movements slowed and she melted around me. My own release came in strong with another deep thrust and I groaned and cursed before falling beside her.

Releasing a breath, I pulled her inert body over mine, loving the erotic scent emanating from her and brushed a few damp hair strands from her face.

She was still panting slightly when she said, "Can't believe I almost left."

I hummed, now tracing my fingers down her lower back. "With all due respect, I was never going to let that happen."

"I had a really nice time."

A chuckle escaped me. "Yeah, me too."

She gave me a look and pushed off me, rolling onto her back. "I meant today."

I turned to face her, pulling her closer. "I know," I said, kissing her forehead. "And still, me too."

I held her close until she drifted off to sleep in my arms. My heart swelled with the idea of waking up with this woman. Regardless of how mesmerizing she was; I was no fool. Whether or not she was hiding something remained to be seen, but there wasn't a doubt in my mind that there was more to her story. I knew I risked losing her if I pressed too hard, so instead I chose to spend every moment she gave me, trying to prove to 'just Isabel' that she could trust me with her life.

22

ELLE

My eyes fluttered at the unfamiliar brightness in the room. Grasping the sheets and squinting at the obnoxiously large windows, I sat up. It didn't take me long to take in the stunning view of the glistening river in the sunrise.

Knowing I was alone, I still turned to the empty space where Scott had been sleeping. My clothes were neatly laid out on the edge of the bed on his side. Everything except for… I yanked on the sheets and duvet to check the bottom of my side of the bed.

Nope.

I took a minute to try to remember exactly the moment I'd lost them and lowered the sheets, completely exposing myself as I bent over to peek at the floor.

"Looking for these?" Scott appeared from the master bathroom, shirtless, with a towel wrapped around his waist and my underwear hanging on the tip of his index finger.

Jesus.

By the wicked grin on his face as he took me in, I must

have looked like an utter sex kitten, naked on all fours on his bed. Instead of jumping to cover myself in the unflattering light, I was oddly aroused by the scene.

"Come get 'em," he teased.

Obediently, I slipped out of the bed and walked over to him by the window. His smoldering eyes making me pool between my legs.

I reached for them and he grabbed my hand, tugging me against him, kissing me with a passion that made me melt into him.

His fingers were at my core before I realized and he stroked at the wetness. "Shouldn't we do something about this first?" he muttered against my lips.

"Please." I moaned, without a clue as to where on earth that came from. Had I just begged him to fuck me again?

He wasted no time getting me back onto his bed, hovering over me and taking my mouth in a deep kiss, then pulling back, holding my gaze as he sank into me.

"It must be magnificent waking up to this every morning." I said as I walked out into his living room, remembering he had a corner apartment with floor to ceiling windows facing the lower west side.

"It was today," he replied with a smirk, striding toward me with two glass mugs of foam rich coffee.

My cheeks flushed the hot annoying pink they got when he was this close. "Thank you, this looks perfect." I attempted a sip of the hot beverage.

He smiled and thumbed the top of my lip. "Sorry, I get a little overboard with the foam."

I pressed my lips together. "Just hope the coffee isn't cold by the time I reach it," I joked.

"Oh sure, hop on a stage to introduce a clown and now you're a regular comedian."

"It was a magician," I corrected.

"I wouldn't know—I left after the opening act," he winked before pulling me in for another hot kiss.

Scott glanced out the window briefly and I sensed some distance in them. Then remembered something. "I didn't plan on intruding on your solitude Sunday."

He stroked my head and nodded. "My Sundays *are* usually quiet. But unfortunately today, I owe an old friend brunch."

Something tugged at my chest at his vagueness. Was he meeting a woman? An old flame? The reserved look in his eyes may have suggested someone he cared about. And clearly didn't want me knowing.

Silently, I urged myself to snap out of it. It wasn't as if I had any claim to him.

Not to mention that last night, I'd quietly mouthed the words *one night* after I put aside any morals I had left.

I drew in a breath. "Well, I won't keep you from whoever it is you're meeting." My brows jumped and I moved from him, hating how jealous I sounded at the possibility of him being with another woman.

I felt his eyes behind me as I went to set the coffee down on the counter. Warm hands slipped under my shirt and turned me to face him; I was expecting an apologetic expression but instead found his eyes bright with amusement.

"It's not what you think," he reassured before what appeared to be a decisive moment in his head. "In fact, why don't you come with me?"

I huffed. "Scott, you don't have to prove anything to me. You're free to see who you want."

"As a matter of fact, I think I do. But not to prove that it isn't a woman I'm going to see; I just realized it's an opportunity to prove to you that I am not the ruthless and nonnegotiable businessman that *It's Just Business* and *New York Uncovered* articles said about me."

I bit my lip and flushed.

"Yeah, I looked it up," he said. "I want you to meet someone who has a slightly different opinion and is in no way biased."

He was asking me to go to a brunch with an old business acquaintance? No harm in that, I supposed.

What? No. I should leave and think about what the hell I was going to do before meeting any friends of his.

The last thing I needed was to get too close to a wealth-focused billionaire who would only expect equality in a companion.

Or a one-night stand.

I looked up at his waiting eyes and nodded once; remembering I was *Isabel.* The mystery socialite who knew to hold her own in a room full of Fortune-500 CEOs and no one, not even Scott Weston and the deep feelings that were growing for him, would ever intimidate me. Not his strong arms or his deep green eyes. Not even his selective generosity to struggling businesses.

The man couldn't be perfect.

He just couldn't,

There were his exquisite looks—and then there was the way he made me feel when he touched me. Or made my insides flip with a single look. The impossible way he read every expression; noticing what I liked and when I was uncomfortable.

And now I was letting him do the very thing that made me steer clear of anyone who tried; he was finding a way into my heart.

"Okay," I said before reaching to pick up my mug. "But first, I need to get cleaned up, can I use your shower?"

His eyes washed over me. "At your own risk."

After getting cleaned up, I sat on the stool by the kitchen island, watching Scott in front of the stove. In a white t-shirt and dark jeans, he flipped scrambled eggs onto two small plates, insisting I have protein with my coffee.

If this man didn't stop trying to prove he was a Godsend, I was going to seriously lose it.

Because how am I supposed to turn away?

"So, I promised I wouldn't ask about your business-life. But can I ask about family?" Scott asked casually as he sat beside me.

Safe subject. There was not much to tell. Nothing about my life stuck out as extraordinary. I was very close with my father, but avoided my cynical mother like the plague. Conversations with the woman always left a bad taste in my mouth that required weeks of self-motivation and reassurance from close friends to move on.

I. Am. Enough.

"Not much excitement here, I'm afraid. I grew up on the west coast. Moved to the city for school and never went back."

Scott frowned. "Like ever?"

I blinked. "Well, of course for the holidays—" I lied. "But most of the time I'm too busy with work."

Scott nodded. "Sounds like an excuse."

"Why? Does it sound familiar?"

He stirred the last of his coffee in his cup. "You could say that I guess. My parents live in London. I suppose I use distance as an excuse more often than not, but work really does get in the way. And unfortunately, it takes priority."

"You're not British." I noted, barely posing a question.

"No. My mother moved there with Philip years ago."

I wanted to know more but wouldn't pry since he hadn't.

"We're actually from Chicago originally. I moved here for grad school and..." he looked at me thoughtfully, "never went back."

"I guess we're both the types to put our work before anything else."

Something caused his eyes to turn cold. "There were a few times I lost focus of my goals after moving to the city, and I vowed to never let that happen again. Not with family or anyone else."

I swallowed the lump in my throat, but every other part of me wanted to hear what happened to him. "Sounds like there's a story."

"Perhaps," he took the last sip of his coffee and smirked at me.

23

SCOTT

I LED ISABEL THROUGH THE HOTEL LOBBY AND INTO THE MAIN dining hall. The host must have remembered me from a few weeks ago since she didn't bother asking for my party and led us straight to the table.

I thought I was ready for another round with the man, but it turned out, I wasn't. Heck I never was, but especially not today, not when I had *her* with me. It was safe to say I'd never woken up with a woman and wanted to spend time with her, keep her for as long as she'd stay. I wanted to know her, everything and anything she was willing to share.

And all the things she wasn't.

The woman certainly had trust issues. I was well aware of moments she'd chosen to keep details to a minimum but her eyes seemed to say so much more at times.

I just hoped anything she witnessed today wouldn't dissuade her even more.

Second guessing myself, I stopped short, turning to the

host. "We can take it from here. I know where he usually sits. Thank you."

The young woman nodded and turned back to her station.

I looked down at Isabel. "Listen, I don't want you to be surprised or make you feel uncomfortable in any way. Sometimes this man and I get into heated discussions and if either he or I make you uncomfortable in any way please let me know and we'll leave."

"Oh, don't worry about me. I know how things can get heated in business meetings" she waved a hand. "In fact, I can probably referee it," she laughed and walked past me.

I wasn't expecting that. But it would be interesting to watch her try. I shook my head and stepped forward, taking her hand.

Okay. Good. No surprises.

Although it may have helped if I told her one more detail before I brought her here. But it was too late now.

I spotted the man at his usual table with his back to us. Since I never acknowledged the man as my father, I didn't bother introducing him as such. Nor would I ever give the old bastard the credit.

"Sorry I'm late," I called when we reached the table. "I hope you don't mind, I brought a friend."

My father straightened in his chair and turned as I pulled Isabel beside me. "Isabel, I'd like you to meet Ron Brightman."

Isabel froze. The woman didn't extend a hand or utter a single word. If anything, she just looked…ill.

Ron must have caught the strange behavior too; his smile faded and his brow rose slightly.

"Isabel, are you alright?" I touched her arm.

She turned to me slowly, her eyes glassy and her mouth slightly open.

"Of course. Where are my manners?" Ron stood. "Isabel, it's a pleasure to meet you." He took her hand.

Did my father just stand for someone? The man didn't get up or move much for *anybody* he didn't know or care about.

Isabel returned with a very weak shake and an even weaker smile. "Mr. Brightman. A pleasure, of course," she said.

"Please call me Ron," he offered and lifted his head slightly.

Isabel stared for a moment before straightening her back and lifting her head.

She glanced at me and turned back to Ron. "I apologize. It must be the crowded room. It's um...making my head spin a bit."

I relaxed. "Please sit, have some water." I pulled out a chair for her from the round table and waited for her to sit before settling next to her.2

"Ron and I like to meet here to talk about... business...and other things every few weeks. The menu here is terrific."

A waiter approached. "Can I get your drinks?"

I turned to Isabel. "Bloody Mary or mimosa?"

"Oh, neither. Thank you."

"Nonsense. She'll have a bloody," Ron snapped his menu shut. "And I'll take one as well, and please be sure to bring a second when I'm about this much through." He pointed halfway down his water glass.

Isabel caught herself mid-eye roll and I laughed to myself. My father was not a man to be ashamed of his precise demands.

"What kind of business are you in, Ron?" Isabel asked, her eyes still on her menu.

The kind that I ran to the ground. Are the words Ron should say, but instead, I waited for my father's usual response.

"Oh, I don't want to spend a lovely day talking about work —Scott, we should order a plate of the smoked salmon bruschetta, I think your guest would love them."

Isabel scoffed. "Do you always make selections for people you've *never met*, mister—sorry, Ron?"

Now that was more the woman I thought I'd brought with me today. I smiled to myself.

"Apologies my dear. Of course, you have a mind of your own."

"Actually, I do want to talk a little bit about business, Ron," I started.

The man inhaled deeply, grabbing his thick beverage directly off the server's tray as he brought it over.

"Let's not today," Ron insisted, naturally.

I shook my head. "Don't worry; I'm not going to try to convince you to re-open." I noticed Isabel stiffen beside me. She took a sip of the drink she'd insisted she didn't want and muttered something quickly to the server—which apparently Ron heard since he chuckled quietly. Was I imagining it, or did Isabel shoot him a glare before turning back to me?

"I asked for an extra shot," she told me, wearing a tight grin.

Okay, I was definitely missing something.

Hoping the confusion would sort itself out, I turned to Isabel for the quick background. "Ron closed up shop a few months ago after my countless efforts to help him."

Her head snapped to my father. "You turned his offer down?"

"It was time to close." He waved a dismissive hand.

"I'm sure your employees would disagree." Isabel muttered before taking another generous sip. The comment didn't seem to faze Ron at all.

I leaned forward in my chair, grinning. "Isabel is a big advocate for the working class, Ron. She'd give you a run for your money if you ever dare to get into your business ethics with her."

"I don't doubt that," Ron agreed, stirring his drink.

"Anyway, I wanted to pick your brain about that firm I

told you I was looking into. You're the only one I know with the knowledge."

Ron's eyes flicked to my date before he answered, "The *only* one? I should put you in touch with one of my best workers from Brightman Events. She practically ran the place with me. I'd even go as far as saying she was the reason I stayed open longer than I planned."

I released a breath in frustration. "Why would I ever take advice from one of your old employees?" I needed my father to share details of what made him the number one event planning firm in the city and what was his ultimate downfall.

But as usual, he was being difficult. "I'm sure you led a good team, but I highly doubt they'd be—"

"So where'd you two meet?" Ron asked, clearly finished with the topic.

Fine, we could change the subject for now. Perhaps my father didn't want to discuss the details in front of a woman he knew nothing about. Knowing the type of women I usually see, it could be anyone that had connections all over the city.

"At an event actually," Isabel answered.

Ron's head popped up with interest. "Oh?"

I smiled at my date. "At one of Donovan Hayes' personal parties a few weeks ago."

Ron gave Isabel what looked like a knowing grin. "And you couldn't help but notice the beautiful mysterious young woman, if you don't mind my saying, wandering the elaborate affair."

Isabel blinked and smiled politely.

"Actually that was exactly it. But Isabel doesn't like to talk about her work much. So we've agreed not to discuss it."

"Well eventually everything needs to be discussed." he eyed us both. "Surely you two know that."

"Would you both excuse me for a moment? I need to return a call I missed."

"Of course dear," Ron said. "Although you should really try Scott's radio-silent Sunday. You seem like someone way too focused on work."

Isabel ignored the observation and walked away with her phone.

"What are you doing? I happen to really like her," I snapped. "You're making her uncomfortable."

"How am I doing that?"

"I don't know." It was true. I had no idea what he was doing, but Isabel was particularly uneasy around him. "But she's not usually like this," I added as if to reassure him I didn't date strange women all the time.

"You always find ways to blame me," Ron shook his head, then cocked it in Isabel's direction. "She seems terrific," Ron agreed. "Don't screw it up."

"Even if I were serious about this woman, what makes you think I would?"

"You've never brought a woman to our lunches, and I think that you have serious trust issues."

That might have been true so I didn't argue. "I've never met anyone like her," I admitted. "I just wish I knew more."

"Like what?"

"Like where she's from, what she does, how she's connected to Hayes Enterprises."

"Why is that important?"

"Because it's suspicious that she refuses to tell me."

Ron nodded, and took a deep breath. "Sounds like someone else I know."

Here we go.

"You don't know that much about me."

"I know that you're exactly like I am. I made mistakes being single minded. Focused on business before anything else."

"What am I supposed to do to prove she can trust me?"

"That might not be as hard as you think." Ron shrugged. "But I will tell you one thing; what that woman might be hiding has nothing to do with who she is. And because I know you, I know it wouldn't matter," he paused. "At least I hope it won't," he added under his breath.

24

ELLE

O<small>N</small> F<small>RIDAY AFTERNOON</small> I <small>FINISHED OFF MY SECOND HOT AND</small> censored that day, placing my new tumbler in the empty space near my computer.

Focus. Focus. Focus.

I was handed the biggest gig of my life a week ago. At this point, I would have had samples delivered, tastings scheduled, quotes from vendors dropping like hail in my inbox. But all I could do was stare at font styles for the invitation and think about how dreadfully awful last Sunday had become.

After a painful brunch with my old boss and a man I should have avoided from the start, I raced home and sulked until Char arrived.

Pouring my heart out to my best friend should have helped, but it only made things worse when Char outright confirmed my bleak reality.

"You need to walk away," Char reminded me as if it were the simplest thing in the world. "You're going to have to pull a 'Josh' and not return his calls...or you need to come clean."

I felt nauseous.

My initial instinct to keep up my charade with Scott because of his connection had become less of a concern. I wasn't worried about losing my job anymore.

That was until Dean handed me the gala event Empire Fashions was calling the *Winter Ballard*; raising the stakes immensely for me. It was the biggest event of the year. Throwing it all away now would be foolish and I'd be a bigger disappointment to myself than I was to my own mother.

I'm a professional. I won't fail.

"I'd go with the classic font," Mimi commented over my shoulder.

"Oh, I wasn't really looking anymore." I minimized the screen I'd been staring at all day.

"I know." Mimi grinned and leaned leisurely at my desk. "Want to talk about it?"

I looked up at her, considering the offer, and wanting so much to open up to someone who's heart was slightly bigger than that of my ice queen bestie's was. But I'd already wasted enough time daydreaming, and I certainly wasn't about to give anyone the impression I was losing focus on the job.

"I'm really glad you're working on this event with me, Mimi." I smiled, re-inviting my one rule that I wasn't here to make friends. That's how distractions happen. That's how people learned your weaknesses and ultimately, used them against you.

"It's an honor, and don't worry; I'm not an amateur. You won't need to babysit me. Just tell me when and where you need me."

Instantly, I felt bad for comparing Mimi to the rest of the staff here. She was clearly different, and noble. "I appreciate that," I said. "I have a lot of calls to make this afternoon, maybe we can split them up?"

Mimi jumped off my desk. "Let's do it."

I glanced back at my screen. "And you know what? I think you're right—let's go with the classic."

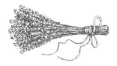

"No, I need this on better paper. Triple cardstock won't do. It's too thick. It needs to *scream* luxury. I want the guests to pick up the place-cards and do a double-take. Do you understand what I'm asking for here?" I growled into the line.

The man on the other line muttered a response, but I was already drafting my next email for an entirely different item on my to-do list.

"Great, send me samples," I demanded before hanging up.

This is good. This is where your mind needs to be.

Always.

It was Wednesday, and I was busier than I'd been in months working on the details of this event. After I had an earful from Claudia Heart on Friday evening about everything needing to be perfect and she couldn't afford mistakes, I'd been a nervous wreck. Even planned on working through the weekend just to make sure I was on track.

But of course, Scott had better plans for us. We'd spent the entire weekend together, both in and out of his bed, shower, and the kitchen counter. We'd gone out to dinner on Saturday night, but on Sunday, he'd taken my phone from me and showed me what radio-silence for a day feels like.

I had no idea what it was like to go silent on your own, but having spent one with him, without thinking or checking on work, I had a feeling I'd been missing out. Though I doubted it would be the same if I pranced around my apartment half naked, making eggs, and watching Cheers *alone*.

But now, it had been two days since I'd spoken to him. On

Monday he called to 'hear my voice' and apologize in advance for the upcoming busy week he was going to have. The gesture was sweet, even though I knew I'd miss him, but it had also set off red flags.

He was apparently closing that deal this week he'd been working on and needed to spend every bit of his time reviewing contracts and negotiating terms.

Just as well. Besides, I needed my focus too. I finally snapped out of my moment of weakness from the other day when I'd spent hours thinking about Scott and how I couldn't bring myself to tell him that the night he'd met me was all a big...misunderstanding.

Or...you know, a flat out lie.

Last Friday was a close one. I trusted Mimi, but what if it got around that I wasn't thoroughly engaged or being inefficient? The gala was less than four weeks away and I needed to get with it.

There was still so much to do.

I glanced at Dean's door; eager to get his sign off on the budget before lining up the vendors. But it had been closed nearly all afternoon.

I shook my head again and stood. "I don't care who's in there, I need to get these signed so I can move forward."

Marching to Dean's office with the file, I raised my knuckles to the door but was interrupted by his assistant.

"He's in a meeting," Layla said.

I turned to the young blond behind the desk by his office. "I get it. But I'm sure he won't mind if he knew why I needed these signed asap."

She rolled her eyes. "Look, I can ring you when he's out so you can sneak a peek."

My brows drew together. "What?"

"All the girls on this side of the floor are gossiping about the hottie who went in there to meet with Dean and Starr. It's like the third or fourth time he'd been here and they're still acting like school children." She rolled her eyes again, "I mean if you like that stiff suit type."

Curious, I looked back at the door, not that I could see anything. The blinds were down, and it was quiet as hell in there. I shook my head. "Whatever, just have him sign these when he's out and I'll pick them up later, okay?"

"Will do."

"Soft-touch in matte," Mimi said when I returned.

Her indifferent tone made me look up. "What?"

"The cardstock you're looking for. Try soft-touch matte. Has that silky velvet feeling you might be looking for. It's pretty impressive. And *very* expensive."

"That sounds perfect, do you happen to have a sample here?"

"Not recently. They're not popular because of how expensive they can get, and not a lot of vendors carry it. But I'll look into it, if it's in the budget."

"It's in the budget," I assured. "Claudia Heart made that very clear when I spoke to her. If it's impressive, it's not off limits."

Mimi winked without another word and turned back to her screen. "I'm on it."

I watched her for a moment and bit my lip. Had been practicing my apology for the past twenty-four hours and would probably still screw it up. "Hey. I'm sorry about yesterday. I shouldn't have blown you off when you were trying to chat."

She shook her head before I'd even finished. "No, no. I shouldn't pry into your personal business."

I decided there was no harm in telling one person about my insecurities. Heaven knows I'd never admit them to Char, even though my best friend probably already knew.

"To be honest Meem, when you asked me about my personal life, I felt like I got caught losing focus on a project I had no place to be given since I'm the most recent hire here. At Brightman, you didn't make friends; everyone was a competitor. So I got a little defensive. Also, it's totally something my mother would see and call me out on, which is probably why I have major trust issues, but we won't get into that now."

Mimi laughed. "Thanks," she shrugged. "I'm not judging. Honestly, I'm just happy to see that you're human. I'd read about your past events when you started. Pretty spectacular; and also very back to back. Probably didn't leave much room for a social life. So I'm glad you found yourself a hot distraction."

I bit my lip and smiled. "He is pretty hot," I caved.

"You have to spill deets soon. We all need a time out from the insanity that goes on here and to be honest, lately you seem like you really need to talk about it. And honey, you can allow yourself time to get lost in your thoughts… otherwise… you're just a robot."

I laughed. "My old boss used to say things like that," I relaxed and moved back to my seat. "It's stressing me out. Things have just gotten so complicated, I'm afraid it's not something I can make go away right now."

Whether I broke it off with Scott or told him the truth, it would directly impact my job.

Mimi leaned in and whispered, "Then don't," as if it were the simplest solution in the world.

My eyes narrowed at her.

"Postpone it. At least until after the event next month."

There was an idea.

"Clearly this has to do with Mr. Wonderful not knowing your real name—and whatever else there is to *that* story…but my point is Elle, it can wait. This opportunity can't—and it's got a real tight schedule. So whatever is stressing you out about it—save it until after the Winter Ballard.

I nodded like she'd just found the ultimate root of my issues. Of course. I couldn't afford this distraction.

What was a few more weeks?

Maybe it wouldn't be that terrible. I would just have to try and see less of Scott until the event and then pray that I hadn't made a bad situation worse by waiting.

"Thanks for this, Mimi. You have no idea how much I needed someone to see both sides for me." I glanced over her shoulder. "Geez," I muttered. "Door's still closed."

"Oh yeah, that VIP is here again," Mimi whispered. "Hey, maybe Starr will walk him over again at some point. You think your guy is hot, wait until you meet this tall, dark and deliciousness." Mimi fanned herself and I laughed.

"I'll just email Dean for his approval later. I need to get out and clear my head anyway." I grabbed my jacket and headed for the elevator.

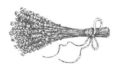

Finally—fresh air.

I definitely needed to soak some up before spending hours collecting options for centerpieces to send to Claudia, who was one frightening individual. By this point, I'd had three different occasions where I almost told her where to shove her "screw this up and you'll never work in this town again" speech. Her demands had been outrageous and her attitude even worse. It was no question the woman wanted us to know who we were dealing with.

The sun was in my eye when I looked to one side of the street before crossing the intersection. Not seeing anything but glare and a red light, I started across and heard an obnoxiously threatening loud horn. I turned, to find a city cab flying over a speed bump and coming at me with no sign of stopping.

Before I could even think to sprint out of the way, a body slammed into me with his arms gripping my waist, hurling us both to the other side of the street, safely.

Setting me back on my feet, I spun to face my rescuer, but had sensed him almost immediately.

I stared into Scott's confused eyes and fought to catch my breath.

"Isabel, what were you doing? I saw you look up in that direction before you crossed, how did you not see that cab coming?" he was breathless, almost angry.

"I—I don't know, I'm usually...I guess I thought I could make it."

His hands dropped from my coat, still confused. "Didn't you hear me call you?"

I didn't remember hearing my name. Although when lost in thought, I didn't typically respond to *Isabel*.

I shook my head. "I didn't, but...thanks for the save, Superman," I answered, still catching my breath.

He moved us all the way to the sidewalk and stared at me in wonder. "What are the chances you're on this side of town again visiting the same client? Or are you finally going to admit that you do indeed have an office near here?"

I shrugged and strode forward, tossing him a backwards glance. "Manhattan's not that big of a city, I get around quickly."

He caught up to me and grabbed my waist, twisting me. "Well, I'm certainly glad to run into you in any part of town." He leaned down and kissed me gently on the lips, some of the day's stress already dissipating somewhere behind me.

I was so thankful for him at that moment, not just for

saving me from oncoming traffic but for...existing. For being there in the moments I'd needed him before I even knew I needed anyone.

I broke our kiss and held him back with one hand on his chest, catching my breath. "I was just going to take a walk to clear my head; it's been... a crazy week. Want to join me?"

He swiped a hand over his face, suddenly appearing exhausted, "Actually, that sounds like a stellar idea. I just survived an intense meeting just across the street and my brain hurts," He rubbed at his temples and looked down at me. "And nobody better to do it with."

We strolled through the park in silence for a few minutes.

"I take it you were at Blue Reserves?" I asked.

"Actually not today, I mean yes, I did stop in for my usual and to check in but I was actually here on other business today."

"Oh?"

"The old friend's business I told you about."

"Ahh. By the looks of it, it's not going as smoothly as you'd hoped."

"I actually just closed that deal; they've done very little to impress me with any changes, but I've given them some time to come up with something before we revisit the idea of any cuts."

"That's a start," I said but at the same time, not thrilled with the fact that he'd been ignored and still signed with them. "Aren't you concerned that they couldn't come up with anything?"

"I suppose, but maybe it's not as easy as I might have thought." He shrugged.

I shook my head at such nonsense. "An agenda I'd recently put together for um...my team... took me less than twenty minutes to put together, and I honestly didn't know where to stop. How can a struggling business not be able to come up with a single idea in a matter of weeks? Maybe the focus doesn't have to be with changing business plans or number of employees to save money. It might be worth starting with— helping the help. Managing staff and each of their efficiencies. Eliminating waste and tracking hours spent on projects. I mean it doesn't matter what business they're in really, a little bit of oversight goes a long way."

I hadn't realized that we'd stopped walking at this point. Somewhere along the small planked bridge that led across the pond, Scott had stopped us to listen to me rant about how easy it can be to figure out what was wrong.

No one ever listens to me.

Except Scott. He was listening. Or watching. Yep. He was just watching me. His eyes searching mine as if he'd seen flashes of gold in them.

My initial instinct was to apologize. But that wouldn't be like Isabel. That was Elle. Isabel needed to be more prominent, not the type to hold anything back or apologize for what she thought. Isabel was the woman I let out when I wanted to have my voice heard.

My brow arched instinctively and I rolled my shoulders back before continuing on our path.

He caught up, clearing his throat. "Thanks for that. I'm afraid that might not work for another investment I'm looking into; the guy has been incredibly difficult. The firm appears to be adequately staffed, but it's more about his laziness that bothers me. His efforts have been minimal. We've met a number of times, but he's convinced he's fresh out of ideas and wants me to do the thinking for him. It seems strange since the guy appealed to me to save his family's legacy. You would think he'd give it a flying chance to try."

I thought about it, but the red flag was hard to ignore in that one. "Sounds like he's not very interested," I mumbled.

"What do you mean?"

I looked up at him, "Just curious, have you ever offered to buy anyone out?"

He jerked back. "Why would I do that? I have no interest in running a firm. I just want to make a profit and move on."

I nodded, suspecting that was the case. "Maybe you should let him know that."

"Hmm..." He pulled me off the bridge when we reached the end and held my hand to help me step over a puddle. "So, can I ask what's been on your mind? he asked.

I shrugged. "Nothing specific. I'm working on a project that's um...launching in just a few weeks...and then, I don't know. Might be time for a change of pace."

He nodded, pushing a strand of hair away from my face. "It's not who you are anymore."

I looked at him in surprise. "You remembered."

"Every word," he assured me softly. "I'm here with expert advice if you ever feel like sharing." He took both my hands. "Isabel, I hope by now you know you can trust me. But I'm patient if you still have... reservations."

I bit my lip, wishing so badly that I could. My chest squeezed as a cool November breeze rustled the leaves off the trees and sprinkled around us.

I stood on my tiptoes and kissed him, silently deciding that giving him up now was not something I trusted myself to handle. Not without adversely affecting my biggest event ever. "I'm getting closer, I promise."

But there was one thing that had been on my mind since Sunday. "What's the story with you and Ron Brightman? Are you...related?"

"Why would you think that?"

"You just seemed to have a very informal interaction. It wasn't exactly business."

He laughed. "Can't get one past you," he rubbed his face again. "Uh...distantly—oh so much distance."

"Distantly related." I released a slow breath. "A story for another day, I guess."

"Aren't they all, *just* Isabel," he raised an eyebrow.

A stronger breeze hit my veins and I slid my arms through his jacket, embracing his warmth. He raked his fingers through my hair and held me.

We stood there for a moment before he kissed the top of my head. "Will you come by later for dinner at my place?" his voice was low.

I smiled at him. "Cooking or take out?"

"Depends on how the former goes," he winked.

25

SCOTT

I spent most of Friday at Hayes Enterprises working on my end of the deal. Donovan had nothing to gain out of the agreement, but offered me his contacts, use of resources and to be present during any follow up meetings with Claudia Heart on the Ballard event.

I shook my head. That man really was beginning to resemble a dirty old man.

"Kat," I called from my old office on the executive floor, which Donovan never bothered to fill after I'd left his firm. Heck my nameplate was still on the door.

She stepped in, her expression professional as always, but there was a hint of something else there. If I didn't know any better, she appeared to be slightly annoyed.

I couldn't decide what bothered me more, the fact that I might have done something to agitate her, or the fact that I even noticed. I rephrased the original command in my head and softened my tone. "Would you mind letting me know when his meeting is over? I need to get his thoughts on something."

She blinked and jerked her head slightly. "Um...of course, yes, will do," she replied and walked back to her desk leaving my door slightly ajar.

The young woman didn't work for me but I made a mental note to get her a Christmas bonus next month.

A few minutes later I heard the elevator ding and then some commotion out in the hall. Frustrated, I bolted outside my office, slamming the door shut behind me.

Three women turned in my direction. Claudia peeled herself off of where she'd been leaning over Kat's desk and stood tall, rolling her shoulders back. Her overly made-up face and unnecessary heels approached me.

"Scott, finally. Will you please tell the assistant to do her job when you have visitors?"

I pushed my jacket back, placing my hands on my waist, glaring at the vixen before me. "Her name is Katherine," I barked. "And I think I heard her ask you to take a seat."

"Mr. Hayes asked to not be disturbed during his meeting," Kat nervously explained to me.

Claudia's head shot back to Kat. "That's because you haven't told him I'm here. My colleague Rebecca is here as well," she turned back to me with a softer expression, pointing out the other woman. "She's one of my leads on the Ballard event that we need to urgently catch up on."

I ignored the introduction. "Kat will let you know when we're ready. After the two of you offer your apologies to her; she'll usher you in," I turned and walked back to my office, "Unless I made myself clear, you can reschedule." I knew they wouldn't. Claudia needed those names. Her timeline depended on it and her senior partners were no doubt pressing for the source of the funds. My connections were crucial to her little project.

About twenty minutes later, Kat pushed my door open. "I just brought Claudia and Rebecca into Donovan's office."

"Great, I'll meet them there in a minute. Thanks so much, Kat."

"Thank *you*," she said smiling. "But you know, I'm usually pretty good at handling—"

I held up a hand. "Oh—no need. I'm well aware you can hold your own. But it's still not something I am willing to tolerate. And I'm going to make sure Donovan doesn't either."

She nodded and I followed her out of my office and into Donovan's.

"And then he made us apologize to her," Claudia whined.

Donovan chuckled just before I shot him an unamused expression. My old boss immediately cleared his throat. "Well, I'm glad you did. Kat holds an important position and we can't have our guests coming in here and asking her to break the rules for them."

So he did understand. Or just knew how to appease me.

I walked to the center of the room and tossed a folder on the glass table in front of the two women. "A few options," I placed both hands in my pockets and strode to the window— an old habit of mine when I felt highly irritable or when I wanted to be anywhere but where I was. Usually, Donovan would pick up on it and take over.

"My recommendation is the top two, they're offering top dollar for a spot at the entrance; not sure how fitting that would be; given the industry. The second might be a better fit, and they claim to have the capacity in the coming weeks to make custom samples for the gift bags."

Claudia and her colleague scanned the rest of the short list of names on my list. They exchanged a few looks and muttered a few words before Claudia stood.

"Works for us. We'll draw up the contracts ASAP. I'll need logos, locations and main contacts from each firm as soon as possible; we'll need to add them to our lineup of sponsors on the website."

I shrugged from where I stood. "Don't look at me, my job is done. The rest is you and the event planner," I smirked. "I suppose if you were nicer to Katherine, she might be willing to take time out of her busy day to email you the contact info."

Claudia huffed and turned to Rebecca, who stood immediately.

"Becky, call Elle and tell her to track these contacts down immediately and get the ball rolling."

Rebecca grabbed her phone and stepped out.

Claudia sauntered toward me at the window, ignoring Donovan's heckling. "Scott, this is very important. No screw-ups," she warned.

I smirked and turned away from her. "Then I suggest you bring your A-game, Claud."

"I'm serious. I'm not sure I'm liking the attitude I'm getting from this Elle when I speak to her so I want to make sure you didn't purposely set me up with a total ditz just to spite me."

I whipped around. "You think I'm playing games with you? Get over yourself Claudia. This is big for me too. That's why I made sure Dean got the best on the job. Besides, I've just signed on as a temporary partner. This has my name all over it too. If anything goes wrong, trust me, she'll have someone much bigger than you to answer to."

Claudia nodded. "That's comforting," she hesitated then ran a finger along my tie. "So I guess we'll be seeing each other there. I'm sure I could arrange for us to sit at the same table."

I almost laughed, but instead, looked at her with empty eyes. "There's no need for that. I already have a date."

Her hand dropped. "Oh. Can't wait to meet her," she shrugged a single shoulder and turned, walking over to

Donovan and offering him a kiss on the cheek before joining her friend outside.

I ran a hand through my hair and walked over to the bar, pouring scotch into an ice filled glass.

"You know you'll need her last name to be on the guest list, right," Donovan mocked.

Unamused, I shot back, "She'll be my plus one."

Donovan shook his head and walked to sit behind his desk. "Having doubts about your investment with Starr-Bright?"

"Why would you say that?"

Donovan watched me. "You oversold it."

I rubbed my jaw. The man knew me too well. "Dean told me they handed the Ballard event to the newbie again." I swallowed down the liquor.

"So?"

"It's risky and reckless."

"Maybe she's pretty."

I shot him a cold glare.

"Okay, okay, I agree…it's a little optimistic and perhaps daring, but maybe she'll surprise you again."

"Because that's something I could afford."

"So why not insist on someone you all know and trust?"

I let out a breath and stared absently at the tall building across the street. "Because that would be too…demanding."

"You're losing me here," Donovan said.

My recent efforts would never make any sense to my old boss so I decided to move on. "You know I went to see Harrison yesterday. For kicks I threw out the idea to buy out the business that he tells me is a family legacy, and he nearly jumped out of his chair with eagerness. Suddenly, he was overloaded with an offer and a timeline to close the deal."

"I don't get it. You say he was never interested in your investment?"

"Nope. He was hoping for a buyout. Wanted to make it look like he tried for the family, but that my offer was too good to turn down. Apparently, he wants no part of the business. He just wants out."

Donovan chuckled. "He's barking up the wrong tree." He swirled his glass. "Pretty brilliant—you testing out his intentions."

"It was Isabel's idea."

Donovan pointed a finger at him. "I told you I don't work with idiots. Why don't you bring her by one of these days, I'm sure if I see her again, I'll remember the connection."

I swallowed down the last of my drink. Doubt tugged at my chest.

And it was starting to become painful.

"Listen, I need to finish up some calls in the other room. Thanks for your help today."

Donovan held up his empty glass waving me out and turned back to his desk.

"Kat," I called as I crossed to her desk out in the hall.

She looked up instantly.

"Could you pull up the guest list for the Hayes' anniversary party from last month?"

Kat clicked away on her computer, and turned the screen towards me. "Here you go."

I scanned it quickly, recognizing most names. But not the one that I was looking for.

She's not on it.

She wasn't on the guest list? How was that possible?

"Thanks Kat,"

Back in my office, I leaned back in my chair and rubbed a hand over my face.

How did you get there?

I crashed. I remembered her teasing, before I implied how unlikely that was.

26

SCOTT

"I NEED TO ASK YOU SOMETHING," I SAID AFTER I'D PLATED OUR dinner on my dining room table later that night.

Isabel looked up from my kitchen counter where she was hovering over her laptop shooting out some follow ups that had apparently been on a mile long to-do list for work.

We'd been spending most evenings together and the last three weekends, so it was no surprise she'd turned down dinner with me tonight to catch up.

But since I had a business trip to California planned for a few days, I had to see her, so insisted she work while I cooked.

"What's up?" she asked before shutting her laptop and joining me at the table.

I handed her a glass of red, and waited until she took a sip. "Do you remember when I asked how you knew Donovan or Elaine?"

She gulped on the wine and set her glass down. Avoiding my eyes.

Not a good sign.

"Yes."

I wanted to make her look at me and tell me how she got there without being on the guest list, if she used an alias and why. I wanted to know why the topic made her nervous. Then and now.

But I hate doing that to her.

I hated the idea of making her anxious. The man in me wanted her to feel safe with me, to trust me.

But the ruthless businessman in me wanted answers. Needed to know if I was being lied to. Needed to understand the unexplainable.

"Were you a plus one?"

"Excuse me?"

Hell if I knew where I was going with this. I just knew my next words couldn't be; *What the hell were you doing there? Tell me the truth.*

"Donovan asked me about you and said he doesn't remember an Isabel on the guest list, so I figured you were just someone's plus one." I kept my voice as even and unaffected as I could get it. She wouldn't feel threatened.

Not by me.

She looked up at me. "I wasn't a guest."

I blinked. Waiting for more.

"When I told you I crashed…I was telling you the truth."

"How? Why?"

She closed her eyes briefly, but not before I caught a glimpse of regret in them. "I needed to get in touch with Mr. Hayes about an opportunity but when I realized it was a personal event for his wife, I changed my mind and decided to reach him another way. When you found me at their table, I was trying to leave…my card."

I waited for a long moment. As did she for my response.

"Would you like me to give him your card?"

"No."

"Why not?"

"I'm not ready. I need more time to...figure out what I'm going to say."

I cocked my head and smirked. "He's not as scary as he seems."

She watched me with so much sincerity in her eyes that it broke my heart to have doubted her. "I don't think so either. At least I hope not. But it's just not something I was ready for then or believe I am now. When I approach him, I want to make sure...I can give him a solid reason to...give me a chance."

I nodded slowly. *What am I missing here?*

"I can help you with your pitch, you know. After the Todd Harrison matter, I think I owe you one."

She grinned and picked up her glass, ignoring my offer.

But I kept my eyes on her. "Just tell me what you're selling."

She took a long sip of her wine. "I'm going to miss you this weekend."

Dropping the subject. Okay.

"Fine. I'll take what you can give me in pieces, sweetheart." I leaned in and pressed my lips to hers, feeling her tension release instantly.

It wasn't until after dinner that Isabel was herself again. And I hated that I felt guilty for confronting her. It wasn't a familiar feeling for me so I didn't know how to deal with it.

How to fix it.

After clearing the dishes together, I pulled her onto the couch. "What's been on your mind tonight?"

"Work, mostly."

I stroked her hair, needing her to feel free to open up to me. "What else?"

She glanced up at me. "I'm sorry I let you believe I was a guest at the party."

Did she think I was mad at her? I chuckled and kissed the top of her head. "Please don't be. I'm in no position to judge artful business tactics. And to be honest, it makes a lot of sense. Somehow you didn't seem like you belonged."

She pulled off me, an unreadable expression on her face. "What do you mean?"

"That entire room was filled with obnoxious, opportunistic, fake or devious business acquaintances of Donovan's, plus a handful of Eileen's yacht club friends. You didn't fit in any category."

She smiled, her eyes brightening instantly. Her fingers slid under my jaw and she kissed me. "Thank you."

"You can tell me anything."

She nodded, her eyes distant again.

Her hand moved to my inner thigh and she climbed over me. A distraction I happily welcomed. I leaned back and gripped her waist, settling her hips to straddle me. She lowered herself, tracing light kisses down my jaw and neck while her fingers worked to undo my belt and zipper.

She shimmied down my legs, tugging at my jeans until she reached what she wanted.

When her cool fingers wrapped around my length, I bit my lip. God I wanted to enjoy this. But the nagging doubt in my chest was too thick to ignore.

I couldn't help but feel this was partially motivated by guilt.

And that made me angry. Because unless you'd been completely up front at dinner, what the hell else are you hiding?

My phone rang from the coffee table two feet away. Normally I'd ignore it. But I didn't mind the excuse to take a minute before Isabel did something that might not have been from pure lust.

"Sorry I just need to see who that is," I whispered and she moved aside.

It was Craig Casing, my contact for the investor I was meeting with Saturday afternoon in L.A.

"Craig, what's going on? He's not thinking of canceling, is he? I'm halfway to the airport," I lied. I'd been waiting for a meeting with Spencer Friedman for months so there was no way I'd let him cancel without a fight.

"No, no. But he did want me to give you a message. Some of the firms he wanted to discuss tomorrow night work with a lot of vendors so he needs someone with this expertise. He needs thoughts on managing, eliminating, and outsourcing type of stuff."

"Okay. Thanks for the heads-up." I muttered. These were the types of questions I planned on asking Spencer myself. He might have been someone I'd been looking to partner with, but this was by no means a hands-down deal I'd sign. I still had standards that he'd need to meet—as would I.

"Spencer caught up with Donovan earlier today and he mentioned you might have an associate in mind you might consider bringing along."

My eyes flicked to Isabel. "I might."

I wrapped up my conversation with Craig, irritated once again that Spencer sent his sous-chef to make his business calls rather than himself.

"That was about my meeting this weekend in L.A."

"Is everything okay?"

"Other than my ego being kicked once again, I'm actually pretty good. Spencer Friedman, I'm sure you know the name, he's the biggest venture capitalist in the U.S. I'm meeting with him tomorrow night to discuss taking over some of his accounts. Or...rather...the opportunity to."

She blinked. "Wow. That's huge."

"This would put me ten steps ahead of my plan to expand on the west coast."

"Incredible. So what's the issue?" she asked, reading the tentative expression on my face.

"Apparently you came up in a conversation between Spencer and Donovan earlier today."

Her eyes widened.

"One of the factors of discussion for these firms will be how we'll plan to handle vendors after I join as a private investor. Donovan mentioned a close 'associate' of mine who might be useful. What do you say? Come with me tomorrow?"

She stood. "Wha—me? Oh no no, I couldn't—this sounds like—it's not really my…"

I peeled my back off the couch and caught her arm. "Isabel, relax. I'm obviously not making you do anything you don't feel comfortable doing, but if you're trying to prove yourself to Donovan before you pitch him, turning this down might not be the best impression."

Personally, I would have handled it just fine on my own, but if Donovan took the time to personally recommend her, and she turned it down, he'd have a personal grudge against her.

"Scott I can't," she snapped.

I stood and reached for her. "Okay. But tell me why," I couldn't hide the edge in my voice. This woman was not making any sense. She went out of her way to attend as a fake guest to one his private parties just to get his attention and now she was turning down what could be the opportunity of a lifetime?

She looked into my eyes and took a moment, forming her words. "I have an important project to work on this weekend. I'm already very behind and—"

"Work on it on the plane. And I promise I'll leave you

alone for the weekend in the hotel to focus. Just come to the dinner meeting tomorrow night and let him pick your brain on the topic. I'm sure it's a lot easier than you think."

She blinked up at me and released a breath. Sheer panic etched all over her face.

"Listen, I wouldn't pressure you into this if I didn't just find out you wanted to go into business with Donovan. One meeting, sweetheart. I promise it won't be the end of you." I winked.

She swallowed. "And it's just this Spencer guy, no one else? I'm uhh...not great with crowds."

I smiled. "Just the three of us."

ELLE

W<small>E WERE STILL TEN HOURS AWAY FROM OUR MEETING WITH</small> Spencer Friedman and my heart was already racing.

How the hell did this happen?

I was supposed to be spending my weekend working on the event of the year—which not only my job depended on, but my entire career. Somehow my little lie over dinner last night got me into a colossal mess.

What am I supposed to say?

What if Spencer Friedman looks into me? Asks about my background?

Overthinking. *You are overthinking this, Elle. Just breathe, and wing it.*

Scott's arms wrapped around me from behind as we stepped up to check in for our flight. "You're not afraid of flying are you?"

"Hmm? Oh no. Just got my mind on work, that's all."

"I know. I appreciate you coming with me. I imagine it will be a little bit of a power play tonight over dinner. Spencer will grill me, I'm going to grill him and by the end of it, it'll look like we got nowhere but I assure you, I never waste my time."

"Thanks for the warning."

"Think of it as good practice for when you meet with Donovan. I'll even go with you if you'd like."

I handed my driver license to the attendant and turned to Scott in an effort to distract him from looking at it. Smirking shrewdly, I replied, "I don't need help with my pitches Mr. Weston, but appreciate the offer."

He laughed. "Ouch. Okay, noted. But in all fairness, I was thoroughly prepared to handle it, but it would be selfish of me not to spread the opportunity out to you."

The woman smiled and handed my I.D. back to me. "Here are your boarding passes. Enjoy your flight."

"Thank you," Scott took our bags and led me away from the line while I held our tickets.

First class. Of course.

Well, at least I'd be able to take the edge off with a drink before we land.

"How did you get us seats together up here when you already had your flight booked?" I asked, settling into my window seat in the second row.

"I always book out two seats when I travel for a meeting. I do a lot of work on the plan and it's all highly confidential. I can't risk anyone peering at my screen."

"Good morning, can I get you both a drink or breakfast just after takeoff?"

"Two Bloody Mary's please," Scott answered for us.

The attendant nodded and disappeared behind the curtain.

After what was probably another twenty minutes, the plane started to rumble and move backwards slowly. My breath caught when it picked up speed and I gripped the hand rest. Heavens, how could I have forgotten about my fear of flying?

"There's good Wi-Fi on this airline, feel free to work on your proj—Isabel?"

I shook my head. I had no idea what for. If it was turning down the offer to work or that I was letting him know that I was not okay.

"W-why are we moving so fast? Why is it so loud?"

"Jesus, is this your first time flying?"

I shook my head again aggressively. "No. I just remembered I'm not a f-fan." Speed picked up massively and I felt Scott lift my fingers off the handle and into his, squeezing it tight.

"Look at me." I turned to his soft voice, his eyes holding mine. "Breathe." He tucked a small strand of hair behind my ear but kept his hand on my face just as we began to takeoff. I sucked in a breath just as Scott leaned in to kiss me. Pressing his lips hard against mine. Releasing only to whisper "You're okay," before returning with a softer kiss.

He held onto me until the plane leveled out. His eyes were everything. Unjudging, compassionate, gentle. I released a calm breath. "Thank you," I whispered.

"I won't let anything happen to you."

I smiled at the sentiment. But I rarely took promises like that seriously.

"What?" he asked, as if reading my thoughts.

"I appreciate it, but it's an unrealistic vow to make."

"Why's that?" he frowned.

"Because there will be things out of your control."

His face fell. "As long as I can help it. As long as I am with you, near you, I won't let anyone or anything hurt you." He promised again, more specifically this time.

"You're very sure of yourself."

He shook his head. "I'm sure of you. I know I don't know a lot about you. But over the past few weeks, I learned enough to realize that there won't ever be anyone like you. And if you give me a chance, I'll prove to you that there won't ever be anyone like me.

I already know that.

Perfect. This man was perfection and I was only setting us up for disaster.

The flight attendant brought our drinks and I reached for it instantly, taking a large sip.

I heard Scott whisper to keep them coming and laughed to myself.

"I rarely fly," I admitted. "The last time had to be over four years ago for my sister's wedding. It was also the last time I saw my family. Before that, I only flew once—when I left California."

"When was that?"

"When I dropped out of UC Berkeley in my second year."

"You went to Berkeley? Seventeen percent acceptance rate. I'm impressed."

"I wasn't. That's why I checked myself out and found a life in New York. Took a few classes in something I was interested in and..." I shrugged. Deciding to skip the part where I'd met Ron and quickly became the city's most wanted event planner.

"I take it your parents weren't thrilled."

"My mother might as well had disowned me for leaving Berkeley. Mocked me for every choice I'd made ever since, from job to boyfriend to the gifts I'd send for her birthdays."

He frowned. "I'm sorry. That's got to be rough."

It would, if I cared anymore.

"I have my fathers support and he's enough."

Scott seemed genuinely satisfied with that bit of information. As if the support of one of my parents was sufficient for him.

The second round came and I wasted no time on that one

either. I frowned. "They skimped out on the olives this time." I held up the toothpick with one crushed olive on it.

He laughed. "Here, take mine." He pulled out an olive with his pick.

I held out my glass but instead of dropping it in, he moved it to my mouth popping one in.

"Tell me more."

I couldn't believe how fast we flew across the country when the captain announced we were landing soon. Neither Scott nor I got any work done on the plane. We tried, but ended up talking most of the ride. A little while after we leveled out, I couldn't get over my freakout during takeoff.

Real smooth Elle.

Scott picked up on my embarrassment from fear of flying and told me all the things that still scared him.

"Not getting a deal, doesn't count, Mr. Weston." I had teased before he had a chance to share his fears.

But he surprised me. He told me he was afraid of small spaces, dark small spaces in particular. Which he believed to be a result of his first closet kiss in the fifth grade where he'd accidentally kissed Ralph Shephard instead of Rachel Miller.

When I finally stopped laughing, he told me about his fear of geckos, centipedes and Tuesdays.

I was confused about that last one until he told me he was just referencing a Tom Hanks movie, The Terminal.

And that wasn't the only Tom Hanks movie reference on this flight. There was another one involving an airplane malfunction he just had to tell me about. That one was revenge for my hysteria over his make out session in the fifth grade, I was sure of it.

"Ladies and gentlemen, prepare for landing." The voice announced through the speakers.

I gripped both arm rests, when Scott calmly took my left hand in his.

"Hey, there's something I've been meaning to tell you. About the man I introduced you to a few weeks back, Ron Brightman."

I turned at the mention of my old boss, my mentor, the man I'd looked up to for seven years until he gave up and folded, laying off forty of the city's most talented event planners.

"Is this about your…distant relation to him?"

He blinked. "Yeah, that." He rubbed his forehead and nearly winced as he spoke. "Ron... is my father."

Chills coursed through me. How was this possible? Life certainly was having a ball with me these days.

Wait a minute.

Ron didn't have children. Since there was no way I could say that, I stayed silent.

"I'm sorry, I know I should have told you before, I just didn't want you thinking I was introducing you to one of my parents. Ron hasn't been that for me...in a very long time." His voice didn't have a hint of regret or sadness. It was more factual.

"I don't understand, your parents aren't in London?"

"My mother is—with Philip. Who she met some time after Ron left us." His voice was cold and void of emotion.

My heart pounded and I couldn't breathe. Ron sat there, knowing I was lying to his son and said nothing? Why wouldn't he have called me at the very least? He still had my number, heavens knew the man had it memorized.

"Between ages nine and eighteen, I saw him twice and received four birthday cards."

"Why did he leave?" The question sounded more like a demand rather than concern.

He took a deep breath. "On business initially. He insisted

he didn't want to uproot the family and left us behind." He glanced out the window past me. "He never came back. My mother met Philip when I was eleven and he's been more of a father to me since."

I shook my head in disbelief. Ron—the same man who urged me to find happiness and start a family rather than work my life away—abandoned his own? "How did you...reconnect?"

Scott stared at me, a hint of amusement in his eyes. He opened his mouth but I cut him off.

"Sorry, I'm asking too many questions."

"No, it's completely fine. Once I was old enough, I moved to the city myself and kind of kept tabs on him. One glorious day Donovan tossed a new deal onto my desk. A developer was very interested in Ron's building and asked us to pursue."

"What? When was this?" I jumped then settled back into my seat. "Sorry—not the point, please go on."

"Nearly three years ago, before I'd ventured off on my own. Anyway, that's when I finally paid the man a visit at his office. He recognized me the second I walked in. I assured him Hayes Enterprises was going to advise the client against the location but warned him that if there was one, there'd be others," he shrugged. "I gave him my contact in case he needed it. You know, for advice."

I nodded slowly. "So now you two get together to talk about...business?"

He laughed. "That's what Ron likes to call it. At least once a month. It was his idea. Especially after folding. I had the means to save it, Isabel. I did. But he refused. Said he didn't deserve the company if he couldn't keep it up himself. But I could tell he was done trying. So I didn't push."

As much as I had no idea what this meant for me and Scott, how much bigger a mess this made, how much bigger a lie. A lie that I'd now brought his father into—I was grateful for the story he shared with me. That the man I was falling hard for trusted me enough to share it.

People around us started to stand and I looked up, confused.

"What's going on?"

Scott smiled and winked. "We've landed. Welcome to L.A., beautiful."

28

SCOTT

I HOPED THERE WOULDN'T BE A POP QUIZ ON WHAT THE DAMN hell this man was talking about all night because I'd likely get a big fat zero.

Spencer Friedman's eyes were pinned on Isabel from the moment we'd approached his table at the hotel restaurant.

The man and I had spoken on two occasions a while back and I knew he was interested in my work. He'd done his research, knew I had a knack for turning sinking small businesses into thriving corporations. Most in less than two years.

I knew I had this account—or rather several of them—if he hadn't even considered anyone else. If he had, he would have told me what they were offering by now.

"And in my opinion, it's all pointless unless you've tried it both ways and know exactly what works one way versus the other," Isabel explained to a highly agreeable Spencer.

"Brilliant, can you give me examples?" He grabbed his wine glass and gave it a twirl before leaning back. "How does it work in your company?"

Isabel glanced at me. "I'd much rather use an example of one of your firms. Which one comes to mind?"

He grinned. "Shadow Enterprises," he rattled off the top of his head. Then explained what they sell and a little bit about their strategies.

"Well, that's either a terrible example or a great one, Mr. Friedman. Because they shouldn't be using vendors. Everything should be done in house and if they don't have the means, then something else is wrong. It's a giant red flag when everything is outsourced in small to mid-sized businesses, surely you know that."

Spencer's eyes wandered before he sat up, uncomfortably. "Yes, yes of course. I had the same thought. The place is too authentic to be outsourcing half the company."

Spencer and I talked logistics about what these transactions would entail, how often I'd fly in to meet with various CEO's and if I were to hire a crew. After that he was all over Isabel's personal life, which she dodged as skillfully as she had the day I'd met her.

I was as impressed as I always was when it came to her and even a little amused.

"I'm sorry, I don't believe I caught your last name."

"And respectfully, Mr. Freidman, you won't, I'm here to assist Mr. Weston. To be quite honest, my being here is a conflict of interest and I prefer not to discuss anything outside of my expertise."

Wow. I tried to contain my brows shooting up but failed miserably.

He nodded and flashed a bright smile. "That's too bad."

I cleared my throat. "Spencer I'm not going to lie, you've made a really good offer to join your quest, but there is one thing that is a drop dead deal breaker for me," I started.

Spencer leaned back. Waiting for the shoe to drop.

"I'm not interested in hostile takeovers. Everyone gets their fair share and a chance to refuse and/or negotiate."

"Of course, of course, I know your morals, and I'm willing to work with them. Except for one or two accounts, possibly. They've been nothing but difficult from the start and we have the means for a takeover."

I hated to brush him off with a simple "out of the question", since I wanted the other accounts, so I chose my words carefully. "Tell you what, send me some details and I'll...consider them."

Spencer watched me and rubbed his chin. Not buying a word of it. "Excellent. I'd love your opinion as well, Ms. —Isabel."

"Sure I can take a look and give Scott my thoughts." She smiled politely.

The waiter approached me. "Mr. Weston, there is a phone call for you at reception."

I blinked. "Do you know who it is?" No one but Donovan and Ron knew I was here this weekend. And both had my mobile number.

"I don't, sir," he answered simply.

"I'll be right back," I muttered to Isabel.

ELLE

I sipped my water nervously. Spencer Friedman was a good-looking man, but somewhat frightening. And he wouldn't stop staring at me.

"So, how did you and Scott meet?"

"At an event."

He nodded once. "Donovan's party, right?"

"Yes. That's right."

He twirled his glass and I felt the room get hotter. Especially each time the man looked up and pinned me with his gaze.

"Amazing, that party, eh?"

My eyes shot up. "You were there?"

"Of course. That's where Scott and I connected. I remember seeing you there, too."

Hot. Very very hot. "Oh?"

He nodded again and leaned in, whispering. "Except when I saw you, you were sneaking back into the venue through the back door. Poor thing, I thought you were lost," he paused. "I waited for you... thinking you forgot your purse or something... planned to offer you a ride back. Until you came out of the kitchen, looking like one of the servers."

I blinked.

Holy shit. "You were the drunk I escorted out of the building."

His grin was wide. "I wasn't that drunk. Listen, Scott isn't going to be long unfortunately, Craig can't B.S. him for long on the phone call he just got. But tell you what. I'll keep your little secret, if you convince Scott to take on those two accounts."

"What?"

"It's a good deal. He'll turn millions in a year. Goes against his morals, but a gold-digger like yourself shouldn't care. Tell him you'll look into it yourself—keep certain ugly details to yourself and get him to sign." His voice was razor sharp with those last four words. Spencer leaned back. "In return, he'll get all the other accounts too. The ones he wants. The reason I know he's here. Oh...and you can keep your man."

"Mr. Friedman, I'm sorry you went through all this trouble. I won't be helping you." He didn't need to hear about my plan to tell Scott the truth after the Ballard event in two weeks.

"That's unfortunate."

But I did know that he needed Scott to sign more than I needed to keep my secret for two more weeks. Just until I got this one event done.

I glanced back to make sure Scott wasn't near before I leaned in, my voice low. "If I were you, I would reconsider. If there's anything Scott hates more than liars, it's blackmail. You won't just lose his funding on those two accounts, but on all the others. If you're smart, you'll forget what you saw and accept his business."

Not that I wanted Scott anywhere near this sleazeball, but even I knew you don't always have to like everyone you work with, As long as it gets you where you need to be.

"I underestimated you. It's too bad I didn't meet you first at that party. But still, it's simple, Isabel, tell him you've checked it out and it looks good and I promise, you'll both be happy. I'll cut you a slice of the profits. Scott never has to know."

I laughed and shook my head. "You're a piece of work," I muttered as Spencer glanced past me and then back to wink at me.

"Am I interrupting?"

I looked up at Scott and he pulled his chair out to sit.

My instinct was to shake my head and let him know everything was fine. But I didn't want Spencer to think he had the upper hand. So I simply raised my brow at the evil man with a tiny smirk and let him answer.

He grinned back and looked at Scott. "No. It's nothing. I was just getting to know your friend here on a more personal level."

"Really? Took me more than one evening to get to know her so I doubt you got very far."

"Are you curious?" Spencer asked Scott, half looking at me.

Bluff. *You're bluffing and I'm going to call it.*

"At the moment, I'm more curious as to why you had me called away from the table." Scott glared at Spencer.

"What on Earth are you talking about?"

"Craig was on the phone. He had a bunch of nonsense to talk about. That call was to pull me away. And I want to know why."

Scott looked at me before turning to Spencer. "Either way, I'll find out from her."

"Alright, I'll tell you." Spencer started, and I didn't know if it was my imagination or if his eyes turned dark as they brushed past me and focused on Scott.

Heat blazed through me again and I touched Scott's arm.

"There's an account he'd like me to look into for you. He wanted my opinion without hurting your feelings. And he thought that I'd turn it down with you sitting here." I swallowed.

Shit. *And I was doing so well.*

Scott's jaw tightened in the slightest way as he watched me. He licked his lips before softening. "I'm very sorry if he made you uncomfortable." He turned back to Spencer. "Of course, if there's anything you wish to share with Isabel for her thoughts, I think that would be a great idea. I don't mind it at all."

Spencer turned to me. "Well?"

"I'll think about it," I practically bit.

"I'll follow up," he said joyfully, letting me know he was holding me to it.

"I'll need at least two weeks to complete my research."

"Done."

. . .

Scott and I went up to our room in silence after dinner. I had thought we might go out on the town for a bit after but I was exhausted from the flight earlier and this meeting had taken a lot out of me.

What the hell kind of mess have I gotten myself into? And what was I doing to keep making it worse each freaking day?

I was ready to burst into tears for three days with all this emotional distress. It had to stop. I wasn't going to make it these two weeks.

No way.

I heard the door close hard behind me when we entered the hotel room and flinched before turning.

Scott was glaring at me. "What was that really about?"

I shook my head. Unable to speak. Because I couldn't lie anymore. I couldn't do it.

"I don't know if I ever told you this, Isabel, but you're not a very good liar. I let you get away with a lot, but I need to know about this one. It's important."

My defenses kicked in and I narrowed my eyes at him. "Why?"

He blinked.

"Because it's business?" I answered for him, partly hurt and part angry. Even though I had zero right to be either at the moment.

He stepped forward, his voice softer. "No. Because I don't want to push you. I don't want to *make* you open up to me. I really like you, Isabel and I know—I can see the conflict in you—I don't know what it is, if it's someone you're still getting over or if you have trust issues or if this is more serious for me than it is for you…I don't know. But I do know that I don't care enough to let it get in the way of whatever is happening here."

Tears pricked my eyes and I wanted to let them loose and

run into his arms. But the tug of war between my body and my conscience paralyzed me.

He stepped closer. "Not yet at least."

I took in a breath, knowing what that meant. And was grateful for the time he was granting me.

"Just tell me it's not someone else."

I looked up at him. "It's not someone else."

He released a breath and took my hands in his, bringing them to his lips.

"About Spencer. When are you planning on signing with him?"

"If I do, it won't be until after the new year." He swiped gently at a tear that fell down my cheek. "But let's forget about that for now. It's not important, and I'm sorry I said it was. The truth is, I was jealous that you two shared something I didn't know about."

"You're the only one I want, Scott. More of you, that's what I want." I reached up and ran my fingers through his hair.

"Hmm...can you handle more of me?"

A flurry of excitement went through me at his seductive teasing voice.

He pulled me to him, my back arching as we kissed long and deep. Like we were old lovers now, there was no discovering each other through our kiss, it was just the way we kissed now—only next level. Familiar level. A connection we hadn't shared before.

And it gave me butterflies.

As if sensing me growing weak in the knees, Scott scooped me into his arms, his strong muscles flexing around me as he carried me to the bed, setting me down on my feet beside it. He wasted no time bending to lift the hem of my dress and pulling it over my head.

He sat me down and unbuttoned his shirt, peeling it off

him, revealing that heavenly upper body I'd come to obsess over. I fought the urge to take the lead, to push myself onto the bed and pull him along with me, and just waited for his next move. I wanted him to own me. To do anything to me.

"What are you thinking?" he asked softly.

I bit my lip. "It's going to be another lie."

He rolled his eyes. "Then just show me, wise ass."

I pressed my lips together. "I want you to take me, to have me every which way you want me."

He narrowed his eyes. "That was no lie."

I shook my head slowly in response, letting him hold my gaze.

"Get up."

I stood as he stepped back. "Take it off," he said, glancing down the black lace undergarments I had on. I did as he asked and let the pieces fall to the floor. "Perfect. Now mine."

I smirked before undoing his belt and lowering the rest of what he had on, licking my lips and stepping back when I was done.

"Good. Lay back."

I pushed myself onto the bed and hoped he would cover me with his body now. My core was burning with an aching need and desire for him.

He sheathed himself seamlessly before moving over me and I loved feeling the heat of him again.

"You're so incredibly sexy, Isabel."

I swallowed at the name and wanted to cry.

"Are you okay?"

I nodded, feeling stupid for getting emotional.

It's just a fucking name. Get over it.

"Good. Now relax, that's your final command."

I giggled and felt myself unwind under his touch between my legs, closing my eyes when his fingers entered me. He moved them in and out of me, slowly, torturously, hitting my spot just enough to make me come undone any minute.

"No," I moaned. "Scott. I need you. Now."

"I'm in charge here," he grunted in my ear.

"You're a terrible boss," I teased, my voice filled with need.

"Insulting me isn't going to get you a promotion, young lady."

"Women in the workforce are stronger than you give us credit for, Mr. Weston." I pushed him onto his back and flipped myself on top of him. "We take what we want."

His grin was wide as he took back control, wrapping a strong arm around my waist, he flipped us both and pressed me against the headboard, holding both my wrists over my head.

"I see you're going to be a problem," he said, his playful yet gruff tone exciting me.

"Teach me a lesson I'll never forget," I challenged.

"Just the opposite, baby, I plan to make you forget everything tonight." Scott smiled, wrapping his fingers around my neck and pressing his lips to mine. Even though I knew it was coming, I gasped when he entered me, tightening all over. Excitement bloomed in me at this all-alpha behavior. I wanted more of it.

The intensity of his seduction, playful but powerful, overwhelmed me, making me wetter and desperate for him as he continued with slow movements. I wrapped my arms around him, gripping and pulling, throwing my head back. He groaned something against my neck before growing into full hard thrusts.

I'd never wanted any man the way I wanted Scott. The way he had me at this moment, the way our bodies connected—it was all that existed, and all that I wanted.

I writhed in pleasure and he slowed his movements, but his thrusts were strong and exactly where I needed him. I screamed through my orgasm, completely letting myself go. Scott let out a deep long groan and I watched his eyes roll back, smiling, knowing I was able bring out such an erotic expression from the sexiest man alive. He collapsed over me before rolling to his side and pulling me against him to kiss me deeply.

I was completely and utterly in love.

And one hundred percent screwed.

29

ELLE

"WHAT ARE WE GOING TO DO ABOUT THESE FOURTEEN additional guests?" Mimi paced my living room the following Thursday afternoon. With only ten days until the Winter Ballard, we didn't have a moment to waste. Details needed to be finalized and our list still had too many unchecked boxes for my comfort. As usual, my coffee table was covered in plans, samples, checklists and chocolate bits.

Fitting in last minute RSVP's was typically something I enjoyed. But now, it only frustrated me to no end. I picked up the eleven by seventeen chart and examined it. "Move those side tables with gift bags and banners to the back wall and add a round table of ten on either side over here."

"But we only need—"

"Oh, there will be others," I assured.

Mimi scribbled away on her staging notes. Her hands shook. "What's our game plan for the floor? I know we got clearance from Starr to be on it when necessary..."

"I'll be in and out of the floor. We'll both do a pre-check, mic the vendor leads and hopefully, when the doors open, we'll just watch the perfect evening play itself out."

Mimi rolled her eyes. "As if that's a thing."

I feigned a shocked expression. "Miriam! Are you not a buyer of my planned to perfection history?"

"Not for a second."

A slow smile spread across my face. "I knew I liked you."

Mimi grabbed her wine off the table and sat on the sofa. "So, I take it things have been pretty smooth in romanceland?"

"What makes you say that?" I pushed aside the planning materials and pulled up the bowl of chocolate.

"There's been no muttering or hair pulling. You also have a goofy smile when replying to text messages."

I laughed, nearly spitting out my wine. "Really, I feel like my privacy has been violated here."

"Okay, swallow—then spill," Mimi instructed.

I shrugged. "I took your advice. Things could have been absolutely dreadful for me the last few weeks if I hadn't." I breathed out a steady breath and stared at the materials in front of me. "I feel like we've done really well. I honestly don't think we've missed a beat and we won't next week either."

"Oh Lord, the pressure," Mimi stood, setting her wine down. "Let's save the drinks for after the runway for the devils."

"Agreed." I stood to walk Mimi out. "I'm going to be working from home tomorrow, so I'll see you Monday."

Nearly an hour later, I'd cleaned up the mess we'd made of my coffee table and fixed myself a small dinner plate. "Finally, the weekend...technically," I breathed. Not that the weekend before a huge event would mean a day off, but now that I had help, it wasn't so overwhelming.

I had been spending most nights for the past few weeks at

Scott's; it was enough to make me feel as though we were in a real relationship.

And soon enough, I'd be giving him that choice—to have something real. Screw the job. Screw his connections and ability to quite possibly sabotage my professional existence.

He wouldn't do that.

I poured out the remains of my wine glass. I needed to stop feeling so guilty. I was as honest about as much as I could be. One might argue even my name. And ninety percent of the time I was just *Elle* with him. I'd given him my thoughts and ideas anytime I heard him on a business call. Called him out when he was being too rash. Though most of the time, commended him on deftly handling every situation.

I did love it when he was a shark. But there was something extraordinary when the man stepped back and showed an open mind.

Scott had seen more in me than anyone else ever had. I was certain he'd understand. I needed him to understand.

My phone rang just as I reached for the remote. I sat back and checked the screen, hoping it was Char.

But instead, it was the last person on earth I'd want to share anything with.

"Mother," I answered.

"Why do you insist on calling me that?" the woman whined.

Do you prefer shrew?

"What is it? I'm working," I lied.

My mother paused. "Are you coming for Christmas?"

"I can't." I said flatly. "I'm working."

"I thought you lost your job. Don't tell me you went and got one just like it, Isa."

"Mom, would you stop. It's a perfectly fine job. I'm paying my Manhattan rent, I buy decent wine, and you know what else," my voice rose to an angry level it typically did when speaking to this woman, "I happen to be one of the best in the city."

"Well, you know the saying; when you're the smartest person in the room…leave."

"Why do you do this?"

"What?"

"For years you criticize everything I say or do. I can't sit at a family table or provide my opinion without you laughing at how silly I sound," I shouted into the other end. "Now you're telling me I'm the smartest person in the room?"

"It was just an expression, stop being so sensitive." My mother insisted, back in her usual cutting tone.

"Tell dad I miss him, I don't think I'll make it this year."

"Elle, you can't keep avoiding us."

"I'm not. Tell dad I'll call him later this week." I hung up before my mother could get in her last words. The woman always had a way of making me feel guilty. And I'd grown tired of it in our last few calls.

"How about a movie tonight?" I called from the couch after dinner on Sunday night at Scott's apartment. It was exactly one week before the Ballard event and I was on cloud nine. In just a matter of days, it would all be over, the lie—well, lies to be precise.

But hopefully Scott wouldn't see it that way. He'd understand that all those other things were just a ripple effect of the first one, wouldn't he?

I had to believe that.

The thought of losing him over this terrified me, it broke my heart a little each time I thought about it.

I loved the idea of cuddling up next to him while we watched a movie—any movie really, just to keep from being in a position to have to lie again.

I was so close. And with Scott going away for most of the week and my working round the clock on the event, we wouldn't see each other until next weekend.

An innocent movie and falling asleep in his arms would be the ideal way to spend our last night together before I rushed back here to tell him the truth next Sunday night.

The *hilarious* story of how we met.

"Do I have to promise to sit through the entire thing?" He cocked his head at me from behind the kitchen counter.

I took the moment to check him out again. I loved him in his suits, but tonight, he looked incredibly irresistible in a faded olive-green long-sleeved shirt and worn blue jeans. And his just-washed hair screamed for me to run my fingers through it.

"I won't blame you for falling asleep in the middle of it." I flicked through the selection of channels that were overpopulated with Christmas romantic comedies. "Looks like our genres are limited this time of year."

Scott strode over with a bowl of popcorn just as I paused at a selection.

"A Chance Meeting?" Scott drew back as he read the title of a movie I happened to watch many years in a row.

"Sure, why not? Cute couple," I shrugged, "snowflakes falling around them, skating their hearts away on a frozen lake."

"The only skating I'm interested in is hockey, a bunch of people roaming around each other in cold weather is odd and not a sport," he commented.

"Okay." I flicked past it, and pressed play at the next holiday romance.

"You want to watch a Christmas romance, I suggest Die Hard."

"That's not a Christmas romance."

"Of course it is. It takes place during the holidays and I'm in love with it." He shrugged and I laughed.

"Fine." I started flicking through the row of movies. "Where is it?"

He snagged the remote from my fingers. "I'm kidding. I'm not going to make my girlfriend watch Die Hard when she clearly had her heart set on a romcom."

I smiled and yanked the popcorn from him.

He used another remote to lower the lights and I leaned into him. Exactly how I pictured our evening.

During the opening credits, I looked up at him. "I'm your girlfriend?"

With his eyes still on the screen, he smiled and kissed the top of my head. "You are, if you don't mind me being your boyfriend."

What I said next wasn't meant to be said out loud yet somehow it was. "But you don't know my last name."

He nodded. "True. It could be hideous and then what would I do? I'd have to introduce you as my girlfriend, Isabel Wrenchenheimer."

I burst out laughing, drying tears from my eyes. "It's Wrenchenheimer-*opolous*, and you have to learn to spell it, or this won't work out."

Scott hurled over in laughter, then stroked my cheek playfully. "Sweetheart your last name, no matter how long it takes me to learn to spell it is not a deal breaker for me."

How about my first name?

I dried more tears from laughter, sobering up too quickly and reached for the bowl of popcorn. He raised his arm so I could rest my head on his chest. I settled into him again, resisting his musky smell. I needed to behave today. Claiming more of what wasn't quite mine seemed wrong and would only hurt that much more if things didn't turn out the way I hoped.

As if sensing my doubts and fears, he cupped the side of my face. "You okay?"

I nodded. I wasn't sure when it happened, but I had fallen hopelessly in love with Scott Weston. The realization made my stomach churn and the high from earlier quickly faded.

The man sitting beside me was going to break my heart. I knew it and wasn't running for the door. Instead I would be selfishly soaking up every minute with him until it'd be time to let go.

Stop being so negative.

This had my mother written all over it. Like I said; weeks to get past even the smallest conversations with her.

I hadn't noticed the movie was paused until Scott pulled himself off the couch. "So, what are you doing next Sunday?"

"Hmm?"

"I'm attending the Winter Ballard and I was hoping you'd be my date."

My face fell and I could feel all color draining from it as I stared back at him.

I heard it wrong. Please tell me I heard him wrong.

W-where?

"Surely you'd heard of it. Empire fashions is putting together the biggest fashion event of the year next week. Some of the country's greatest designers will be attending. I usually sponsor these types of things, but I'm—"

Think, think.

"I would love to, but I—" I stood, feeling as though I would come out of my skin if I didn't move. My hands were shaking and I took a breath.

Isabel, how would Isabel turn him down?

"Unfortunately, I'm otherwise engaged that evening."

His brows creased and I could tell he wasn't buying it. What killed it for me, I wondered. Was it the 'otherwise engaged' remark?

"I see," he said after a minute. "Why don't you meet me over there if you get free?" The invitation wasn't as inviting as the first one. This one was more testy, as if he was waiting for another excuse.

My heart broke for him. For us.

Jesus, I just need one more goddamn week.

"Why don't I meet you here after it's over?" I countered, forcing a smile.

His eyes searched mine for a moment and he stepped closer. My heart raced as I willed my hands to stop shaking. For the sweat beads on my forehead to disappear. For him to just not notice me falling apart inside.

"Sounds like a plan," he said, unconvincingly. "Come on, let's rewind a little bit and see how this love story pans out."

I would prefer to fast forward.

30

ELLE

T MINUS THIRTY-SEVEN MINUTES UNTIL THE DOORS OPENED TO the city's biggest event of the year. In my black pant suit, I stood above the grand staircase of the second level in the atrium-styled venue, admiring the impeccable staging of the main hall. The theme was *Winter with a Splash of Gold*. White columns stretching to the third level were draped with green wreaths spotted with white roses. Each rose gently sprayed gold. The railing of the staircase was fully lined with ever-green twigs with over a thousand gold beaded snowflake ornaments. Sponsor banners hung from the ceiling exactly where I had instructed them to be.

I turned behind me once again to admire the display of the place card table. I picked up Scott's card, thumbing the gold lettering of his name on the black velvety card. A fresh pang of nerves hit me all over again. Last week had changed all my expectations for how tonight was going to go. Now, not only had I lied by omission about myself for the last six weeks, but I had also worked for and had a close relationship with his estranged father, which was sure to complicate things all in itself.

Restless, I walked down the stairs, double checking my list.

"All clear down here," Mimi called from the main floor, waiting for me. "The vendors are all mic'd up."

"And they know—"

"Keep on mute unless checking in," Mimi finished with a nod.

"Good. I hate it when the chefs go off the rails and forget the mic."

There was some commotion from the stage crew and I rushed over with Mimi. "Gentlemen, what is going on?"

"All good, we're all good." Ryan, the event's main lighting designer turned to us, holding his hands up as if we'd walked in on a private crew freakout.

"Doesn't sound like it's all good, what is going on?"

He sighed. "We're short one crew member. We're trying to decide who will cue each set."

"Um...that's kind of important," Mimi pointed out.

I glared at the guy. "Figure it out in less than twenty-two minutes. I need an update before the doors open." I seethed.

Nothing can go wrong tonight.

I marched off to double check that no one else had been keeping any possible disasters from me.

To make matters worse, I kept getting texts and calls from Claudia and her assistant checking in on things. Even Dean and Starr weren't this overbearing. I finally told Ms. Heart that if she wanted my clipboard and run the damn night herself, she could have it.

That was when they finally got off my back.

I took the last fifteen minutes to check in on everyone and everything either through my mic or a run through.

Everything appeared perfect.

Typically, that would bother me, because I thrived on a

good last second problem solve, but tonight I was too distracted.

Was Scott mad at me for not coming with him tonight?

Was going over tonight a good idea? I'd certainly need a shower...

"Elle," I heard my name called again, snapping me out of my daze.

"What?"

Mimi smiled. "It's showtime."

I grinned back. "Perfect. I'm ready."

The doors opened promptly for the procession of the exclusive guests. I ran a lot of corporate events in my career, even some small magazine fashion shows. But I have never seen the level of attire that the women attending tonight were showing off. It was royal wedding worthy. Fancy hats, silks, taffetas and chiffons detailed in a variety of winter themed tones.

"Wow," I heard Mimi breath through the mic.

"Mm-hmm," I agreed.

"Kinda raises the stakes for tonight, huh?" she commented.

If they weren't before. They sure as hell are now. I released a steady a breath as I could muster, remembering that I was a professional. And I've never screwed up at an event. Not to a level that I couldn't fix, anyway.

"Nah. We've got this," I replied, half meaning it and half remembering there were over a dozen vendors and staff with a mic listening in.

"Marcus, are you all set with the hors d'oeuvres?"

"On the way out now," he replied promptly.

"Ryan, let's raise the volume a degree," I instructed. Hearing the level rise slightly, I added, "Perfect."

Someone else came onto the mic. "Ladies, we have a situation with a missing place card."

"What's the name?" I moved to a nearby table and scanned

my last-minute guest list as the venue's concierge repeated the name I heard mumbled in the background. "Not on my list. Did they have an invitation or a ticket?" I pulled out the blank spare place cards I had requested in the initial order and my calligraphy pen, ready to transcribe, if needed.

"Ticket."

Thinking quickly, I pulled out my own ticket sample. "What does the back say?"

He sighed, realizing he should have checked. "It's blank."

My shoulders released. "Please let him know he was sold a fake and remind security to check this at the door." I shut off my mic. "Amateurs."

Making my way backstage where the models would be lining up once the cocktail hour was over, I found Ryan. "What's the story?"

"We're good," he assured. "I've set up the light cues to automatic, so if there's any delay, I just need a heads up so I can stall it."

I nodded once, thankful for his skillful resolve. "I can do that."

"Awesome, I'll keep the volume up on this thing." He tapped his mic.

"Sounds good," I rattled off and raced away. "Mimi, we're good on the stage lights. How's the kitchen?"

"Right on schedule."

Good. Now time to disappear.

I hadn't seen Scott anywhere on the floor just yet. Then again, I'd been too focused on the overall operation of the night to notice.

My hair was in a high tight ponytail instead of down like it usually was when I was with him. Even if he'd caught a glimpse, he wouldn't recognize me. Would he?

Once the reception started and all guests were seated, I felt free to roam and focus on the evening's schedule. It was much easier to keep track of three hundred and thirty people when they were stationary and all facing one direction.

Scott was seated at table five. And what was strange was Claudia, who was supposed to be at table one, was sitting next to him.

What the hell?

I wondered how much she knew about the man she conveniently chose to sit next to.

A speaker was up on the stage and by the sound of it, wrapping up soon. I checked my schedule and looked up, searching from my hidden spot for the next speaker—who was nowhere in sight.

I hit my mic. "Ryan let's hold on that next cue until we find the next speaker."

"Holding," he confirmed.

"Mimi, could you look for a Robert Saint Patrick? I think just ask Rebecca out on the floor. Andrew, could you please play some light music as soon as this one's off the stage so it doesn't look like we're waiting for anybody?" I suggested.

"Ready," Andrew assured.

I breathed out another sign of relief. Fighting the urge to glance over at Scott's table.

Stop it. It'll only throw you off. You're at work.

"Elle," Mimi found me and raced up. "There's someone asking for you."

I held up a finger, focusing on the stage. The next speaker was walking up the aisle and climbed the stairs just as I instructed Ryan to release the light cue he'd been holding. Once he was set, I turned to my eager partner. "Who, Starr?" I knew Starr was planning to attend, but not for the entire evening. Still, my boss could have just texted me.

"No. He said he was going to wait for you by the gift bag table in the back of the hall," Mimi explained. "He said you'd know who he is."

"Thanks," I murmured and stalked through the side doors to cross to the back of the hall.

I spotted the waiting man and sighed. Surprised to feel relieved. The man was like the next best thing to home for me. And I could have really used the support right about now. "If you're looking for someone in a lacey black dress, you're not going to find one here."

My old boss tossed a compact back into one of the gift bags and turned to face me. He scanned my black suit with a smirk across his face. "Elle, my dear." He opened his arms and I walked into his embrace.

A pulled back to take a good look at the retired man and smiled. "How are you, Ron?" I asked before glancing at the seated crowd facing the opposite direction.

"We're out of sight from his table," he reassured.

I let out a shaky breath. "Thanks," I paused and looked at him. "You never told me you had a family."

"I didn't really have them anymore," he said grimly. "I'm sure Scotty told you the only version he chooses to believe. That I never wanted a family and ran off to build my empire."

"He told me the only version that counts. That you've reconnected and he enjoys spending time with you," I fibbed.

He grunted. "You made that last part up."

I laughed, caught red-handed. "He didn't have to say it."

Ron snickered. "I planned on coming back, you know."

I shook my head, facing away. "It's none of my business."

"In that case, I'll withdraw the question I was going to ask you," he arched the same brow whenever he questioned my tactics.

"Good."

"I'll just skip to my advice. Elle, I made the mistake of putting my career first. And I lost everything in the end."

I frowned, still facing the crowd. "It got carried away," I mumbled, then shook my head. "I was going to tell him after the event tonight." I watched Scott at his table, listening intently to the speaker. "But now I'm not so sure."

The difference between us was so vivid when it was like this. When I was standing back here, practically checking coats and he was seated next to some of the most important guests of the evening. When it was just the two of us, when we weren't so separated by a crowd like this, it felt as though we belonged. That was why telling him tonight felt like it was going to be painlessly seamless, but now…

Ron followed my eyes. "Don't mind where he's sitting and where you're standing. I've never agreed with the persona you always thought you needed."

Doubt consumed me in the worst way, and I felt my eyes water. "At this point he'll just see me as a liar. And I'd only confirm his initial theory, that the working class can't be trusted."

Ron huffed. "Or he'll see the same Elle Rybeck that is able, brilliant and forceful all on her own."

I turned back to him with a bitter smile. "You still think I'm worthy of your son?"

"I think you're more worthy of him than he is of you."

That made one tear escape and I swiped at it. "You've always given me too much credit."

"Somebody has to," he muttered.

I straightened and cleared my throat. "Get back to your table, Mr. Brightman. Runway's about to start." I turned on my ear piece as my old boss mouthed *good luck* and walked back to his seat.

On my way back, I was stopped by yet another guest. Rebecca.

I threw on my best smile. "Hey, everything okay?"

Rebecca pulled me aside. "Yes, listen before the last model is presented, we need to pause for an announcement from our CEO regarding the designer she'll be showcasing. Could you make sure the stage crew and the last model knows? It's very important."

"Of course, so she should be cued to enter when the speaker is done?" I confirmed with a question.

"And the applause."

"Right."

"Thanks much." Rebecca stalked away, as I rolled my eyes.

I found Mimi and relayed the instructions as I scanned the schedule. "Could you please let...Adrienne know to listen for her cue and then take the stage. They're moving kind of fast, so she'll already be standing by."

"Start her strut when the applause ends...I'm on it," Mimi murmured before disappearing backstage.

I turned on my mic and instructed Ryan to pause on Adrienne's light cue.

"Noted. Just give me the signal to release," Ryan reminded.

I shut my mic off and breathed a sigh of relief. The night would be over very shortly after the final showcase. Dessert was already being served, which meant that in less than one hour, I'd be closing up here and make my final decision on talking to Scott.

Maybe Ron was right, maybe I did deserve a chance, but not without the truth.

I sighed. I couldn't think about that right now. Instead, I focused on the CEO's speech and praise on the extraordinary work of this last but not least designer who they plan to feature quite a bit in the coming new year.

Ugh, get on with it.

Unable to control myself, I looked over at Scott's table, but he was gone. I frowned, unsettled by the fact that I didn't have eyes on him. Especially since I was already spotted by Ron. My eyes searched and found him leaning by one of the pillars. I froze.

He wasn't alone.

Claudia was with him, in her stylish gold and black gown, sparkly heels and long blond hair draping over her shoulders. She reached up, dusting the shoulder of his suit jacket. Scott didn't seem to welcome it but didn't walk away either. Instead, he gave her a wicked grin and leaned in closer only to disappear behind a crowd that stood and applauded, covering the discreet duo.

My heart stopped. The noise in the room was like thunder and I looked for an escape.

How could I be so foolish? *That* was the kind of woman Scott belonged with. Prominent, elegant, upscale; a genuine version of *Isabel*.

Finally, the thunderous applause stopped and the room returned to a light chatter, which stopped almost abruptly with confusion spread across the guest's faces.

What the hell is going on?

It took all but my name being urged twice in my earpiece before the adrenaline flooded and my eyes were wide as reality hit me.

My head spun to the stage. A flushed and angry model stood on the dim, lifeless runway.

31

SCOTT

THE LAST MODEL EMERGED ONTO A DESOLATE STAGE.

I tore my eyes off the frozen woman showcasing the evenings most talked about designer, and glanced around at the confused audience. Empire Fashions' CEO stood from his chair and waved at the DJ who just shrugged back at him.

Beside me, Claudia, who was just very politely reminded she wasn't free to touch me whenever she felt like it, rushed forward, grabbing Rebecca. "What the hell is going on? Where are her lights?"

"I don't know, I gave Elle very clear instructions. I'll go find her."

Before Rebecca could get away from Claudia's wrath, the lights came on suddenly, in full effect. The model recovered and moved gracefully down the runway, posing a bizarre yet remarkable gown with confidence.

"Forget it, Bec, I'll go find her," she turned on her heel then swiveled back, "Which one is she again?"

I rolled my eyes and approached Claudia, placing a hand

on her shoulder. She froze at my touch and looked up at me. "Why don't you leave my staff to me," I spoke coolly.

She released herself from my hold. "Elle might work for you, but she owes me an explanation on what the hell that was, all the same." She turned again. "Come on, you can help point her out for me."

How was I going to tell Claudia, I'd never met her?

"Claudia," the edge in my voice stopped her in her tracks. "I'm not going to repeat myself. I will deal with her. Stay out of it."

She huffed and brushed past me. "Come on," she turned to Rebecca, and they both raced over to a hysterical CEO and someone else I assumed was the eminent designer.

"Fuck," I muttered under my breath and rubbed my forehead. I was not in the mood to deal with this tonight.

"Friend of yours?" Ron walked up to me, handing me my drink.

I took a hefty sip. "More like a foe."

"Sure didn't seem like it." Ron cocked his head and turned to wave at one of the parting guests.

"It's not what you think," I said breathlessly. Claudia was the last person I needed to worry about.

"I'm not thinking anything. I'm just letting you know," he turned to face me, "what it might look like to someone."

I shook my head and finished off my drink. "Right. Like it matters to me if someone got the wrong idea here." I set my drink down and rubbed my eyes, considering the tempting thought to call it a night and deal with the problem in the morning.

"I need to get out of here. Get some rest so I can fire someone in the morning," I mumbled.

Ron raised his glass at me. "Good luck with that," he chuckled and walked away.

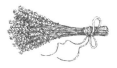

I took a long hot shower. The evening's disaster played over in my head. What are the chances that Starr-Bright Events logo being displayed on every table would turn out to be something I now regretted?

I threw on a clean shirt as my doorbell rang. It was well after midnight at this point, but it didn't matter because I knew who it was. A smile spread across my face before I opened the door and saw the miserable expression on hers.

My face fell. "Isabel, what's the matter?" She stood at my doorstep dressed in an all-black pantsuit, which she in fact looked amazingly sexy in. With glistening eyes, she opened her mouth to say something but then hesitated.

I frowned, pulling her inside. "Hey, what is it? Did something happen?"

She nodded. "I had a long night."

The pained expression on her face tugged at my heart and I wrapped my arms around her. She released a breath and melted into me. After a moment she tensed and stepped back.

"Scott," she started, shakily, "I don't think this is going to work."

I glared at her. She was here to break up with me?

I shook my head. "I don't understand. You came here after midnight...to end it?" That couldn't be right. There was something else. Something she wasn't telling me. Still, I felt my heart ripping at the seams.

"I was afraid I'd change my mind tomorrow," she said softly.

"Still not making sense, sweetheart," I snapped.

"I can't explain it. Not tonight anyway. Maybe someday." She seemed as confused as I was. "I just realized tonight that...we're not compatible. Your lifestyle. It's very different from mine."

I couldn't believe what I was hearing. "This is all very funny, Isabel, because I'm unable to agree or disagree with you. I have no argument since you've told me so little about yourself to begin with," I growled.

She winced and I pulled her into me, softening my voice.

"All I can do is stand here and try to convince you that we sure as hell do belong together because I've never felt this way about anyone, and I *know* you feel it too."

She looked at me bitterly. "You're wrong." She turned to leave and I grabbed her arm.

My voice was low. "Give me a reason I can hold on to, baby." I searched her eyes. "Is there someone else?"

"Definitely not."

"Then it's not good enough," I whispered.

She looked utterly exhausted so I refused to pressure her any further.

I released a deep breath. "Can we at least talk tomorrow? When...we've both had some rest?"

She nodded, her head still low and her eyes red.

I lifted her chin and kissed her softly. "Whatever it is, we need to talk about it."

She blinked but there was no response. God how I wished my kiss would be enough to convince her to stay. "I've got something I need to do in the morning, so maybe afternoon?"

She nodded. "Okay. Let's talk tomorrow. At the park across the street from Blue Reserves?"

"That's perfect, I'll be right around there in the morning."

She swiped at a tear and pulled my door open. I placed a hand over it, stopping her. Still refusing to look at me, I whispered in her ear. "I don't know what's going on. But I hope we can figure this out tomorrow."

With a weak smile, she turned and left.

32

ELLE

I avoided a text from Ron that morning checking in on me. The last thing I needed was a lecture from my old boss when I was no doubt about to endure one as soon as I got upstairs. I guzzled my coffee before even hitting the elevator bank at the lobby.

Maybe caffeine was a bad idea today. My heart was already up in my throat, and I couldn't breathe. It was the screw up last night.

That had to be it.

I was upset over the screw up.

My stupid—distraction-caused—colossal mistake.

I froze.

I actually froze.

Claudia Heart. Of course he'd find *her* at the party.

I sighed. Who was I kidding?

No matter the load of caffeine or mascara, my eyes still felt like glass. I was more than tired. More than annoyed at myself. There was a black cloud over me that even the best of problem solvers couldn't fix.

I was heartbroken.

I took a breath and rubbed the back of my neck as the elevator reached the floor to my office. I reminded myself why I always put my work first; distractions were a hazard. And I let it happen because of a man.

Oh hey. It was Monday. I was supposed to lead my *planned to perfection* meeting today. I laughed to myself as I reached my desk.

Mimi rolled over to me in her chair. "Are you drunk?"

"What?"

"What are you laughing about? We're going to be in serious trouble today. I'm astonished that someone didn't hunt us down last night," Mimi whispered.

"Oh it's coming Meem, don't you worry. But seriously; don't worry. Last night was on me."

"No. We're partners." She put a hand on my shoulder. "We stick together."

My new friend warmed my heart. "Thank you. But you did your part flawlessly. And mine would have been too if I hadn't..." my voice trailed off.

Froze from jealousy.

"You're human," Mimi shrugged and gave me a soft smile and then frowned, taking me in. "Not that you don't look terrific otherwise, but I'm going to recommend an eye cream that does *wonders*," she offered, sliding back to her desk and reaching for a notepad.

"Thanks." I glanced at Dean's door, expecting anxiety to consume me. Instead, all I felt was infuriated that after everything I'd accomplished in my adult life; I had to explain myself to anyone.

I was better than this. And maybe it was time I stopped being afraid to declare it.

My desk phone rang.

I bit my lip. Maybe today wasn't the best day to claim my Godliness.

SCOTT

A few minutes earlier...

"What the hell happened last night?" I barked when I stormed into Dean's office first thing Monday morning. After barely sleeping the night before and being in the dreadful mood I was in, I needed a reason why there was a major screw up at one of the biggest deals I'd handed this struggling company. Now that my name was all over this event planning firm, I had a great deal to lose.

Dean jumped out of his chair. "Scott, Starr called me this morning and told me about the fumble last night." He ran around his desk nervously. "Look I can't imagine what happened, but this never—"

"Where the hell was your team? Where was she? I didn't see anyone working the floor last night."

"That's how we like it, Scott." Starr walked in and hung her coat up. She appeared so casual and unaffected.

"What? That doesn't make any sense." I turned away from her and faced Dean. The only one who seemed to care about the business at all.

"It's part of our image," Starr announced proudly.

Dean eyed her tiredly, then turned back to me. "Look, we will find out what happened and we'll fix it."

"This is irreversible damage, Dean," I shouted, knowing full well where part of my frustration was coming from. I rubbed at my forehead and walked to the window, lowering my voice. "Dean, I just signed to protect you guys from sinking as a firm because you showed me that you could handle anything after Donovan's party."

"Same person," Dean mumbled, staring absently out the windows of his office, regardless of the shades being down.

"I don't give a damn." I seethed, turning to Dean and pressing a finger against my chest. "Do you know what she cost me last night? Why don't you both show me you mean business; I want her gone. Now."

Dean looked alarmed. "I don't think that's necessary. We don't fire people for a mistake." He held his hands up. "Listen, I get it, it was a big one, and I'm not sure why, but I'll talk to her."

Dean's loyalty to his staff was honorable. Something Isabel would appreciate. The thought of losing her angered me again and I glared at my new partner, my tone not to be misunderstood. "This is my firm now too. Those are *my* employees just as much as they are yours until I feel like you can handle it on your own, Dean."

After a moment of hesitation, Dean looked at Starr. "Call her in," he turned back to me, his eyes filled with regret. "I'll do it."

Starr picked up her phone and dialed a few digits. "Oh hi, Elle. Would you mind coming by for a moment?" her eyes flicked to me. "Great, thank you."

I crossed to the sofa and sat, rubbing my hands together to control my anger. I didn't typically get like this. Screw ups happen and perhaps my anger was displaced. But I didn't care. If this Elle would be on the receiving end of my rage—then so be it. Someone needed to be.

A short moment passed before Dean's door opened swiftly

without so much as a knock. My heated eyes shot up and my breath caught when she walked in.

Isabel?

Either I'd completely lost it, or Isabel just walked into the room in place of whoever this Elle was.

She was dressed in a white blouse and blue mini skirt. She looked at Dean and opened her mouth, prepared to say something until she spotted me on the sofa, all the color instantly drained from her beautiful features. She looked about as ill as I felt.

Dean scratched his forehead and went to stand in front of his desk. "Elle, this is Scott Weston. He's our new...partner. Scott was also the one to land us the fashion event you ran last night."

Isabel's mouth dropped open again and her chest hitched.

No. Impossible.

Physically, I was frozen, but my mind blustered with a mixture of confusion, doubt and hell...more anger than I thought possible moments ago.

"He was highly invested in this firm and the Ballard event was a big deal to us Elle," Dean continued, his words somewhat a blur, much like my vision.

Isabel tore her eyes from me and faced Dean. Seeming as though she lost her words, she swallowed and took a breath as though she'd been drowning.

I wanted to jump out of my seat and breathe life into her, but instead I stayed where I was, watching it all unfold.

"Elle, I've known you for a long time. You were one of Brightman's best. You plan to perfection. What happened?"

Isabel winced.

"You worked for Brightman?" My hard tone carried in the room.

Isabel bravely turned in my direction. "Seven years," she answered flatly.

My jaw flexed as I held her gaze before she blinked away. Mentally shaking my head, I tried to snap out of the nightmare I was living. But it was useless.

She turned back to Dean, raising her head slightly. "I don't plan to perfection, Dean. Whoever told you that was fooled. That's what I do. I fool people. I fool them into thinking that everything is running smoothly, but it never does. I completely flaked on the Hayes party, but the Winter Ballard was indeed planned to perfection."

I watched her eyes wander and she swallowed. "There was a cue that… needed to happen towards the end and—well I got distracted." She glanced at me.

I frowned, knowing instantly what she meant. Ron's comment about Claudia and how it could appear to someone. He must have known Elle was there.

"What are you talking about? Donovan's event went smoothly," Starr argued

Elle laughed wearily. "Nothing ever goes smoothly, Starr. If you ever worked in the field and were a true professional, you'd know."

Dean's solemn features turned angry as he took a step toward Elle, and I stood instinctively. Dean seemed to recover and continued. "I think we've heard enough. Elle, last night's screw up was too big for everyone in the room and…we just can't have this at our firm, especially since—"

I blinked. *Wait. No.*

"Hold on a minute, Dean, maybe this is—" I interjected before I was cut off.

"No Dean, please continue," she demanded, without so much as a glance at me.

Both my new business partners looked at me questioningly, considering moments ago I'd insisted this employee be terminated immediately. How would I explain a change of heart without damaging her career and reputation? I'd have no power over what these two could do to her in this field.

Apparently, I had taken too long to answer and Dean took that as his cue to continue.

"We're going to have to let you go. I'm sorry Elle; I thought you were better than this."

I stalked to the window, for once, not knowing what to do. Because all I fucking wanted to do was whisk her out of this nightmare, talk to her, will the life back into her eyes.

But that wasn't who I was. I was no hero. I was tricked, lied to, made into a fool. Firing her was the least of how to deal with people like her.

Behind me, I heard Elle let out a short, shaky laugh. "No apologies necessary. I *am* better than this. Not in the work I delivered, but this firm. I do plan to perfection. It won't always appear that way to me, but it will to my clients."

I turned and looked at her. This time, she looked back at me.

"I did what had to be done in order for both events to go smoothly. And sometimes you have to get creative—like wearing a fitting dress to remove an accidental raspberry from the guest of honor's plate so she doesn't burst into hives."

The napkin. I shook my head.

"Or hire an old flame who happens to be a photographer and owes you a favor. I guarantee you, Dean, Starr, it was done with every single job you ever booked," she proclaimed without a trace of doubt in her voice.

Her eyes were on me again. "But if you're going to let some V.I.P. investor—who doesn't even know how it works, come in here and tell you I'm not good enough—I thought *you* were better than this, Dean." She blinked rapidly and took a breath. "It's been a real pleasure," she murmured before turning and leaving the room.

I moved from the window as soon as Elle shut the door behind her. My chest heavy with guilt and anger. Emotions whirled inside me, clouding my thoughts. Why should I feel guilty? I owed her nothing. She lied to me from the start and continued to spend weeks deceiving me. For what? Had she known who I was? The surprised look on her face suggested that she didn't.

Dean watched the door regrettably, "Well, that was—"

"Dean, is there a private conference room where I can speak with Ms. Rybeck alone?"

Dean glared at me for a moment before answering. "You can use room B."

33

ELLE

COMPLETELY FLUSHED AND RUSHING TO GET THE HELL OUT OF that building as fast as I could, I speed-walked to my desk to gather my things. Thankfully, there was nothing that didn't fit in my everyday tote bag.

Leave everything else.

"What's going on?" Mimi jumped out of her chair, alarmed.

"Mimi, I've got to go. I'll call you later, okay?"

"Oh no," she mumbled. "It was that VIP guy who'd been here a few times, wasn't it? It's always the hot ones who turn out to be jerks."

"Can we talk later, I've got to go."

"Call me," she whispered as I raced to the elevator.

Grateful to have finally reached the front of the floor, I pushed the button and willed myself to ignore the peering eyes. How much of this was going to ruin my career?

How much did I care?

I wanted to care. I wanted to worry more about my career

right now than think about Scott. And how any chance of us working things out was now burnt to a crisp. How had I not known how heavily involved and invested he was in the company I worked for?

"Come on," I urged, pressing the button again. I couldn't wait to get in the elevator so I could bang my head against the door seventeen times. Heartbreak combined with utter humiliation will make you do that.

Like music to my ears, the bell chimed and the stainless-steel doors opened. I stepped in and released the breath I'd been holding. I turned in place just as a familiar hand grabbed hold of one of the slow-moving doors.

"Ms. Rybeck, could we have a quick word in conference room B please?" Scott appeared a foot from me, holding the doors in place. His tone was even and his expression blank.

"I—I'm sorry, I need to be going. I've said everything I needed to."

"Oh I don't think you have." With only a slight twist of his head, he glanced at the surrounding cubicles and drafting tables with people watching us. He turned back and pinned me with his eyes. I didn't miss the warning promise that he wouldn't hesitate to cause a scene.

I swallowed and whispered, "Maybe I could spare a minute."

I followed him inside the corner conference room.

Scott didn't bother sitting, he crossed to the opposite end of the room, and stood facing the windows. I'd witnessed him do the same in his apartment after a disagreement with a business owner.

I took a deep silent breath.

"Close the door," he ordered, his tone as sharp as ever.

Fixating my jaw tightly, I swallowed some words and closed the door lightly. "Scott, I don't think—"

He spun around but didn't face me; instead he strode past

me curiously observing the staff through the aggravatingly spotless glass walls.

"Tell me," he began, in a formal, authoritative tone, "which of these loyal and tenured employees—my employees—is your assistant?"

"None of them," I answered flatly.

With his eyes still wandering around the crowded floor, he nodded, then placed his hands in his pockets and turned to finally face me. His eyes were cold, not hurt as I would have expected. He didn't even look disappointed. He looked as if HR had just caught me laundering money from his company, or as if I'd been caught to be a mole that he trusted. Either way, it was a look I'd imagined he'd give to business associates. Not someone he claimed he belonged with less than twelve hours ago.

If his attempt was to make me feel as inferior to him as possible, he was regrettably succeeding.

I avoided calling out his name again, since he was making it clear, it wasn't like that. "I was planning on telling you when we met today."

Scott glanced at his watch. "Well it looks like your morning just freed up," he glared at me, "You're on *my* time now."

"No I'm not," I shot back, lifting my head and raising my voice to make that clear.

"What exactly *were* you planning on telling me?" He leaned against one of the window columns.

"Everything."

He huffed at me. A moment went by before he spoke again. "You saw me at the event with Claudia," he stated matter-of-factly.

"I did."

His eyes shot to me. "Why couldn't you just tell me that last night?" he breathed.

I took two steps closer. "That's not why I ended things, Scott; I don't break up with someone over jealousy. You know me better than that."

"That was really the wrong thing to say right now, *Elle*," he practically shouted.

I glanced back at the glass walls toward the onlooking staff, then looked down. "Why did you call me in here if you're not going to let me explain?" I asked quietly, hoping he'd take the hint to lower his voice.

"Because I can't believe a single word you say," he answered gruffly.

My heart sank and words became hard to form. I swallowed the ball in my throat. "Can we go somewhere and talk?"

"Why then?"

I took that as a no. "You already know that I was not a guest at Donovan's party."

"People will start to get curious. Get to the point." His voice grew.

"We're...from two different worlds."

"What world are you from, Elle?"

"Stop it, Scott, you know what I mean." I took another step toward him. "Let's say I told you last night; I'm not the successful entrepreneur, socialite, high dollar event goer you assumed I was."

"Assumed?" He shook his head and turned away, but not before I caught the glimpse of hurt I'd expected before.

I stood frozen, unable to move, because all I wanted was to reach for him. Make him look at me and let him know everything else was real. Why couldn't I just screw everyone watching and just do it?

This might be the only chance I get.

But that wasn't who I was. I wasn't affectionate in public, especially in sensitive situations.

He knew that and he was using it.

"I'm sorry. Whether it was at Elaine's chair or waiting for the cab outside the venue, or the next morning at the cafe... I should have told you. But it kept getting harder..." when my voice cracked, I knew it was time to get the hell out of there and fast.

He turned back to face me, the hurt plain on his face. "So it was easier to break up with me?"

I folded my arms in an effort to keep myself from reaching for him. "Please, let's just go somewhere to—"

"Answer the question."

I looked down and answered in a low voice. "No, that part was nearly impossible."

He breathed out an unamused laugh, which hurt me to the core. "And now I find you here. Living your true life..."

This life hadn't felt true to me for a while now. But he probably wouldn't have remembered me sharing this sad reality with him weeks ago. I fought the tears that threatened to escape. "If we're done here, I'm going to go."

"We most certainly are," he confirmed.

I turned to start the short walk to the door.

"I can get you your job back," he muttered, facing the window.

"I appreciate that. But maybe you haven't been listening. I'm more than this. I have been for a while and maybe this is the push I needed."

His head fell to his side as if he wanted to turn back to me but caught himself.

"Goodbye, Scott."

SCOTT

I took a seat at the narrow end of the conference table well after she walked out. I buried my head in my hands for only a short moment before running a hand over my face and urging myself to pull it together. Since my staff was no doubt still peering into the room from a distance.

I snickered at the consideration of my own interest. More than I'd afforded Elle. I was keenly aware of her dislike of public displays of anything.

But I didn't let it stop me, in fact I basked in it for a moment there. But all it did was drive her out of here as quickly as possible.

The door opened slowly. I didn't have to turn to know it was Dean. No one else on this floor would dare walk through it right now.

Dean closed the door behind him, cautiously. "Everything alright?"

I glanced in his direction but didn't respond to the stupid question.

Dean nodded slowly, then turned to push a button by the door, near the light switch. A humming noise sounded and silver shades gradually rolled down each glass wall. In a few seconds, we were in complete privacy from the rest of the floor.

I sighed and shook my head, wondering how much more I would have gotten out of Elle if I knew *that* was an option.

Dean crossed the room to sit. After a long silence, he finally leaned back. "So, how do you know her?"

I rubbed my temples and looked up. "The party," I replied miserably.

"This weekend?"

"Hayes"

"Hayes?" Dean pushed off the back of his chair in surprise.

I lifted my head. "The raspberry."

Dean threw his head back in laughter. "Oh man. What are you going to do?"

I frowned and jerked back a little. "I just did it."

Something shifted in Dean's expression and he stood abruptly. "Well I'm going to undo it. You forced my hand back there and put Starr and me under pressure to fire one of our best. One of the *city's* best," he shouted. "She had a point, you may have the money but you don't know anything about the business. If you did, you would have given her a chance to explain before letting go one of our biggest assets. He moved to the door. "I'm calling Elle. Hell, I'll give her a promotion if that's what it takes."

"Don't bother," I muttered. "She doesn't want it."

"What are you talking about? I've known Elle for years; she loves this job. She's remarkable at it. Last night was just—"

"Last night was my fault," I rose to my feet and buttoned my jacket. "I haven't known Elle very long. But she was probably right about one thing; she *is* better than this. And I wish her well." I crossed to Dean, who was holding the door open. I stopped before him to make myself clear. "But she won't be coming back here."

In the elevator, all I could think was that Isabel had been in the same one just a few minutes ago. I pushed down the annoying sting of regret of not taking the ride down with her instead of forcing her into the goddamn fishbowl.

The truth was, this shouldn't have been a surprise to me. I was always good at reading people; I knew when I was being lied to. In fact, thinking back now, I could have probably pinpointed exactly at what point she was lying.

But it was never about who she was or what she was passionate about, it was all superficial stuff. Stuff, as she correctly suspected, I would have guessed from someone I met at Donovan's party.

I ran my hand through my face again as the elevator doors opened to the bright lobby and stepped out. My face burned when I found an angry tall blond shouting at the small-framed brunette.

"What do you mean you no longer owe me an explanation."

Elle rolled her eyes and turned toward the exit. Claudia grabbed her arm, shifting her back. "Do you have any idea—"

"Claudia!" I barked from the elevator bank.

Both women turned at my voice. Elle took the opportunity to break free of Claudia's grasp and raced out through the revolving doors.

Claudia stalked towards me. "I can't believe you hired that woman. She's an absolute ditz, Scott. I want answers for last night and someone better give them to me."

"The hell do you think you're doing putting your hands on anyone?"

That only seemed to have frustrated her even more. "I was really looking forward to yelling at someone today, Scott."

"Get a grip Claudia."

"Excuse me?"

"You had some ridiculous demands for their planning and they came through, unbelievably. Which reminds me why I should have never gone into business with you again. You set one foot upstairs or make any kind of threats against Elle, my business partners, or any of my staff, I will make sure that all my contacts are generously warned."

Claudia opened her mouth, a rebuttal prepared.

"And that's not slander, sweetheart, that's business."

I walked out of the building. Dark clouds had spread across the late morning sky and the wind grew strong. Thunder rolled in the distance. I hated that my first instinct was to search for her, but I knew she'd been long gone.

And it was probably better that way.

34

ELLE

I IGNORED ALL CALLS FOR THE REST OF THE AFTERNOON. I DID eventually acknowledge a text from Mimi shortly after I got home.

Hope you're okay. Let me know if you want to talk. But I have to know...is that the guy you met at a party that didn't know your real name?

I replied with a yes, and tossed my phone aside. I was done with people for the day.

I finally made my way to the shower after coming home drenched and drained. What little battery I had left after an endless and unrelenting Sunday night, I'd used up in Dean's office.

God that felt good. It felt right.

At least I'd gone down feeling proud. Defending myself. Since it was clear no one else in that room had my back.

I forced a glass of water down my throat and sprawled across my sofa, giving myself this time to be alone and sulk.

Eventually, I was bound to be so consumed by everything I'd have no choice but to fall asleep.

Sometime later, it had appeared to be exactly what happened. I walked to my kitchen for another glass of water, grabbed three stale pretzels out of a bowl left on the counter, and a multivitamin.

That should do the trick for now.

I fell asleep for what seemed like a day and a half when I heard footsteps in my apartment. I sprinted up and found Char tiptoeing in.

"Hey," my friend whispered, setting the spare keys I'd given her on the table.

"Hi." My voice was hoarse.

"You never called me last night to tell me how it went. It's barely six o'clock, how long have you been home from work sleeping?"

I held myself up by my elbows and stared at Char for a moment before tears sprung out of me like a loose fire hydrant.

Last night's events and this morning's calamity poured out of me in somewhat audible intervals. I wasn't sure at what point Char had squeezed onto the couch and wrapped an arm around me, but I was grateful.

"I carried this on for much longer than I should have. I avoided the truth because I was afraid to either lose my job or lose him and consequently lose focus during one of the biggest moments of my career." I blinked in confusion. "What kind of sick joke is it that all of those things happened anyway?"

She scrunched her nose. "That is kind of funny."

"Char, what am I going to do?"

"You're going to start by having some real food." Char stood and walked to the kitchen. "Then we're going to get online and find you work ASAP."

I scoffed. I didn't want to just *find work*. Obviously, that would be the appropriate course of events: lose a job, find another, pay rent, live. But how long would I need to keep *working* these mediocre jobs to prove that I was capable of so much more?

"Until you're dead." Char approached me with a cup of hot tea.

"I have got to stop talking to myself." I shook my head. "Hey maybe there's something to that party planning hotline idea…"

"A what?"

"Never mind; no one was around to hear that one." I half-joked.

"You have nothing in your freezer and I don't know how long those leftovers have been in your fridge, so I put on some pasta."

I nodded.

"Alright, I came here straight from work so I need to go home to feed my pets. Please promise me you'll go to sleep as soon as you've eaten."

"I won't have much of a choice; I've slept a total of three hours in the last two days."

After Char left, I swallowed down most of my dinner but there was no way I could sleep. At nearly ten o'clock, I was still staring up at the dark ceiling in my bedroom listening to the unwavering pattering at my window. Deciding to endure it rather than tune it out, I pulled aside my drapes and opened the window, breathing in the mist penetrating the screen.

"Useless," I groaned. Heartache struck again as I pictured his face. I wanted to hate him for not giving me the chance to explain in private, for shutting me down, for humiliating me.

But instead, some low, pathetic part of me just ached for him.

I inhaled deeply, pushing down the doubt, and let out a shaky breath.

This was a tremendously bad idea. But I saw no other way to get through the night, especially when my anger and adrenaline to set my record straight was so high.

Forty minutes later my hair was once again soaked. I closed up my hopeless umbrella against the strong wind and pushed my way through the doors of Scott's apartment building.

I smiled at Fredrick at the lobby desk who typically had the night shift and he greeted me right back, calling for the penthouse elevator.

Quietly, I cursed the determination that disappeared and was replaced with a hammering heartbeat. Deep breaths were proving to be pointless as I reached his floor.

The fuck was I thinking?

Before I could turn back, I pounded at his door, wiping the raindrops from my forehead with the back of my hand as the door opened furiously.

My breath caught. It was unfair how massively tense I was while Scott stood there, shirtless, staring at me without as much as a blink. His eyes washed over me but there was no warmth in them.

I opened my mouth and his jaw flexed as he pushed the door open, stepping aside.

I stepped in hesitantly, removing my raincoat while he disappeared wordlessly through the corridor. He returned a moment later, handing me a white towel and pulling a t-shirt over his head.

"Thank you," I whispered and patted my face. I tried my first words again. I had them—accusing him of not giving me a real chance to explain, diminishing my existence. I reminded myself that I had nothing else to lose.

"I couldn't sleep," I blurted.

Seriously? That's what you start with?

"Guilty conscience?" his tone was flat.

"That's not what I meant. I needed to talk to you, without…" my voice cut off again, dammit.

Scott rolled his eyes and went behind his kitchen counter.

I turned away taking a few more steps into the apartment, rubbing my forehead; willing myself to get it together. Feeling ready, I spun and found him standing before me, handing me a glass of red wine.

"What's this?"

"It's a glass of wine," he nodded at the half-poured stem glass, "please have some."

I gritted my teeth and gave him a cold glare, but took the glass because he was right. I needed this. I swallowed down more than half of it and handed it back. "You think you know me so well," I muttered, barely posing a question.

He twirled the glass and the corner of his mouth twitched. "Maybe a little."

"I'm sorry it's late."

He shook his head slightly, setting the glass down. "The evening? The truth? Be more specific here."

I sighed. "Both. Okay?"

He slipped his hands in the pockets of his sweatpants and leaned against the wall. His glare came off as if he were giving me the chance to say more but not to expect anything of it.

"I'm sure it didn't go unnoticed that I still owe you a reason. I want you to know that it wasn't at all because I didn't think you'd like me if I weren't equal to your status."

"First of all, only a handful of people in this city are.

Second, I'm not an idiot, Elle. I'm aware of the amount of times you tried to get away from me when I was in full pursuit." He pushed off the wall, irritated. "Maybe I should fix myself a drink since this is clearly going to take a while."

Okay. He is getting impatient.

"I didn't think I'd see you again. I had this outstanding reputation. If it got out that I'd often dress to fit in with the crowd to do damage control at my own events, I'd be the joke of the industry rather than a role model."

"You'd make a terrible role model," his voice wavered but I still nodded at his words.

I swallowed knowing it was time for the hard truth. "At first, I was afraid of what you, in your position, could do to someone like me in this city." I shrugged. "If I didn't have my career, I had nothing. I don't *know* anything else."

He frowned and his mouth opened slightly.

I continued, holding up a hand, "I have *never* been the type to put a relationship before my work. But when things became serious between us, I wanted nothing more than to drop the stupid charade no matter what it cost me just so that we can have a fair chance. And even though I trusted you, I was still willing to risk it all for you."

The creases on Scott's forehead smoothed. "Not all."

"You're right. When Dean handed me the Ballard event, that...complicated things because I really wanted that gig and I needed it to be perfect."

He glanced down as if he was the one with regrets.

I rubbed a hand over my face, almost ashamed to admit it. Losing focus is unacceptable in my world as you well know now, so I put off telling you."

Scott looked down and nodded slowly. "Well, lying is unacceptable in mine, *Isabel,* so if you've said everything you needed to..." he implied but made no move toward escorting me out.

"That actually is my legal name."

"Yes I know, I was making a point."

"I will leave but not before I say one more thing," I paused and softened my tone. "Please don't blame Ron for my lie."

Scott laughed. "Oh don't worry—I'm saving all this blame for you, sweetheart," he stalked forward. "But while we're on the subject of my father, this actually made a lot of sense. Because you see, I swore I was losing my mind the day I introduced you." He shook his head and paced around his living room. "Let me tell you something Elle, I am awfully good at reading people, and I could tell that something was up but I pushed it aside because I didn't think it would be possible for both of you to be hiding something from me."

I bit my lip and grinned anxiously. "Ron never questioned my tactics...perhaps he should have."

Scott glanced away then placed his hands back in his pockets, looking at me. "Anything else?"

My eyes watered, realizing I had yet to say the words. "I'm so sorry," I whispered. "I should have told you everything last night."

He swallowed. "I bet seeing me with Claudia was really convenient for you; you could end it with a reason and feel no remorse."

"Would you forget about Claudia? Okay, yes, seeing you with her was a big push in breaking up with you but it wasn't jealousy or anger. It was because I'm not one of those women. The class, the social standing," I paused remembering a quote in one of the articles I'd read. "I'm the person you don't bother mentioning did all the work behind the scenes."

"Those were not my words, Elle, you know that," he shouted.

I shrugged defensively. "What does it matter? It was probably paraphrased." It was a low blow, but I was angry that he had little regard for my apology and after I'd poured out my excruciating six weeks, he'd simply asked me to leave.

He rubbed the stubble on his chin. "I think I liked it better when you were nervous."

My teeth clenched. "I think I liked it better when you were ignorant." I pushed past him and grabbed my coat off the hook.

I barely heard the footsteps behind me before he spun me in place and pushed me against the foyer wall. He gave me only a fraction of a second to push him away before he crushed my lips with his, kissing me furiously. There was no passion and it didn't feel like he just wanted a last kiss. It was filled with anger and possibly a power play.

"I should fuck you senseless," he growled.

"Do it."

His eyes flicked to mine. "It will be goodbye, Isabel."

But what if I could change your mind?

I couldn't help but replay the words he'd said to me just last night. Standing at this very spot, pleading with me to see that we belonged together when I was ending it. When he'd seen the pain in my eyes and wanted nothing more than to fix it, to convince me to stay, to talk to him.

I had to believe that it wouldn't be goodbye. I swallowed the painful and almost shameful acknowledgement if he meant those words and made my choice regardless.

"Then make it good," I said flatly. The words felt like fire in my throat because I knew this was a bad idea. But I wanted him. Even if it was the last time. "And the name is Elle."

His eyes swept me wickedly and he grinned. "Not tonight."

Sweeping me off my feet, he led me to his bedroom, our mouths connected and hungry for each other.

I expected him to move us to his bed, but instead, he'd pulled us to a spot across it, to a narrow wall between two large windows. The drapes were open, the city lights illuminating the darkened room.

"Were you expecting something else?" he asked as he pulled his shirt over his head.

My jaw clenched and my chest burned. "This will do."

"Good." He tugged at my sweaterdress and I pushed off the wall slightly to let him lift it off of me. "Hmm," he leaned in, kissing my collarbone. "You smell like rose petals."

"Maybe you shouldn't talk."

His eyes met mine and he grinned. "Fine. Maybe you shouldn't look at me while I fuck you either. Turn around."

I did as he asked and felt him freeze behind me. A moment later, his lips pressed softly on my shoulder while his hands roamed my body slowly.

He stroked me for a moment before entering me. Slow and careful at first, then harder with rough strokes.

"What about this part, baby?" he asked against my ear. "Was this part real?"

I whimpered. Tempted to say *it wasn't* just to anger him more. But I'd told my last lie yesterday and I was done.

I nodded.

"Did you lose your voice?"

"Yes," I cried. "Every part of it was real."

He bit down on my shoulder and pumped harder, bringing me closer with each thrust. I cried out, tears at the brink as I came.

He followed with one final thrust and a curse before emptying inside me and pulling out slowly.

We stood like that for a moment, him breathing at my neck while I urged myself to pull it together before I had to turn around.

He won't see me cry.

"Come to bed with me," he whispered tenderly after a long moment.

"What?"

"Elle," he turned me. "Stay the night."

"Why?"

He took a moment before answering. "Because I'm not ready to let you go."

My eyes welled again. It wasn't because he was in love with me. It was because he wanted to have his cake and eat it too.

I pushed him off of me and picked up my dress. "You don't get a round two to say your goodbye."

"Isabel."

"Don't call me that," I shouted before slipping my things back on and racing out of his room.

I heard him mutter a curse behind me. I slipped my shoes back on just as he caught up with me in the foyer, shirtless but with his sweatpants back on.

I couldn't hold my tears any longer. Screw my dignity, I'd already lost it ten minutes ago. I released them when he twisted me to face him.

"I am not a liar. I am not a fraud. I made the mistake of putting my career first," I swallowed, "instead of trusting the man I'd fallen in love with."

His expression softened but I had heard enough tonight to know there was no hope for us. "I should have known better than to think I could make it all work out in the end." I tried to push past him but he held a tight grip. "And I should have known better than to come here tonight. So please let go of me."

His mouth opened but he was speechless.

"Don't bother," I said, wiping at my tears. "You've already said your goodbye. And I heard it loud and clear."

I pulled the door open and waited for him to hand me my coat.

His eyes roamed over me, regret clear in his eyes but

nothing else about the way he watched me was readable. And no words were being said to support it.

I had my answer.

He gently placed the coat over my shoulders. "For what it's worth, I couldn't sleep either," he said in a husky voice before I strode away.

35

SCOTT

MY NEW OFFICE HAD BEEN A REVOLVING DOOR SINCE I'D MOVED in. The location was temporary; I leased out an entire floor at the Hayes Enterprises building. As much as I wanted to venture away from where I'd started, I still had quite a bit of accounts open with H.E. and knew Donovan would only want to hold meetings at his building. So it served a purpose to rent the space.

I closed the binder prepared for my review by Dean's assistant and handed it back to him. "Plans look great. Let's just hope we didn't miss anything. How's New Year's Eve looking?"

Dean pushed out of his chair, eagerly. "Our entire staff is booked for new years."

"Excellent." I noticed other new implementations from my review that sounded strangely familiar. "I like the new time management system you've set up for each planner,"

Dean nodded. "Tracking project hours will help us

improve efficiencies, and figure out where time is being wasted and unnecessary money being spent. It was something Elle started, and my office manager fine-tuned."

I should have been satisfied at the progress on staff efficiencies since it was one of the key issues I noticed and immediately needed to rectify. Instead, I stood, irritably. "Have you spoken to her?" I asked in my most disinterested tone.

As though I could get one over on Dean.

"She finally answered my call a few days ago," Dean replied, and then chuckled. "She was very pleased to hear that our staff won't be getting away with half the shit they used to. I needed some advice on the new plans and also to…"

I turned. "To what?"

"To apologize," Dean said straightforwardly. "I urged her to come work for me after Brightman folded and she accepted. Only to fire her less than two months later."

My chest ached again.

I walked to the window, fighting the urge to ask him how she sounded. It had been two weeks since Elle walked out of my apartment. A stupid thing I let happen.

For days I was convinced the woman had shown up that night simply to curse me. Because since then, at exactly that hour each night, I lay awake in bed picturing an entirely different outcome. I'd have said all the right words and kissed her in all the right places, taken her to my bed and made love to her the way she deserved instead of letting my anger and frustration, my constant need for power get the better of me.

Of us.

I belittled her after she poured her honest heart out and practically manhandled her; a reality that haunted me mercilessly.

There was no denying it; I missed her.

"Do you know if she found a new job?"

"Not something you ask someone less than two weeks

after firing them." Dean admitted. "Besides, her saying no would only tempt me to do what you told me not to."

I cleared my throat, keeping my tone even. Since apologies weren't something I did well. Or ever. "Surely, she'll be alright. She would still be getting a year-end bonus, correct?"

"No, she hadn't worked for us long enough to be eligible," Dean answered flatly. No doubt the man was trying to get a reaction out of me.

My jaw tightened. "Right."

Dean strolled to the door and shrugged. "But you know I did just get a new partner who I suppose could bend the rules."

I shook my head and let out a short laugh. Soon, I was going to be his only partner. A week ago, Starr had proposed to sell her share of the company. Dean accepted and came up with a plan to buy her out.

The financial setback would only cost him a few more months of my involvement before Dean bought back his entire company.

"Have HR make the arrangement, please."

Dean turned. "I can't do that."

"Why not?"

"Because there is still a policy, Scott. I meant if you wanted to cut her a check, it needs to be under something else. Like…additional gratuities from the last event she planned."

I deadpanned him.

"Okay, maybe not the last one she planned."

I shook my head. My heart broke for Elle having to live with the reputation of screwing up the years biggest event. Because she had done an incredible job. It was too bad no one else believed it. She was right. No matter how hard you plan, how meticulous you are, things will always go wrong. And people will only focus on the screw ups.

In her case, it was a missed cue, one that she shouldn't have been responsible for in the first place.

One that she was more than prepared for.

One that I was largely to blame.

"So what are our options?"

Dean walked over, opening up his checkbook and writing out a figure. "Split this with me?"

I looked at the figure that was a fairly large bonus, but not too much for it to be suspiciously too generous. "I'll cover the whole thing. Just sign it."

Dean smirked and signed the check.

"Alright, I'll have this delivered in a few days, when she's back."

"What do you mean? Why not send it now?"

"I spoke to Elle yesterday, she's out of town. She won't be home to sign for it."

"Where'd she go?"

Dean shrugged and headed for the door. "I didn't ask, figured she was visiting family for the holidays."

"That's unlikely," I muttered as he walked out of my office.

Two days before Christmas Eve, I met Ron at the hotel for a quick breakfast before rushing back to my office to work on…anything. I'd avoided working out of my home for the past week since all it did was remind me of all the nights we'd spent together there.

Ron was late which was strange. The man was never late except when trying to be a father.

I finished off my first cup of coffee when Ron finally

showed up and dropped a heavy folder on the white tablecloth.

"What's this?" I asked.

"Your Christmas present." Ron nodded at the thick stack. "Sorry it's not wrapped."

I hesitated, then reached for the folder, scanning its contents and frowned. "Still not clear on what this is and why you're giving it to me."

"You've been asking me for my plans, policies, and everything that one might need to know about how Brightman Events operated; well, here it is. All of it."

"Why now?"

"Because you're going to need all the help you can get. It's a tough business. Especially with Starr Howard leaving."

"Not to a competitor," I stated.

"But she had the business management, knowledge and the experience," he paused. "Unless of course you call someone else who would be twice the asset Starr was."

I'd already been toying with an idea but no one but my lawyer would be privy to it. Especially considering I still had my doubts.

Anger settled in me again. Why couldn't I just get past it?

Every time I asked myself this for the past two weeks, I couldn't figure out which part I was desperate to get over? Elle? Or the fact that she'd lied to me. She had kept in the dark about so much. I'd told her about my family while all along, she'd known a whole other side to the story and said nothing.

It was the doubt that had kept me from hitting the dial button every night. The one that kept me from getting out of the car when I reached her building.

"You could have told me about her."

"Elle had been loyal to me for seven years. I trusted her reasons...her timing could have been better."

I scoffed. "Her timing was non-existent."

"Or that," Ron shrugged and reached for the menu. "Doesn't matter anyway. You broke it off regardless, and can consider it a dodged bullet."

I winced. "And it's not because she's not who I thought she was. It's because she's what I hoped she wasn't."

My father sighed. "Then probably not worth bringing her up again. Have you ordered yet?"

I tapped my finger on the table. "Besides, even if I did plan on reaching out, which I'm not, it would have to wait. I heard she's traveling."

Ron laughed. "Elle doesn't travel."

I shook my head. "Well she was this week, but you're right. Let's just forget it."

Ron was clearly not the one to talk to about Elle. I should have been as angry with him as I was with her. But the man would argue me to death about who was really to blame here.

Ron frowned. "Traveling?" he muttered to himself. "Oh she was probably in Chicago for an interview. She should be back by now though."

"You talk to her?"

"No, Chicago Weddings magazine called me for a reference."

"Why?" That was a dumb question. I knew why. And I didn't want the answer to it.

Ron watched me for a moment, and finally shrugged. "Not your problem now, is it?"

I leaned back in my chair. As usual, the conversation with Ron utterly exhausted me. I ran my fingers through my hair and blew out a heavy breath and leaned in. It was time to get real answers out of this man. And if that was going to happen, I needed to be upfront. I leaned in. "Elle told me she hasn't seen her family in years, so I know she doesn't go to California for Christmas." I paused. "Do you know what she usually does?"

Ron's response didn't surprise me as much as it hurt that I didn't know this little fact about her.

36

ELLE

THE WAITER APPROACHED, PLACING ANOTHER CAPPUCCINO IN front of me.

"Oh um... I didn't realize I ordered another one."

"You didn't." The waiter glanced at me and rushed away before I could thank him.

I blinked. It was, after all, Christmas morning in New York City. Who was I to question someone's generosity? I turned back to the skaters on the rink at Rockefeller Center. Even watching them from the inside of the quaint little café in midtown somehow warmed my heart. A ritual that Char would tease me about since I started it four years ago. Each year my best friend would insist I spend the holidays with her and her family in Texas. But I preferred to spend it alone in the city. I refused to spend another painful holiday listening to my mother ridicule my life choices.

I pushed my hair to the side, picking up the spoon to my fresh hot...and free beverage.

Heaven knew I could have used all the free coffee I could get my hands on these days.

At least until I started my new gig at Chicago Weddings Magazine. They had called with an offer for a part time remote position—which meant I could stay in New York—to write articles about weddings and event planning and recommend the trendiest spots to hold such affairs all over the country.

The pay was just enough to cover my living expenses, but this totally beat my hotline idea. I didn't even have to talk to anyone this way.

Which was probably for the best, since I didn't make many friends at Dean's.

The snow started falling lightly over the glossy oval ice and its surrounding trees. This is what Christmas meant to me; snow, laughter, peace.

Spending it with people you love.

"I hear it's much more fun on the ice."

I froze in my chair before turning and locking eyes with the last person I expected to see.

Scott stood merely a few short feet from me, wearing an open black wool coat, ivory sweater and blue jeans. Even in the most relaxed attire, the man captured my heart.

I turned back to the window as if I hadn't known him. As if he'd mistaken me for someone else.

Because he had.

No one had ever disturbed my Christmas mornings at the rink. Only Char and one other person knew about my sad little ritual.

Ron.

I sat there, facing away from him, willing him to just go away.

Because even if I could get rid of the lump in my throat; there was nothing left to say.

His voice drew closer. "Mind if I join you?"

I pushed the filled mug aside carefully. "I was just leaving."

"But you have a fresh new cappuccino. One sugar. Easy on the foam." He took a seat across from me at the small round table. "What I have to say won't take longer than the time it will take you," he pushed the round mug back in front of me, "to finish this."

I carefully wrapped my hands around the piping hot mug. I felt trapped. What else could the man possibly want from me? A better apology? My first born? Perhaps that was a bad example; I'd have happily carried the man's child.

I refused to look at him, but something told me he was waiting until I would.

Glancing up for a second, I found his beautiful green eyes gazing softly at me. I nearly winced at the sight. A painful reminder of what I'd lost.

Say what you came to say so I can get out of here. I let out a breath and took two large sips of the scorching beverage and glared at him.

His brows jumped. "Message received. I'll make this quick," he swallowed. "You were right. It's nearly impossible to always get it right when you're working alone," he swallowed hard.

I frowned. *What?*

"I'd never second guess myself or miss an important piece to the puzzle. I don't typically underestimate anyone, or be completely inconsiderate of those that matter. That was never me." He took a breath. "Sometime after venturing out on my own, I lost the qualities that got me so far and the ones that made me proud to be the type of businessman I'd become."

Great. He's here to remind me how I fooled him.

"In the short weeks that I'd known you, you reminded me of the man I used to be. The one I thought I was. On top of that, you taught me more than you could imagine."

I tensed as hope tugged at my heart. Even though it was over, at least there was the slightest bit of dignity and respect I could take with me after all this.

But I pushed it aside, remembering the bitter words that crushed me. I took another long sip. Needing for this to be over.

He glanced at the near empty cup and reached into his coat pocket, pulling out a thickly folded document.

He slid it slowly across the table. "I don't want to work alone anymore. I need someone by my side. I need someone like you; someone who could hear a quick summary of a roadblock in one of my new investments and figure out that I might be getting hustled. I might have the funds and the vision for opportunity," his tone softened significantly at his next words, "but you have just about *everything* else."

I glared coldly at the papers he set in front of me, not bothering to touch it. Was he seriously asking me to *work for him*? A pity job? I'd heard enough. I finished off the cappuccino. "Time's up. Thanks for the cap." I pushed off the table to stand and he reached out and caught my arm.

"Please," his voice was soft. "Just open it."

I ran a quick hand over my forehead and picked up the document, scanning its contents. My mouth opened before I spoke. "This is an offer for…"

"Full partnership. Fifty-fifty," he stated. "And I'm not asking for an investment or buy in; I'm not interested in your money."

"Very funny," I muttered.

He smirked. "I'm interested in everything you have to offer…intellectually."

"That's all?"

He studied me with a slight lift of the corner of his mouth, then cocked his head. "What else is there?"

I grinded my teeth. He was still cold and unforgiving.

I stood. "I don't understand, first you try to fire me...now you're offering a partnership?"

He rubbed the stubble on his chin. "I suppose that would be accurate." Scott stayed seated and looked up at me. "I'm a patient man. I'll give you time to think about it."

I glanced down at the tempting offer to not only live out what could possibly be a dream job but do it side by side; equally, with the man I loved.

And who didn't love me back.

Pain stabbed at me again and I needed to get away. I glanced out the window and saw a place where I could cool off with a guarantee he wouldn't follow me. "Don't bother, I'm not interested," I muttered and strode away.

I ran through the doors and hoped to have disappeared in the crowd that surrounded the rink. I zipped up my puffer jacket and walked up to the booth, handing the attendant my boots.

I breathed a sigh of relief to have gotten away from the man that had the ability to shatter me with anything he said. Tying up my skates, I tried to remember the last time I'd been on the rink. It had been at least ten years and I wasn't that good at it to begin with.

Perhaps I hadn't thought this through. I was heated, hurt, and confused as all hell. But the cold air blowing at my face was just what I needed to snap me out of it all.

Scott had caused my adrenaline to spike when he showed up out of nowhere, looking at me the way he did and then having the audacity to offer me endless days of suffering working side by side with him while he what? Went out with the Claudia's of New York City?

No thank you.

The rink had a fairly small crowd on Christmas mornings. I grabbed on to the handrail along the edge and watched for an open space to roam free.

The flurries continued to fall around me as I took off, attempting my first lap around the ice. After a few slow and steady strides, I picked up the pace and managed to get halfway across the rink smoothly. I breathed in and let my mind wander back to his tender eyes, letting mine falter for just a moment.

I looked up to see a figure coming toward me. An older gentleman holding a little girls' hand. He was watching and guiding her, his head down.

Oh no. How do you stop these things again?

I braced myself for impact just before a hand caught mine and tugged me out of their way.

I gasped as Scott skillfully slid across the ice, pulling me into an even glide alongside him.

"I thought you didn't skate," I called, gripping his hand more than I should have.

He glanced down at me. "I said I thought it was an odd sport—not that I didn't know how."

I clutched his arm with my other hand. At this speed, there was no way I could balance on my own.

He was frustratingly quiet as we made our first lap together, and I got the feeling that he was silently letting me know that if I needed to cool off this way, I wouldn't do it alone.

"I can't work with you," I called through the wind.

"Why not?" he asked simply, without bothering another glance at me.

I pushed aside a strand of hair that flew over my face. "Because... you wouldn't trust me."

He didn't say anything and kept focused ahead.

"I lied."

"Did you? About what?"

My cheeks were getting cold. "You know about all of them."

He guided us to a halt, and twisted me to face him. "Good," he breathed. "Then there aren't really that many."

I searched his eyes trying to figure out what on earth he was telling me. Are full sentences no longer part of his abilities?

Frustrated, I took the opportunity to skate away from the man that only confused the hell out of me.

But he caught up. "Because I remember nearly every word you said to me, Elle."

God I love it when he says my name.

"And I'm not as ignorant as you think I was. I can tell when I'm being lied to. I just didn't care to question it until it was thrown in my face."

I wavered for a moment and shot him a glance. My eyes stung and I skated past him praying the wind would cease any tears in their tracks.

He slid effortlessly beside me. "I know you tried," his voice was gentle and a bit desperate. "I know you fought to be as honest as you could be."

A lump caught in my throat and the first tear fell. "Not hard enough," I kept my voice even and swiped at my cheek.

"I made mistakes too." He caught my waist and pulled me against the rounded wall. "All starting that last night you came by."

I looked up at him. "Really? What would you have done differently?"

"Not much, probably. It was still too fresh. But when I kissed you, it would have been sweet and gentle, the way you're meant to be kissed," he brushed my lips with his thumb and swallowed hard, letting his eyes fall. "I wouldn't have taken you the way I did. And when you told me you'd fallen in love with me," his eyes were back on mine. "I would have held onto you... and made you say it again."

My breath caught.

"Then I would have swooped you off your tired feet and laid you down in my bed. Kissing you right here." He brushed my forehead with his fingertips. "You would have argued that it wouldn't be right to stay and I would have assured you we could continue our screaming match in the morning."

I smiled, then pressed my lips shut immediately. "And do we?"

"No. Dean comes over first thing, so I hide you in the closet."

A laugh escaped and I nearly lost my balance on the ice. He caught me and held me close.

Tiredly, I fell into him, resting my head on his chest. "What about the rest of it?" I asked.

"You want to know what would have happened if you were honest from the start?"

I closed my eyes. "Not really."

He pulled me off him and cupped my jaw. "Neither do I. Because I like our story just the way it is. Comical, entertaining, and quite suspenseful, no?"

I laughed lightly and shrugged. "I should have trusted you anyway."

"Do you now?"

I nodded.

"Then give me another chance; say it again."

I breathed in the cool air. "I love you."

He closed his eyes, releasing a relieved breath. Something flashed in his eyes when he opened them. "I am so in love with you, Elle. Probably since I saw you jump off that stage; flushed yet confident as hell."

"Yeah, I have intense stage fright, but I take joy in setting people straight."

His eyes were smiling before they fell. "I'm sorry it took me so long to get here. Weeks ago I promised you that as long as I could help it, I wouldn't let anyone or anything hurt you.

That I wouldn't let anything happen to you." He took my hands. "I broke that in Dean's office."

I began to protest but he stopped me.

"Not only didn't I defend you, I made a bad situation worse by whisking you off into a glass box instead of doing what I should have."

I bit my lip, hiding my smile. "What was that?"

He sighed. "Getting you the hell out of there, bringing you back to my place, where we could just be us—even if it was the hurt, angry, heated version of us."

A cool wind blew past us, and he warmed my lips with his. I clung to him, sliding my arms in his coat. "Can we go be that version now, minus the hurt and angry, leave in the heat?"

He smiled down at me. "I can pretty much guarantee you heat. You've seen my fireplace." He winked.

I slipped my arm in his and let him lead us across. "Well, what if I'm still cold?"

"Then I'll throw in a hot coco to really warm you up." He shrugged.

I pursed my lips. "Oh."

He leaned down and whispered. "In the morning."

37

ELLE

I STROKED THE FABRIC OF MY NEW BATHROBE. "THIS WAS amazing. I can't believe you did all this."

When I walked in, Scott's apartment was unrecognizable. He had a massive Christmas tree, fully decorated and lit. The fireplace was completely decked out with throw pillows and blankets set in front of it and a pair of fuzzy slippers set aside. His sofa was covered with a red and green plaid blanket and his usually bare table was pre-set with candles and Christmas themed place settings.

There were several wrapped boxes under the tree which I thought was cute, assuming he threw in empty wrapped boxes the way they did in lobbies for decoration. Until he asked me to open a few.

There was a luxurious bathrobe in one, an overflowing basket of toiletries and facial creams in another and a large shawl.

I sensed a theme of which he eventually admitted of

having an ulterior motive to give me gifts that were items I'd need if I were to spend a few nights with him.

He also confessed he had help from Kat and the building staff with the decorations.

He wrapped me in his arms. "You haven't been home for the holidays in years, and I don't think I've had a Christmas tree since I was in high school. I thought it would be fitting for us to spend the holiday the way it was meant to be." He kissed my temple. "With the people you love."

I snuggled into him. "Thank you."

"Besides, when had anyone ever planned anything for *you?*"

"Never," I admitted, then frowned. "But I didn't get you anything."

"There is one thing I want." He wiggled his brows and reached over to the tree, handing me a small box.

"You're ridiculous, what is this?" I opened the box and pulled out a silver pen. But there was something printed on it; my name in italic font and *Weston Capital Ltd.* engraved underneath it.

When I looked up, Scott was holding out the partnership papers to me. "Just one thing," he repeated.

"Scott," I groaned.

"Isabel," he said sternly. Scott had joked that he still planned on using my full name when he meant business and I found myself surprisingly turned on by it.

I shook my head, laughing. "But I just got a new job." I had told Scott about my part time remote columnist position with Chicago Weddings, and that I was quite excited about it.

"You can do both."

I bit my lip. "Forty nine percent."

His shoulders lowered and he sighed. "Do you know how much it's going to cost me to have this redrafted, just sign it, dammit."

I took the pen and held it against the signature line, then gasped, my head snapping up.

"What is it?"

I held my hand to my chest. "Oh my God, there's something I forgot to tell you."

He tossed the papers aside and dropped down on one of the pillows. "You're killing me. There's more?"

"Spencer Friedman," I started.

He lifted himself off the floor, glowering at me.

I winced. "You didn't...did you sign with him yet?"

"No. I turned him down. There was something off about some of the accounts I looked into and I decided I'd find another way to branch out on the west coast."

I breathed a sigh of relief.

"Isabel?"

I looked up at him. Then quickly rattled off the conversation between Spencer and me when Scott was called away, assuring him that I had no intention of convincing him of anything, but agreed I'd do it in order to stall the man from ratting me out. If Scott was going to find out the truth from anyone, it was going to be me. I began another slew of apologies, but Scott cut me off.

"He threatened you?"

"Yes, but—"

"That son-of-a—" he ran a hand over his face. "Baby, I am so sorry I put you in that situation. You must have..." he shook his head.

"Scott, I can handle people like him. I just hope you know I would have never—"

He touched my face. "I know. I trust you. Now I'm asking that you trust me the same. Be my partner." He reached beside me and handed me the pen. "In every way."

EPILOGUE

ELLE

Donovan lifted his glass for the tenth time that evening, toasting his loyal wife and beautiful friends. I was pretty sure he meant that the other way around. Or at least I hoped he did. Although his speech was beginning to be slurred and his upper body swaying; even with no music playing.

"Oh jeez," I muttered and searched for Mimi on the floor. I spotted her easily now that Dean finally broke his one rule into a million pieces. I made eye contact with my old colleague from where I stood and signaled her to cut him off for the night.

"Probably a good idea," Dean appeared beside me, clinking his champagne glass against mine. "We're ready for dessert anyway shortly."

"Good, that's on schedule, right?" Dean turned to me and smirked. "Nothing you need to worry about. You're a guest here tonight."

I winced.

"Oh come on, Dean." Scott came up behind me, placing one hand on my back. "You know she can't help herself."

Donovan and Elaine were now celebrating their twenty-sixth wedding anniversary. After the extravagant party he had thrown her last year—or I had thrown her last year, however you choose to look at it—Elaine had insisted on one just like it every year. Down to the very last detail. Same venue, same band and yes, even the same photographer.

Dean set down his flute. "Scott, I know you planned on taking off early, I was just told your car is ready outside." He winked and left us alone at our table.

I turned to Scott, confused. "We're leaving? I mean sure Donovan won't notice, but they're just serving dessert."

Scott took my glass and set it on the table along with his. "Don't worry sweetheart, I made sure there were no rasp-berries."

I rolled my eyes. "Cute."

His smoldering eyes scanned me again. "You know, you didn't have to wear the same dress." Scott lifted my arm and spun me once to admire the black laced gown from the night we'd met.

I shrugged. "Kind of an inside joke. Besides you're the only one who would remember what I wore that night."

"Don't be so sure of that," a familiar voice came from behind me.

Scott turned slowly, his expression unamused. "Hello Shawn."

Despite the insincerity in Scott's voice, Shawn beamed. "Hey, thanks again for the gig. Now let's try a smile." He held up his camera.

Scott pulled me against him and I nudged a grin out of him.

When Shawn slipped to the couple a few feet away, Scott turned to me. "Really? There was *no one* else?"

I shrugged in response and he lifted my purse from the table, then nodded once at Dean who stood a few feet away, talking to Mimi.

Outside, I looked around the empty driveway. The same one where he'd found me "waiting" last year and basically chased me away. "Where is your car? I thought Dean said it was ready?"

Scott turned me and arched a brow. "Well, I guess we'll have to kill some time."

We walked along the pier behind Square Landing. The planked walkway was suspiciously lined with tree lights along the sides. Something stood at the edge. It was a little hazy at first, but as we neared, I gasped at the small round table set for two. A sample of various desserts were spread. Three tall candles within glass cylinder holders were lit.

"I actually think it's completely fitting that you wore the same dress again tonight, one year after the day we met." His voice was soft. "You took my breath away that night and haven't stopped since."

I opened my mouth to let him know I felt the same, but he went on. "This past year, getting to know you, spending time with you, waking up with you and falling more in love with all the things that make up who you are...it's all I'll ever want." He reached into his pocket and pulled out a small shiny object that finally came into view behind my glistening eyes. "For the rest of my life."

Chills ran through me and I gasped as the man I loved more than anything held out a gorgeous diamond setting in front of me. "Scott."

"Elle...Isabel," he let out a short laugh. "Be my wife. And sincerely make me the richest man in Manhattan."

I looked up at him. "Yes. I would love to be your wife."

His eyes shined and he smiled as he slipped the ring on my finger.

I stood on my toes to kiss him. "I love you. It's beautiful."

"Today and forever, I will love you more." He led me to our table. "You didn't really think I'd ever let you skip dessert. Especially since you insisted on skipping to ice cream on our first date."

I crinkled my nose. "I was starting to have my doubts about you twenty minutes ago." I popped a raspberry in my mouth, which Scott and I declared months ago as the fruit of our love.

Barely five minutes went by before the waiter from the venue approached the table, setting down a bottle of champagne and one too many glasses.

Scott looked up. "Um, thank you, but my fiancé prefers tea with her dessert…"

"Nonsense," Ron said from behind the waiter, who was tearing off the wrapping regardless of Scott's request. "Assuming she said yes, I wanted to get one last toast for the evening before calling it a night."

I picked up a glass and kicked Scott under the table to do the same.

"I want to start off by saying that there are no two people in the world that I think belong together, and I'm thankful you two found each other." He turned to me. "I'm toasting today to the very last thing I'll want to see you plan, your own wedding."

"Thank you, that means a lot to us." Scott focused on me for a moment before turning back to Ron. "And thank you for being part of what brought us together," he swallowed, "Dad."

Ron looked down, a smile escaped him.

I stood, saving Ron from any words. "Thank you, but I will most definitely be hiring a planner for this one. Except for the invitations…that's all me. And the venue, of course, and guest list, favors, music—that's important." I gasped. "This would be great for my column, planning my own wedding…you know what, I'll just do it all myself."

Ron laughed, "No one will do it better." He looked at Scott thoughtfully. "I'll leave you two to celebrate."

Scott wrapped an arm around me once Ron had gone. "Speaking of invitations, have you given any thought about visiting your parents soon?"

Talking with my mother had been no different, but I no longer felt as affected by her cynicism. Then again, I told her very little about my new life with Scott.

"I suppose I could accept their invitation to Thanksgiving."

Scott cleared his throat. "Remember, you won't be alone."

"I know. And that's the only thing I'm going to be thankful for this year."

The End.

Thank you for reading
Mistaken
I hope you enjoyed this book and will consider leaving a review.

I LOVE HEARING FROM READERS!

Facebook
https://www.facebook.com/roxanne.tully.3
Instagram
https://www.instagram.com/roxtully.author
Website
https://www.roxannetully.com/
Newsletter
https://www.roxannetully.com/news

.

ACKNOWLEDGMENTS

Thank you to my readers. I hope you all enjoyed Scott and Elle's story. I've gone through multiple journeys with these two and so happy that I could finally give them the story they deserve. They are one of my favorite couples that will always have a special place in my heart.

Thank you to my fantastic Street Team; ARC Team; bloggers, bookstagrammers and everyone in my Reader Group (Roxanne's Rocks). You guys are all truly amazing and make all of this worthwhile.

To Midnight Readers; for everything you do everyday and for organizing the hell out of this release and making this launch such an exciting time for me.

To Betty: for brining my visions to life with this killer cover when no one else seemed to get me! You're amazing!

To Kerri, Emma, Amy, Nicole, Liz, Cassie, Heather, Nedra, Marisa, Felicia, Shawna, Michelle (hopefully I didn't forget anyone) Thank you for all your endless support and encouragement. You ladies are incredible and I'm grateful for you.

OTHER BOOKS BY

ROXANNE TULLY

The Better Bully

(an enemies to lovers sports romance)

https://geni.us/tbbaudus

The Roommate Deal

(a fake relationship sports romance)

https://geni.us/trd2022

Sporting Goods

(a single parent sports romance)

https://geni.us/sg101921

Made in the USA
Columbia, SC
26 August 2022